THE DOUBLE-A WESTERN DETECTIVE AGENCY

HOLMES ON THE RANGE
BOOK 6

STEVE HOCKENSMITH

*ROUGH
EDGES
PRESS*

The Double-A Western Detective Agency
Paperback Edition
Copyright © 2023 (As Revised) Steve Hockensmith

Rough Edges Press
An Imprint of Wolfpack Publishing
9850 S. Maryland Parkway, Suite A-5 #323
Las Vegas, Nevada 89183

roughedgespress.com

Paperback ISBN 978-1-68549-335-6
eBook ISBN 978-1-68549-334-9

For Mar, Buttafuoco

THE DOUBLE-A WESTERN
DETECTIVE AGENCY

PRELUDE

OR, UP THE CREEK

"YOU KNOW when it ain't a good idea to play both sides off against the middle?" I asked my brother.

"Shhh," he said.

"When you're *in* the middle," I went on anyway, "and both sides have guns."

"Shhh," Old Red said.

He stood in his stirrups and craned his scrawny neck for a peek back at the trail that wound around the bottom of the canyon. We'd steered our horses off it and stopped behind a huge rock—a boulder the size of a coal car that had no doubt tumbled down into the arroyo around the time Moses was in swaddling clothes—five minutes before. In all that time, there'd been no sound but the whispering of the wind along the gully walls and the low gurgle of the muddy trickle the locals called Eagle Creek.

Five minutes of silence is a lifetime for me, especially when I've got something on my mind. And I most definitely did—though my brother had been known to say I had nothing on my mind but my hat. So I spoke up again.

"Anybody back there?"

"Shhh," Old Red said.

But he'd answered my question all the same. I am the world's leading authority on my brother's shushes, having experienced them daily—sometimes even hourly and on the minute—for years. This one was Type 1-B. Non-urgent. Annoyed but not yet infuriated.

Old Red had got the itch that someone was behind us, but there was no one to be seen.

Which is why I went on talking. Low, of course, so as not to get the dreaded Type 3-C—which is accompanied by a swat from Old Red's white Stetson.

"If there *is* someone aimin' to back-shoot us, it wouldn't be a surprise the way you been pokin' a stick in the hornet's nest from the first 'Howdy' here."

"Shhh."

It was a Type 2-A. I was still safe from my brother's hat. So on I went.

"I mean, these folks was already itchin' to start pullin' triggers. Then we show up, and they start scratchin' the itch. That body we was lookin' at back in the valley is just the beginning."

"Shhh."

2-A again.

"I'm just sayin' there's about to be a lot more shootin' around here, from a lot of guns, and it's just the two of us to be sendin' any lead the other direction. Maybe we oughta—"

"*Shhh.*"

Type 4-A. Urgent—because our lives might depend on it.

I shushed.

The creek didn't, of course, nor did the cool January wind. So that was all I heard for the next long, quiet moment. Then a new sound joined them. The unhurried *clop-clop-clop* of a horse ambling up the trail.

Old Red was still peeping out over that big rock, so I figured he couldn't begrudge me a quick look, as well.

I pushed myself up, the stirrup leather creaking, to see who was coming.

I spotted him just as he rode into sight around the bend of the canyon. He was sixty or seventy yards off, yet he made a big impression: a dark-skinned man with a broad, square-jawed face and lank black hair. He was wearing a blue shirt, high moccasin boots, a kerchief tied round his forehead, and a breechcloth tucked into the front of his trousers.

I knew straight off what I was looking at—and it gave me a jolt that almost sent me jumping right out of my saddle.

Somehow I managed to duck back down. Old Red did likewise.

"An Apache. Damn," I whispered. "You reckon he's one of the men who killed—?"

"Shhh."

Type 2-C. *Shut up. I'm thinking.*

Impatient to be moving again, my pinto shook his head and snorted.

I stroked his neck and gave him a 1-A.

"Shhh."

Old Red shushed my shushing with another 4-A, then moved a hand toward his holstered Colt.

"What are you aimin' to do?" I whispered.

That got me shushed yet again. Funny thing, though: I didn't recognize the type…and my brother's lips hadn't moved.

The "Shhh" had come from behind us.

I started to turn around and look.

This time I got an actual word in response.

"*No,*" a man said.

So I froze. As did Old Red. And it was back to silence but for the sighing of the wind and the burbling of the water and the *clop-clop-clop* of the slowly approaching horse.

And the cocking of the man's gun.

ONE
A IS FOR ARGUMENT
OR, OUR NEW BUSINESS PARTNER GIVES US THE BUSINESS

I HAD Sherlock Holmes to thank for my impending demise in that New Mexico arroyo. If not for the great detective's example, my cowpuncher brother Gustav "Old Red" Amlingmeyer would never have been inspired to take up detectiving himself. Would never have begun poking his big nose—and the bushy red mustache beneath it—into every bloody mess we came across. Would never have made us more enemies in a year and a half than most folks rack up in a lifetime. Would never have won a bushelful of cash—by our meager standards—in a sleuthing contest at the World's Columbian Exposition in Chicago. Would never have used the money to start our own detective agency, with the existing ones having somehow resisted the temptation to hire us. Would never have got me bushwhacked beside that grubby little creek.

So thank you, Mr. Holmes, and may flights of angels sing thee to thy rest. They best be quick about it, for were you still earth-bound, I would, at times, be tempted to look you up and give you a swift kick to the seat of the pants.

It was the detective agency that sent us into that ravine. Old Red had his own very particular ideas about what it meant to operate one. Ideas built upon a very particular foundation: Mr. Holmes, of course. Yet we had a partner in our agency—one Col. C. Kermit Crowe, formerly of the Southern Pacific Railroad Police—and he had priorities of his own.

"Paying customers!" he ranted at us. "Clients! Fees! *Money*! That is what will secure the long-term security and prosperity of the AA Western Detective Agency! Not fairy tales and snipe hunts!"

Every few words, the colonel would thump the top of his mahogany desk for emphasis. He thumped hardest for "Money!" naturally. The desk and the chair behind it were the only furnishings the Double-A's offices had as yet—we'd taken possession of the space just the day before—so Old Red had to make his case with no tabletop to pound.

"There ain't no payin' customers," he said. "And I don't propose to sit on my ass waitin' for 'em when I could be out consultin'."

Crowe's round face turned red, and he balled up both his little fists as if he meant to go from desk-thumping to thumping Old Red. His fists are little, by the by, because the rest of him is, too. The colonel might have temper enough for two men, but height-wise, he barely has the makings of one.

"*Mr.* Amlingmeyer," Crowe snarled, "if this is the way you propose to conduct yourself..."

His gaze darted to his left. Standing there beside his desk was another partner in the Double-A: his adopted daughter Diana. I treasure every opportunity to look at her—especially if it gives me the chance to look *away* from the colonel—so I turned toward her and gave her an apologetic shrug. She responded with a small, sly smile that said apologies weren't needed.

Old Red apparently agreed.

"Oh, the lady ain't offended by talk of ass-sittin'," he said, swiping a hand her way. "I should think it's the doin' of it she'd be unhappy about, same as me."

"And you'd think correctly," Diana said. "However—"

"See?" Old Red cut in. "It's been two months since the Exposition. Two months of doin' diddly. And some of us are ready to get to work!"

Usually, my brother wouldn't be so rude as to interrupt a woman. And not just out of manners. He gets so tongue-tied around anything in a skirt he can barely talk. But Diana had won a special honor: Thanks to our experiences together, Old Red had grown comfortable enough around her to be himself...with all the moody rudeness that brought with it.

Congratulations, Miss!

"We've got us a case," Old Red went on. "So why keep lollygaggin'?'"

Col. Crowe lifted his right fist and popped out a finger. The index, specifically, though the look on the man's face made it plain a different finger better fit his feelings.

"Point number one," he said. "*I* have not been 'lollygagging.' I have been organizing. Because, despite how you would have it, there is more to operating a detective agency than running off to investigate every tall tale and sob story one stumbles across. Which brings us to point two."

The colonel moved his hand so that his extended finger pointed at the piece of paper I'd been reading from before the arguing started.

"That is not a case. It is balderdash and too absurd even for the penny dreadful your brother writes for."

"I am offended, sir," I said. "The last time I checked, the dreadful I write for costs a full dime."

But Old Red refused to be sidetracked by so trifling a matter as an insult to *me*.

"That," he said, pointing at the letter in my hand just as the colonel was, "is a lady in need of our help. And I don't see why she should be denied it."

Dear Mr. Amlingmeyer, the letter began.

I have read of your adventures in Smythe's Frontier Detective *with great delight. That our West is blessed with as keen a crime-solving mind as can be found in old Europe should have the breast of every true American swelling with pride. Never did I imagine, however, that I would have need of that remarkable intellect myself until this week, when I found myself entangled in as bewildering and grotesque a series of circumstances as was ever faced by your idol, Sherlock Holmes.*

The letter went on to lay out a strange tale involving a ghostly puma, the map to a lost silver mine, a damsel in distress, and a drowned man found dead in his bed dressed as a nun. It had been forwarded to our new home—a pair of adjoining rooms in an Ogden, Utah, boarding house—by my publisher, who appended a note suggesting that we look into the matter "as a kindness to an ardent admirer." Translation: "for the publicity."

"Read what's at the end again," Col. Crowe ordered me.

"Uhh…'Sincerely, Ann Wendell, McCammon, Idaho'?"

The colonel gave me the sort of glare I can only assume he once reserved for privates who tripped over their rifles when told "About face!"

"*The last sentence of the letter,*" he said.

"Oh. Right."

I looked back down at the paper in my hands.

"'Although I cannot offer you any payment should you come to my aid, I implore you to—'"

"A-*ha!*" the colonel crowed. "You don't see why this person should be denied our services? Why, she tells you herself. She has mistaken the AA Western Detective Agency for the Salvation Army. We are a business, not a charity!"

"Yeah," Old Red said, folding his arms across his chest, "but there ain't no business yet."

Col. Crowe snatched a pile of papers from his desk and gave them a shake.

"I am working on that! I've made inquiries to associates from the Southern Pacific, the Union Pacific, the War Department, the Bureau of Indian Affairs, the Marshals Service, the Secret Service, banks, stockmen's associations, and territorial and state governments. If you gathered up all my correspondences from the last two months, it would stack up taller than me!"

Before I could be unwise enough to toss out something like, "That ain't sayin' much," the colonel swiveled his scowl over to me.

"Or even you, 'Big Red'!" he said, using the nickname I earned for my all-around size, but which on occasion applies primarily to my mouth. "Contracts don't just walk into one's office and sign themselves. They must be flushed from the brush!"

"And we do appreciate all the flushin' you been doin', Colonel," I said contritely.

"And you can keep right at it," Old Red threw in, "while my brother and I straighten out this thing in McCammon."

Col. Crowe dropped the papers back onto his desk.

"If you go to Idaho, you won't use a penny of company funds to do it," he told Old Red. "I've made a considerable investment in this new agency, and I don't propose to have my capital squandered on your every vainglorious caprice."

"Father…" Diana began.

"My every what now?" Old Red growled.

"Puffed up whim," I whispered to him.

His eyes narrowed.

"Listen here, Colonel," he said. "It ain't the Crowe Western Detective Agency you put money in. It's the AA. As in Amlingmeyer and Amlingmeyer. And this Amlingmeyer gets to say where he goes on company business."

"I knew it was only a matter of time before you threw that in my face," Col. Crowe shot back. "Do you remember who suggested that name for *our* agency?"

"Of course," my brother said. "It was Miss Crowe."

"Quite so. And do you know why?"

"Cuz of Otto's magazine stories," Old Red said, jerking his head my way. "They've made a name for us."

The colonel gave his desk another thump. "No!"

"Father…" Diana said again.

He ignored her.

"*This* is why our agency is the AA," he said.

He opened one of his desk drawers and pulled out a large,

floppy book. He flipped through it, then spun it around and slammed it down.

"Explain it to him," he said to me.

He was pointing at something halfway down the page. I stepped closer to see what.

"Oh," I said when I saw it.

Old Red stepped closer, too, for all the good it would do him. The page was covered with words and numbers in tiny print. The numbers my brother could work out, but the words would be but meaningless black curlicues decorating the rough, thin paper. He has the finest mind I've ever encountered outside Dr. John Watson's accounts of Mr. Holmes, yet he lacks the schooling to read word one of those accounts himself, which is why it's my job to do the reading for him.

I told him what the colonel was pointing at.

"That there's a telephone directory—"

"I can see that much," Old Red grumbled.

"—and the first listing in this section is for the AA Safe and Lock Company."

The colonel rifled through the pages and stabbed his finger at another line.

"And the first listing here?" he said.

I peered down at the page.

"AA Paints," I said.

Col. Crowe slid his finger across the page to point at another line. "And here?"

"AAA Plumbing and Fixtures," I sighed.

"That's enough," Diana told me.

She turned toward my brother. The look he gave her back was accusing and hurt.

"Our agency's name *was* inspired by Amlingmeyer and Amlingmeyer," she told him gently. "But you do have partners."

"And competition," Col. Crowe threw in not-so-gently. "Chiefly, the Pinkerton National Detective Agency. So we specialize. We cover the West. And we make sure that whenever someone looks up a detective agency, we will be the first listing they see.

That's going to cost money, by the way. But it will pay dividends a wild goose chase in Idaho won't."

Old Red gave the man a long, silent, squint-eyed glare. The colonel's got a fine glare himself, so he returned the favor.

"So you're orderin' me not to go, huh?" my brother finally said. "Well, in case you ain't noticed, this ain't the army, and I don't owe you no salutes. Goodbye, *Mr.* Crowe."

Old Red had been holding his white Stetson by the brim, and now he slapped it atop his head, spun on his heel, and marched toward the door.

Not only was he announcing that the colonel wasn't his commanding officer, it looked like he was saying the man wasn't his partner either.

"Father," Diana said. "Clayton Haney."

Old Red kept stomping away, the sharp clapping of boot leather on floorboards echoing off the bare walls of the empty office. He wasn't *my* commanding officer, of course, but he was my older brother, and I always backed him.

I gave the lady a resigned shrug, then headed after Old Red.

"*Clayton Haney*, Father," Diana said.

Old Red reached the door.

"You're forcing my hand, Amlingmeyer," Col. Crowe said. "There is still much to prepare. Much groundwork to be laid."

Old Red stopped, but he didn't turn around.

"What are you talkin' about?" he said.

"A potential client," Col. Crowe grated out. "A rancher who's having trouble with cattle thieves. He's offering thirty dollars a day for our services."

"Thirty a *day?*" I blurted out.

As cowhands, Old Red and I were accustomed to one.

"With a bonus of five hundred if we stop the losses to his herd," said the colonel.

"Why didn't you tell us this before?" my brother asked without looking at him. He was still standing before the door, seemingly ready to carry on through it should the conversation not persuade him to do otherwise.

"Because I didn't think we were ready," Col. Crowe said.

"Let's say we take the job and rope us that bonus," I mused. "That'd bring in enough for the Double-A to cover a little jaunt up to Idaho, wouldn't it?"

Old Red looked over at me.

"More than enough, I reckon," he said.

The colonel glowered at us sourly.

"So…*quid pro quo*," he said.

Old Red furrowed his brow and frowned.

"This for that. A trade," I explained.

I was the lettered one in the family. Which didn't mean I had that much more schooling. But it's amazing what you can pick up when you read enough *Harper's Weekly*s.

"Yes. A deal. And a fair one, I think," Diana said, speaking as much to her adoptive father as me and Old Red. "You complete a paying assignment for the agency, and afterwards you can take on a side job *gratis*."

"For free," I told my brother.

"That one I know," he muttered.

He went back to staring straight ahead at the door, mulling the offer over.

After a moment, he turned to face the desk again.

"So, Colonel," he said, "where will we find this Clayton Haney and his rustlers?"

TWO
TOWN MARSHAL, ALFRED HINKLE

OR, WE LEARN WHY THE SUPPOSEDLY LONG ARM OF THE LAW DIDN'T STRETCH FAR ENOUGH TO SUIT CLAYTON HANEY

MR. HANEY AND HIS RUSTLERS, it turned out, were to be found near a little, heretofore unknown-to-me town called DeBarge in southeastern New Mexico Territory. Which made joining them a lengthy process.

We'd picked Ogden for the Double-A's headquarters because of the city's reputation as a railhead. From it, one could quickly reach anywhere in the West…so long as said "anywhere" had tracks. The Texas and Pacific Railway hoped to reach DeBarge sometime in the general vicinity of 1896, of this I learned when we began making our travel plans. So, this being January of 1894, the T.P. would be of little use to us. The Iron Horse wouldn't get us there. It was up to the flesh-and-blood variety.

Under normal circumstances, this would have been welcome news to my brother, who would choose to be hurled to his destination via catapult if it would spare him so much as a minute on a train. For him, procuring horses and riding to DeBarge from the nearest railroad station—a hundred miles from the town, in the county seat—wouldn't be an inconvenience. It would be a preference.

But there was a wrinkle. A quite fetching one. Diana had

worked for her father as a spotter and spy back when he ran the Southern Pacific Railroad Police, and he insisted that she join us for this, the first official enterprise of the AA Western Detective Agency. As I saw it, this displayed a lack of confidence in me and my brother on two fronts: as representatives of the Double-A and as suitors. The colonel knew that both Old Red and I were smitten with the lady, and he made no effort to hide the deep and distressing dyspepsia this inflicted upon him. Yet here he was, pushing her on us as a travel companion. He obviously thought undereducated saddle tramps such as ourselves had little chance with the likes of her. I would have been insulted if I hadn't secretly agreed. And there was a silver lining—nay, a solid gold one encrusted with diamonds and rubies. Diana was coming with us.

Instead of covering the last leg on horseback, we accommodated the lady by taking a stagecoach. I spent the long, jolting journey enjoying my view of scrub-covered buttes, plunging valleys, and the brown-haired beauty seated across from me. Old Red spent it doing his utmost not to vomit. He does prefer stages to trains, but that isn't saying much. He'd take cholera, food poisoning, or getting kicked by a mule over a train, too. That our new business was being built on our supposed easy accessibility via the railroads was an irony Old Red had yet to fully appreciate. And regret. But it was early days yet...

Usually, when we had rails or wheels beneath us, I could ease my brother's collywobbles by distracting him with his favorite entertainment/edification: a new dispatch from Dr. Watson. The good doctor's latest—and, I presumed, last—had left Old Red in a funk for weeks, though. "The Final Problem" had appeared in *McClure's Magazine* the previous month, and given that it ended with the patron saint of deducifying going off a cliff, never to be seen again, it was not the mood-lifter both my brother and I depended upon. Old Red didn't ask me to read for him on the way to DeBarge, nor did I volunteer to, for even pulling out our beloved, much-thumbed *Adventures of Sherlock Holmes* would merely be a reminder that those adventures were over.

So my brother suffered in silence through the long stage ride. The second we were within the city limits of DeBarge, however, he could take it no more, and he threw open the door and leapt from the coach before the wheels had even stopped turning. I poked my head out to watch him, fearful he'd fly into a trough or up the backside of a passing drover's pony.

"Whatever happened to ladies first?" I called to him.

He just jogged along behind us till his momentum played out, at which point he doubled over and began clearing his head with deep, rasping gasps. By the time the coach came to a halt and Diana and I were stepping down into the dusty street, he'd recovered some of his color and caught his breath, and he came strolling up as if he might casually ask, "What took you so long?"

"Notice anything funny about this place?" he asked me instead.

Diana and I looked this way and that, taking in DeBarge in all its less-than-substantial glory.

It appeared to be one of those little shotgun shack-style towns that run straight through from entrance to exit with nary a turn. Not only were we standing on their Main Street, it was their Only Street. It extended perhaps 200 yards, both sides lined with the usual stores, saloons, and restaurants.

I spied nothing "funny" in either the amusing or peculiar senses of the word. But Diana smiled and said, "It's a mirror."

"What do you mean?" I asked.

Old Red kept his eyes on me.

"'You see, but you do not observe,'" he said, quoting one of his hero's slights to long-suffering Doc Watson.

He might have kept me standing there ten more minutes trying to work out what it was he wanted me to see. He'd done it before. But Diana was more merciful. She lifted a gloved hand and pointed at the nearest building.

"Hotel," she said. She pointed across the street. "Hotel."

Indeed, the DeBarge Arms Hotel was behind us, the DeBarge House Hotel directly facing it.

My brother jerked his head at Diana.

"*She* observes," he said.

"The town's got two hotels," I said. "So?"

Old Red rolled his eyes.

Diana gestured toward the storefront just beyond the DeBarge Arms.

"Dress shop," she said. She pointed across the street again. "Dress shop."

I shifted my gaze from Miss Claudette's Dresses, Sewing & Alterations on one side of the street to Miss Margarita's Dresses, Alterations & Sewing on the other.

"And two blacksmith shops and two liveries," Old Red said, his pointing finger bouncing from one business to the other. "That's what caught my eye."

"Well, huzzah for DeBarge," I said. "If we meet the two mayors, I shall congratulate them on their...oh. That is odd, ain't it?"

I'd finally seen the mirror.

If the eastern side of town had Darlington's Fine Candies & Chocolates, then the western had to have Cabrera's Fine Confections & Sweets. If one side had Johnson's Barber Shop and Tonsorial Emporium, the other had to have Ramirez Barbering & Baths. Etcetera. There were even rival banks, the First DeBarge Bank versus the First Bank of DeBarge, churches—Baptist vs. Catholic—and hitching posts. The horse turds and dogs seemed to be distributed randomly, but other than that, the town was built upon a tit-for-tat so unswerving that even someone who couldn't read the signs might notice it,—especially if that someone was my brother.

"I wonder what happens if a building catches fire here," I said. "Do they rebuild it or just burn down the place across the street?"

I looked at the DeBarge House Hotel again, almost afraid I'd see another stagecoach out front with three freshly disembarked passengers staring back at us—one of them especially tall and broad and good looking *a la* your humble narrator. This I did not see, though someone *was* looking our way. A short, pudgy man with a mustache and strands of dark hair flattened across a shiny-bald scalp was eyeing us from the doorway.

"Well," I said, "much as I'd love to keep standin' around admirin' the architecture, I'm sure Diana would like to freshen up, and I could probably use a splash of *eau de toilette* myself. So which hotel will it be? We got two to choose from…like with everything else around here."

Old Red looked both places over, then shrugged. "Lady's choice."

"Thank you," Diana said. "But I think perhaps we shall let natural selection do the choosing."

She nodded at the little man across the street, who'd started toward us with a finger in the air.

"Excuse me," he said.

"Pardon," someone said behind me.

I turned to find another short, balding man—this one with reddish-gray hair, where there was still hair—hustling from the DeBarge Arms.

"*Excuse me,*" said the man from the DeBarge House, picking up his pace.

"*Pardon,*" said the man from the DeBarge Arms, breaking into a sprint.

The House man had a head start, but the Arms man was closer. The stagecoach driver had already unloaded our things—a couple of carpetbags for me and my brother, a portmanteau for Diana—and the Arms man snatched up the former and positioned himself proprietarily before the latter.

"Welcome to DeBarge!" he announced. "Do you need a place to stay while you're here?"

"Why, yes, we do," I told him. "I assume you have vacancies."

"Indeed—and they happen to be the best rooms in town," said the Arms man, throwing a triumphant sidelong look at the competition.

The House man had stopped in the street a few feet away. It was a cool day, yet he pulled out a handkerchief and mopped beads of sweat from his forehead.

"I don't wish to be rude," he said to us, "but do you have business hereabouts?"

"We didn't come for the sparklin' waters," I replied cheerfully.

"Who, if I may ask, is your business with?" the plump little man pressed.

One would've thought his rival would shoo him away, but instead, the Arms man merely waited for our answer with obvious interest. Having two of everything apparently extended to the town's pair of overly nosy hotel clerks.

"We're advance agents for a European gentleman who's thinking of acquiring property in the Territory," Diana said, trotting out the story we'd agreed upon before beginning our journey. "We'll be making inquiries with several local landowners."

"Has there been any advance contact?" asked the House man.

"Anyone you're already in discussions with?" asked the Arms man.

They were like a prying Tweedledee and Tweedledum in black frock coats.

"Well," I began, about to toss off a dodge of some sort.

"We was invited down by the gent who owns the Pecos Bend Ranch," Old Red said. "You know him?"

Both clerks nodded.

"Clayton Haney," said the Arms man, looking smug.

"Clayton Haney," said the House man, looking abashed. He had instantly resigned himself to defeat, it seemed, for rather than pelt us with more questions, he jerked his chin at the DeBarge Arms and sighed, "Watch out for bedbugs."

"Oh, you've got bedbugs," the Arms man snapped.

"And don't let him put you on the top floor," the House man went on glumly. "The roof leaks."

"Get back to your side of the street, Julio," the Arms man told him.

The House man offered Diana a half-hearted bow, turned, and plodded off.

"Matthew!" his triumphant counterpart boomed. "Guests!"

A red-haired boy of perhaps eleven came bursting out of the

DeBarge Arms and headed our way. He wasn't in one of the fancy, double-breasted monkey suits of the sort bellboys sport in big city hotels, but he was wearing a blue soldier's cap, which must have been enough to pass for a uniform thereabouts.

"I'm Mr. Yadel, the manager, by the way," the Arms man said as the boy approached. "What sort of accommodations will you be needing during your stay with us?"

He looked back and forth between us, obviously unsure who was in charge of our little party: the alluring lady in the finely tailored traveling suit and cape, the rough-around-the-edges and still a bit 'green-around-the-gills' cowboy with the mustache and the weathered Boss of the Plains hat or the handsome young buck who seemed to be a combination of his companions, having the more refined sartorial tastes of the first and the red hair, broad-brimmed Stetson and Colt-carting gun belt of the second.

I was the handsome young buck, lest there be any doubt.

"Two rooms," I said. "One for the lady, one for us. Beside each other, if possible."

"Certainly," Yadel said.

"And, uhh…not on the top floor, if that's alright."

Yadel frowned but nodded.

When Matthew reached Diana's portmanteau, he bent down and lifted it with an understandable grunt and groan. I'd helped with the case a few times myself and had meant to ask the lady why she'd packed an anvil for our trip.

"This way, please," the bellboy wheezed as he waddled toward the hotel.

"Hold on, Matthew," said Yadel.

I thought he was going to help the boy, but instead he plopped our carpetbags atop the portmanteau.

"Carry on," he said.

Matthew went on his way again, hunchbacked and wobbly kneed.

"I'm wonderin', Mr. Yadel," Old Red said. "Do you know Mr. Haney?"

Yadel chuckled in a self-satisfied sort of way. "I don't just know him, I have the distinct pleasure of working for him. Mr. Haney is one of the owners of the DeBarge Arms."

"You don't say."

Yadel nodded and waved a floppy hand at the eastern side of the street. "Mr. Haney has an interest in most of the finer establishments in town."

"You don't say," Old Red said again, throwing a glance at Julio the House man as he trudged back into his hotel on the western side of the street.

Yadel swept an arm out toward the entrance to the DeBarge Arms, which Matthew was at that moment staggering through.

"Let's get you settled, shall we?"

Old Red turned to Diana. "Why don't you go sign us in and freshen up? Me'n'Otto like to stretch our legs after a ride like that."

Diana stepped toward him and wrapped an arm around his.

"A stroll sounds like a splendid idea, Gustav," she said. "I'm sure Mr. Yadel can get us squared away."

My brother's face flushed and his gaze dropped to his boot toes.

"Fine," he muttered. "Come on."

He led the lady onto the town's plank sidewalk and began walking away from the DeBarge Arms. I tipped my hat to Yadel before following.

"Enjoy your constitutional. We'll have your rooms ready when you get back," the clerk called after us. "And welcome to DeBarge!"

The three of us sauntered along without a word for a while, taking in the town and exchanging friendly nods with the occasional local as we put distance between us and Yadel. Diana broke the silence once we had the boardwalk to ourselves.

"I wonder if we should have mentioned our connection to Mr. Haney quite so soon," she said, voice low. "We are *private* detectives, after all."

She tried to soften the criticism by offering a small smile to my brother, who was still trapped beside her by an entwined arm.

"I know…but we wasn't gonna stay private for long," Old Red grumbled. "The plan is to check in with the local law before we go see Haney, right? Well, just look around. Think folks ain't gonna notice when we rent you a surrey and escort you out to the Pecos Bend Ranch?"

Indeed, we were getting stares from whatever men, women, and children happened to be on the streets of DeBarge. Even the horses at the hitching posts gawked at us as we passed. In a remote little town like this, visitors—particularly pretty ones—were going to be more than noticed. They'd be the day's top entertainment and topic of conversation.

"You have a point," Diana said. "It's something the colonel and I discussed before we left Ogden, in fact."

Old Red shot her a hard stare.

"And yet here you are anyhow announcin' our arrival like a brass band," he said.

The lady stiffened. She remained on Old Red's arm, but the space between them grew a little wider.

"The AA Western Detective Agency's most experienced professional operative has been assigned to our first case," she said. "Would you have it otherwise?"

I took the liberty of replying on behalf of the Amlingmeyer contingent because I was worried about what the rest of it might say.

"Certainly not! We're pleased as Punch to have you along!" I enthused. "'Our first case.' Can you believe it, Gustav? After all those months tryin' to follow in Mr. Holmes's footsteps we're finally on the job as consultin' detectives. Think they got any champagne in this podunk town? Cuz it seems to me we oughta be washin' the trail dust out of our throats with a toast. You see a restaurant that'd serve anything fancier than eggs and coffee?"

"Oh…" Old Red began.

It was an "Oh" I know well. It was the one that paves the way for "shut up."

"I don't see such a restaurant yet, Otto," Diana cut in. "But I have been noticing some interesting differences between this side of the street and the other. I'm sure Gustav has spotted them, as well."

The lady was offering an olive branch. Seeing as it gave my brother the chance to change the subject with some deducifying, he decided, after an exasperated sigh, to take hold of it.

"Yeah, I seen 'em," he said. "Paint's more faded and peeled over there on the western side of the street. Wood's more weathered. And the people...they look like they've seen more sun, too."

Which was my brother's way of saying that the folks across the street from us tended toward the dusky. You were more likely to spy sombreros, ponchos, and colorful peasant dresses over that way, as well. It was as if one could look that way for a glimpse of Old Mexico, while the eastern side of the street offered up the New.

"It will be interesting to see on which side of the street we find the...ah. Speak of the devil," Diana said.

She was looking at a sign hanging outside a squat adobe building.

TOWN MARSHAL
ALFRED HINKLE

It was on the western side of town. There was no opposing lawman's office on the eastern side. Facing it instead was the place of business of one Cornelius Hale—the town's one and only undertaker.

I read the lawman's sign out loud for my brother.

"I hope you hadn't intended to go see the marshal without me," Diana said to him.

Old Red just gritted his teeth and cleared his throat.

"Well, here we are," I said. "Shall we see what Alfred Hinkle has to say about our rustlers?"

Diana nodded. "Why not?"

She looked over at Old Red as if this were a genuine question and not just an expression.

Why shouldn't we—*all of us*—get to work?

I got the feeling my brother had a genuine answer for that, too, but at the time all he did was mutter, "Let's go," and start for the marshal's office.

A moment later we were walking through the door. Inside were two men: a tall, gray-haired, mustachioed gent with his feet up on a desk and a younger, slender, fair-haired fellow standing with a broom in his hands.

"Can I help you?" the older man asked with a solicitous smile.

"We'd like a word with the marshal, if we may," Diana said.

The man swept his feet off the desk and sat up straight, his chair creaking beneath him.

"Certainly. That would be me." He nodded at the younger man. "This is my deputy, Flip Compton."

"Pleased to meet you," Diana said to both men.

Old Red and I gave each a silent nod, mine with a smile.

There was something wary and watchful about the marshal as we made our greetings, though his own smile never wavered.

"I hope you won't mind," Diana said, "but this is a private matter."

Her gaze flicked over to the deputy.

"Of course," Hinkle said. "Flip, it's time to do your rounds, isn't it?"

The deputy furrowed his brow. "Uh…no."

Hinkle seemed to stifle a sigh.

"I'll see you in a few minutes, Flip," he said.

"Uh…O.K."

The deputy leaned his broom in a corner, retrieved his hat and coat from a rack there, and left.

"Flip's a good man," Hinkle said once Compton was gone. "Thick as a brick, but a good man. Now…what can I do for you?"

"We hear you got a problem with cattle thieves 'round these parts," my brother said.

The marshal cocked his head, still smiling. "That depends on who you talk to."

"We heard it from Clayton Haney," Old Red said.

Usually, Diana's a good enough actress to give Sarah Bernhardt a run for her money, but I thought I spied a little flinch she couldn't hide. My brother was tossing our client's name left and right like he was Johnny Appleseed sowing an orchard.

Hinkle nodded slowly in a way that seemed to say, "Of course."

"You friends of his?" he said.

"Potential business associates," Diana told him.

The marshal chuckled. "You'll have to pardon me, miss, but you don't strike me as the sort of person Mr. Haney usually associates with. Your companions on the other hand..." He looked me and Old Red up and down, his gaze lingering on our gun belts. "Exactly what business are you in?"

"Cattle, at the moment," Diana said. "Which is why we're wondering if Mr. Haney has a legitimate complaint."

Hinkle shrugged. "Where there's beeves, there's thieves."

"Do you have any idea who's doing the thieving here?" Diana pressed.

"Well...there's not much rustling going on within city limits, miss."

"So it ain't none of your business?" Old Red said.

Hinkle's expression remained amiable, but his eyes narrowed in a way that hinted at steel behind his smile.

"That's right. It's a county matter, and you can take it up with the sheriff. You'll find his office at the county seat."

"A hundred miles from here," Old Red said.

The marshal nodded.

"*My* business," he said, "is keeping the peace in DeBarge. That's not always easy...and going on a tear about 'rustlers' doesn't make it any easier."

"Haney 'goin' on a tear,' is he?" my brother said.

Rather than answer, Hinkle pointed at me.

"Does this one ever talk?"

It was the first time we'd ever heard that question asked of *me*. Folks usually wonder if I'll ever stop.

"Oh, no, sir. Never," I told Hinkle. "I'm mute."

The marshal laughed.

The man might have been cagey as hell, but I liked him.

"Who *are* you people?" he said.

"Alf!" someone called out.

The door burst open and Deputy Compton hurried back in.

"Mr. Martinez sent me to get you!" he said. "He says the shooting's about to start again—in the middle of his store this time!"

Hinkle winced.

"I'm sorry," he said to us. He sounded like he meant it. "You'll have to excuse me."

He opened a drawer in his desk and pulled out a coiled gun belt holding a Peacemaker. He strapped on the belt, retrieved a flat-brimmed, dimple-peaked campaign hat from the rack, and walked out with Compton.

"I don't suppose you'd wanna go back to the hotel while Otto and I stretch our legs some more?" my brother said to Diana.

"No. I don't believe I would," she replied.

We were *all* mute for a moment. Which didn't keep us from knowing exactly what was going to happen next.

"Alright, then…after you," Old Red muttered to the lady, and one by one we filed out of the marshal's office and followed him and his deputy up the street.

THREE
DANGER IN STORE
OR, WE FIND OURSELVES SURROUNDED BY MEN IN THE MARKET FOR TROUBLE

WE PASSED a blacksmith's shop and its opposite number on the other side of the street, a gunsmith's and its opposite number, and a laundry and its opposite number, then Marshal Hinkle and Deputy Compton turned left and pushed through a door. There was writing across the front of the building: "DeBARGE GENERAL STORE, F. MARTINEZ, PROPRIETOR." Directly across the street was a near-identical door in a near-identical storefront beneath near-identical writing: "DeBARGE MERCAN-TILE & SUNDRIES, M. BAKER, PROPRIETOR."

My brother, Diana, and I followed the lawmen into F. Martinez's place.

It turned out to be pretty typical—canned goods on shelves, barrels of flour and cornmeal and crackers, brushes and watches and tableware in glass cases—except for the customers. There were no women feeling fabrics or debating the merits of this or that patent medicine, and no kids eyeing the candy jars lined up by the cash register. The only folks there, until Diana's arrival, were men.

Lots of them, too. Eleven or twelve were spread out through the store. At first glance, it would've been easy to take them for cowboys, what with their rough clothes, boots and Stetsons—and holsters filled with Colts, Schofields and Remingtons. But if one worked a little harder to observe and not just see, Old Red style by way of Sherlock Holmes, one would notice that most had doubled-up on their shooting irons, with spares stowed in extra gun belts, bulging in coat pockets or simply stuffed into the tops of ratty trousers. One especially squat, slovenly, unshaven specimen was even sporting crisscrossing bandoliers lined with shells—a look more befitting a bandito than a cowhand.

Only one man wasn't a walking armory: a forty-ish, dark-skinned gent wearing a white apron over his shirt and tie and vest. You didn't need to be Mr. Holmes to deduce that this was F. Martinez. The tremulous, wide-eyed way he was watching the men mill about around the merchandise made that plain enough. He was standing near the cash register looking like he was thinking of snatching it up in his arms and diving out the nearest window.

"Hello, *Marshal*," he said, voice loud but nowhere near steady.

The announcement—for that was clearly what it was—turned every man toward Hinkle as he walked slowly to the counter, Compton a step behind him.

"Frank," Hinkle said, giving Martinez a nod.

Usually, Diana's arrival can be counted on to turn a few heads, but no one looked our way as we came to a stop just inside the doorway. All eyes remained on Hinkle.

He turned to face a brown-haired man lingering near the store's potbelly stove.

"It's been a while, Bartlett," the marshal said. "What brings you into DeBarge today?"

Bartlett grinned. Physically, he was nothing special. Average height, average build, average looks. But there was something about his smile that made you look at him twice, like when your gaze wanders over a broken branch lying on the ground then snaps back quick, a voice in your head saying, "Is that a snake?"

"Can't you see?" he said. "Got some new hands. More coming. Need supplies." Bartlett's smile widened, and I almost expected a forked tongue to poke through it and taste the air. "We're shopping."

"Not me!" said the small, grimy fellow with the bandoliers over his belly. "I was hopin' to get me a peek at that sweet lil' chiquita who used to work here. What was her name, Martinez?"

The merchant just kept standing at attention behind the counter, watching Hinkle.

Bartlett answered for him.

"Maria Sweeney."

The little man snapped his thick, filthy fingers. "That's it! There's a hot tamale for you! Where is she, Martinez? Back on the ol' hacienda?"

Again, Martinez said nothing.

"I believe she is, Jody," said Bartlett. "But I have the feeling she'll be back in town soon."

"Well, I'll be lookin' for her," the slob said, and he stamped a foot and yipped like a coyote.

A couple of the other men yipped and howled along, and when I looked toward the sound, I had to blink to clear away my double vision. Which didn't work, because what I saw didn't change.

Further back in the darker part of the store stood a gangly young man with long blond hair sticking like straw from beneath a weather-beaten hat. Beside him was a gangly young man with long blond hair sticking like straw from beneath a weather-beaten hat.

His twin, in other words. Neither looked like a particularly savory specimen of humanity, yet God in his infinite wisdom had seen fit to bless the world with a spare.

As the two of them coyote-yowled some, the tub of guts called "Jody" snatched up a light brown campaign hat from a nearby table. It was identical to the one Hinkle was wearing but for the price tag attached to the band.

"I like your lid, Marshal. It's got personality," Jody said. He inspected the hat a moment, then tossed it back on the table, brim up. "Buy it here, did you?"

"Of course, he bought it here," Bartlett said. "Marshal Hinkle does all his shopping on this side of the street."

The mudball in the bandoliers laughed and looked around at the other men to make sure they were joining in. They did, though it was obvious half didn't get the joke.

I glanced over at my brother and Diana to see what they made of the scene before us. The lady looked grim and tense. Old Red looked boiling mad.

I had to hope Bartlett took his trade elsewhere, and soon. When my brother gets that angry, he's not likely to keep it to himself, consequences be damned.

"You usually buy your supplies over at the mercantile, Bartlett," Hinkle said. "Why don't you head over there and see what's new?"

"But we're not done here, Marshal," Bartlett said.

He squared his feet and hovered a hand over his holster in a way that kept on talking.

You want me to leave? it said. *Make me.*

Jody copied Bartlett's stance, and then men throughout the store were doing it, too. Deputy Compton and Mr. Martinez looked around at them, fear on their faces. They and the marshal were outnumbered three to one.

"Not wasting any time this year, are you?" Hinkle said to Bartlett.

Bartlett gave him another serpent-in-the-garden smile.

"No time like the present," he said.

"Goddamn it," I heard Old Red growl under his breath.

"You know, Brother," I whispered to him, "there is a *door* right behind us."

"And it's time Miss Crowe used it," he said.

Then he moved slowly to his right, putting distance between himself and the lady.

The marshal's odds were about to improve. All the way from *hopeless* to *mostly hopeless*.

"He's right," I told Diana quietly. "You'd best take the air while it ain't fulla bullets."

And I moved to the left.

Old Red's dander was up, and in all my twenty-one years, I hadn't figured out how to get it down. The only thing to do was try to keep him alive until his fit of pique passed and he went back to being simply surly as opposed to suicidally irate.

Some of Bartlett's bunch had noticed us by now. It was time to make sure Bartlett did, too.

I cleared my throat.

"I hate to interrupt a good Mexican standoff, and this one you got here's a real corker," I said. "But I have a question for Mr. Martinez."

The merchant looked my way for the first time, as did Bartlett, Hinkle, and a sweaty, unsteady-looking Compton.

"Excuse me?" Martinez said.

"Do you stock .44/.40 cartridges, sir?" I nodded at Old Red, who'd taken up position before shelves of canned tomatoes, pickles, and peaches. "Me and my brother, we've got plenty of ammunition, but you never know when you might need more."

I stopped by the store's display of books and magazines. If my brains ended up splattered across *The Adventures of Sherlock Holmes* or the latest issue of *Smythe's Frontier Detective* it would be a fitting end, for surely they'd have killed me as much as whichever S.O.B. was about to pull the trigger. No one ever wanted to shoot me before Old Red and I started playing sleuth.

Well...not that many people, anyhow...

"Yes, we stock .44/.40s," Martinez said, voice warbling like a singing magpie. He lifted a shaking hand and pointed at a row of boxes on the wall behind him. "Shall I—"

"No, that's alright, sir. Like I said, we got plenty for now." I shifted my gaze from Martinez to Bartlett. "Won't need more 'less there's call to use what we got."

Bartlett just stared back at me, cool and amused. But his chubby, grubby compadre Jody took it upon himself to spit out the question his boss was no doubt thinking.

"Who the hell are you?"

"Just a couple businessmen passin' through," I said.

Bartlett grunted out a chuckle.

"Well, well," he said. "Looks like we're not the only ones who've been hiring."

He finally turned away from the marshal, and I started to breathe a sigh of relief...until he squared up again facing *me*.

Now, I know how to use a gun, and I am most definitely a man. A gunman I am not, however. Neither am I a gunslinger, a gunfighter, or a pistolero. So to find myself facing down a fellow with a roomful of gunmen, gunslingers, gunfighters, and pistoleros behind him was...what's the word?

Pardon me while I consult my thesaurus.

Ah, yes. Here it is.

Terrifying.

I'd hoped that a little blowhard bluster would be enough to put off the gunplay for another day—one when we weren't around to play along. But Bartlett was calling my bluff.

He stared at me. I stared at him. I could only assume that my brother and Marshal Hinkle and Deputy Compton and Mr. Martinez found their own men to trade stares with. There were certainly plenty to choose from.

"You boys oughta listen to the marshal and move along," Old Red said.

"You boys can go tuck yourselves into bed," said Jody. Only without the "into bed." And we weren't being invited to go tuck ourselves.

I was about to remind him to mind his language in the presence of a lady—and remind the lady to get the hell out of there, if she hadn't already. But before I could speak up, Diana walked out into the middle of the store. Which meant into the middle of the standoff, too, of course. She stopped at a spot that just happened to be between me and Bartlett, between Old Red and Jody, and between the deputy and the marshal and everyone else.

Well chosen, that particular floorboard was. You couldn't have picked a better place to get yourself shot.

"Diana!" Old Red gasped. "Get outta here!"

Deputy Compton jerked his head toward my brother, looking

strangely thunderstruck. He opened his mouth to say something, but when no sounds emerged, he just left his jaw to dangle there like an empty swing from a tree branch.

"But I have a question about the merchandise, too," Diana told Old Red. "Mr. Martinez, do you have any aspirin?"

A quavery "Huh?" was all the merchant could manage.

"Aspirin tablets. Do you have some in stock?" Diana placed a dainty hand to her forehead. "I suddenly find I have the most dreadful headache."

"Oh. Uhhh. I see."

Martinez looked at the dozen or so tense, grim men filling his store, and for a moment, I thought he was going to apologize to us all for breaking the mood.

"We carry Bayer and Dr. Williams' Pink Pills," he said, turning away and walking to one of the shelves behind the counter.

"Bayer, please. And do you have any tooth powder?"

"Of course. We stock Sozodent, Rubifoam, and Dr. Lyon's."

"No Zodenta?"

"I'm afraid not, ma'am."

"Oh, well. Dr. Lyon's then, please."

"Miss Crowe," Old Red grated out as Martinez fetched down the boxes of pills and powder, "what are you doin'?"

"I would think that's obvious. Like Mr. Bartlett and his friends, I'm shopping." She looked over at Bartlett. "Lovely weather for it today, don't you think?"

"Beautiful," Bartlett said with a smirk.

Diana gave him a prim smile in reply, then turned back to Martinez, who was lining up the boxes by the register.

"And do you have anything for…" Diana leaned forward and lowered her voice. "…feminine complaints?"

Martinez's brown face took on a strong undertone of red.

"Oh. Yes. Yes, we do."

"What brands?"

"W-well…th-there are s-several," the shopkeeper stammered. Before he could start listing them, Bartlett burst out laughing. Jody watched him with a frozen smile on his dirty, patchy-bearded face, clearly wondering if he should cue the rest of the gang to join in again. A few of the men tittered along with their boss anyhow, but most kept their eyes on us and their hands near their irons.

"Looks like the lady's got quite the shopping list, and nothing's gonna keep her from it," Bartlett said when he finally stopped his guffawing. "We may as well go enjoy the lovely weather, boys."

He tipped his hat to Diana, gave the marshal an "I'll see you later" sort of nod, then went striding from the store. Jody followed at his heels like a particularly mangy dog, and the rest of the men trudged off behind them. The twins were the last to go, and one of them made sure his bony shoulder clipped me as he tramped past.

"Whatcha gonna do when we see you again," his brother giggled, "and you don't have a woman to hide behind?"

I like to think I'm pretty handy with a cutting riposte when called upon, yet I held back the reply that came immediately to mind.

Good question.

FOUR
NOT JUST ANY S.O.B.S

OR, WE LEARN THAT BARTLETT HAS SOMETHING IN COMMON WITH US, AND IT'S UNCOMMONLY VEXING

AS SOON AS Bartlett and his men had filed out, Martinez placed both hands on the countertop before him, hunched over so he was facing the floor, and took a deep, shuddering breath.

"Thank god," he said hoarsely.

"On second thought, I don't think I'll be needing that other medicine we spoke of," Diana told him placidly. "The aspirin and tooth powder will do for now. What do I owe you?"

Martinez shook his head without looking up. "Take them. They're on the house."

"You got anything for heart attacks?" Old Red asked the shop-keeper. He jabbed a trembling finger at Diana. "Cuz she just about gave me one."

"You would've preferred getting shot?" Diana said.

"I would've preferred doin' what I had to do without you hornin' in and gettin' yourself killed!"

Diana widened her eyes. "I save your life and I'm just 'horning in'?"

"What Gustav means to say," I broke in, "is 'thank you.'"

"No, it ain't," my brother grumbled.

"Alf, we need to talk," Deputy Compton whispered to the

marshal, and when I glanced his way, I found him watching me and Old Red and Diana with the sort of dumbstruck wonderment one usually reserves for observing, say, the parting of the Red Sea.

"Back at the office, Flip," Marshal Hinkle told him. He turned to the three of us, brow furrowed in confusion. "I owe all of you my thanks, as well. So…thanks. But why'd you do it?"

I shrugged. "I guess we're what you'd call law-and-order types."

"I can't stand bullies," Old Red muttered.

The marshal seemed to grow even more bewildered.

"Well," he said, "you might want to get the lay of the land before you do anything like that again."

He took his leave of Martinez and Diana, then led his deputy out the door.

"I don't get it," I said. "He doesn't want us on his side if them S.O.B.s stir up trouble again?"

"They ain't just any S.O.B.s, I reckon," said Old Red.

"You think they're related to our business here?" Diana asked.

My brother ignored her, turning instead to Martinez.

"Who do Bartlett and his boys ride for?" he said.

Martinez was still leaning against the counter like it was the only thing keeping him from crumpling into a sweaty heap on the floor. He lifted one hand and ran it through his dark, thinning hair before finding the strength to answer Old Red.

"A local rancher," he said. "A man named Haney."

"*What?*" I blurted out.

"Oh," Diana sighed.

Yet Old Red seemed entirely unsurprised. Un*happy*, most assuredly, but unsurprised.

"Hang on a tick," I said to Martinez, waggling a thumb toward the door of his store. "Them men that was just in here fixin' to gun down the marshal and the deputy and whoever else happened to be in the general vicinity? They work for Clayton Haney? Of the Pecos Bend Ranch?"

Martinez nodded, and suddenly I had a much clearer picture

of what was going on around DeBarge and what we were supposed to do about it. It wasn't a pretty sight.

"Is that sort of behavior typical for them?" Diana asked Martinez.

He nodded again.

"Haney's feudin' with someone, ain't he?" my brother said. "Has been for a while now."

Martinez nodded yet again.

"Who?" Old Red asked.

The shopkeeper traded in his nods for a cagey shrug.

"Mr. Haney's been 'feuding' with someone, and you don't know who it is?" Diana said.

"He's had disagreements with a lot of people, miss. He's a real…"

Martinez paused. Whatever his preferred words were for describing Haney, he didn't want to use them in front of a lady.

He finally settled on "demanding businessman" as a suitable substitution.

"But there's gotta be somebody Haney's particularly 'demand-ing' with. Somebody who don't take kindly to demands. Other-wise he wouldn't have the likes of Bartlett and his bunch on the payroll," Old Red said. "Who is it?"

Martinez obviously wished he could go back to just nodding or shrugging or preferably, crawling into bed and pulling the covers over his head.

"The Sweeney family," he said, defeated.

My brother noted the name with a grunt.

"And what is your opinion of the Sweeneys?" Diana asked.

"They're…good people," Martinez said reluctantly.

"Good, upstanding, *law-abiding* people?" Diana pressed.

"They're good people," Martinez repeated, more firmly this time. "But they've been pushed too far."

"That doesn't exactly answer the question, Mr. Martinez," Diana pointed out.

Martinez finally remembered how to use his backbone, pushing himself away from the counter and straightening his spine. He looked like he was about to do what he wished he could've done to Bartlett—tell us to get the hell out—but Old Red spoke up before he could get to it.

"Oh, leave him be. The man don't need more badgerin'," he snapped at Diana. "I've heard enough anyhow."

Diana looked surprised, then hurt, then indignant in quick succession. But all she said was, "You have?"

My brother nodded brusquely.

"You and Otto wait here. There's something I need to check on 'fore we do anything else," he said. "Mr. Martinez...I hope your day gets better from here."

And with that he spun on his heel and marched from the store.

"Sorry 'bout that," I whispered to Diana.

She ignored the apology.

"Any idea where he's going?" she said instead.

"Nope," I told her.

"Any idea how long he'll be gone?"

"Nope."

"Any idea why we should just stand here in the meantime?"

"Uhh...cuz he said to?"

Diana gave me a look that made it plain "cuz he said to" might suffice for me, but it sure wasn't good enough for her.

She turned back to Martinez and picked up her aspirin and tooth powder.

"Thank you for these," she said. "I hope your day improves, too."

I made my own goodbye to the shopkeeper with a tug on my hat brim, then started to follow Diana toward the door.

"Uhh, mister?" Martinez said.

I faced him again.

"I don't know what you're doing here," he told me. "But...be careful."

"Thank you, sir. I'm sure that's good advice."

"...that my brother ain't likely to take," I could've added. But I had a lady to catch up with.

I found her just outside, on the plank sidewalk before the store.

"You aren't going to wait with Mr. Martinez like Old Red told you to?" she asked me when I joined her.

"'Wait here,' he said." I stretched out my arms. "I reckon I'm still 'here.' Ish. So long as I don't leave New Mexico."

Diana's lips curled ever so slightly into what was *almost* a smile, and then she turned away to take a good look this way and that. I did the same.

There wasn't much to see. A couple of homesteaders bringing their kids to town in a buckboard. A water wagon spraying down the dusty street. A random smattering of locals sauntering from shop to shop.

And no Old Red.

What was that little so-and-so up to?

"If we're going to continue working together, your brother needs to learn not to disappear like this," Diana said.

I pointed at the bottle of headache pills in her hand.

"If we're going to continue working together," I said, "you're going to need a lot more of those. And good luck gettin' Gustav to change his ways."

"He doesn't necessarily need to change his ways. He just needs to be a little less…"

Diana paused, searching for the right word.

"Ornery?" I suggested.

She shook her head.

"Mulish?" I said.

She shook her head again.

"Cantankerous?"

"That's the same as 'ornery,'" Diana said.

"Not when you're talkin' about my brother. He finds subtle shadings. A day when he's feelin' ornery and a day when he's bein' cantankerous…they ain't precisely the same."

Diana went back to her word search.

"Delphic, perhaps," she mused.

"What now?"

The lady shook her head once again. "No, that doesn't quite capture it."

"Good. Cause I got no idea what it means."

"It's similar to oracular."

"I got no idea what *that* means."

Diana brightened. "Mercurial. That's the word."

"Now that one I know. And you're right: It fits Gustav. But his tetchiness now—that ain't just him bein' mercurial. Or Delphic even, most likely. He's riled up about what we've walked into here. And I don't blame him one bit."

Diana frowned. "What do you mean?"

"Just this," I said. "My brother might not always say what he's thinkin', but I can usually work it out sooner or later. And right now I figure he's…he's…"

"He's what, Otto?" Diana said.

I barely heard her. A motion beyond her had caught my eye: a man riding a calico horse out of town. He was headed away from us, fast, but there was no mistaking his slight build and white Stetson.

"Goddamn it!" I spat. "The son of a bitch is ditchin' us!"

FIVE
THE RANCH OF THE CANYON OF THE COWBOYS

OR, OLD RED RIDES ALONE, AND I RIDE AFTER HIM WISHING I WAS, TOO

I STOMPED up the street after my brother muttering more obscenities. Diana hustled along beside me thinking them, I assume.

It didn't take long for us to spot where Old Red must have gone a few minutes before: There was a livery stable not far from the general store. There were two, actually. One on the same side of the street as us, the other across from it. I kept heading for the closer one.

Off in the distance, Old Red reached the edge of town and kept riding, headed straight south.

"Where do you think he's going?" Diana asked.

"I got two ideas about that," I told her. "And if I were a bettin' man, I'd put my money on the one I like the least."

I was in too sour a mood to tip my hand more than that just then. Old Red's not the only Amlingmeyer who can be mercurial. I said nothing more—not even grumbled curses—till we reached the livery.

"You rent a horse and tack to a little red-haired fella just now?" I asked the brown-skinned, pot-bellied man we found inside.

He gave Diana a smile and a polite nod before telling me yes.

"Did he say where he was going?" Diana asked.

"In a way, maybe," the liveryman said. "He asked me how to get to Cañada de los Vaqueros."

My command of Spanish doesn't stretch far beyond "*Hola, amigo*" and "*Más tequila, por favor*," but I was able to puzzle out what the man had just said.

"The…canyon…of…the cowboys?"

The liveryman beamed at me. A lot of white folks won't even bother learning "*Hola, amigo*," and it seemed to please him that I wasn't that kind of *gringo* myself.

"That's right," he said.

"He knew this canyon by name?" Diana asked.

The man chuckled. "No. *Rancho* Cañada de los Vaqueros is the full name. That's the place he was asking about."

"The ranch of the canyon of the cowboys?" Diana said.

The man looked like he wanted to pat her on the head.

"*Sí*," he said.

"The Sweeney place," I guessed.

"*Sí*," the liveryman said again. "That's where he wanted to go."

I stifled a sigh. If I'd placed that bet, I would've won.

I'd figured Old Red was either off to see Clayton Haney or the folks he was feuding with. That my brother had left Diana behind —and me to look after her—told me it was probably the latter.

Mr. Martinez might have said the Sweeneys were "good people," but even the best will get itchy trigger fingers when they're up against the likes of Bartlett and his men.

"Wait here," Diana told me, and she spun around and hurried from the livery barn.

"I already fell for that once today!" I called after her. But I did as she asked—because I had business at the livery anyway.

"You got more horses?" I asked the liveryman.

"*Sí*," he said. "Always."

Ernesto—that was the man's name, it turned out—had just finished saddling the pinto I'd picked for myself when Diana came back with Matthew, the DeBarge Arms bellboy, in tow. Draped over the boy's hunched back was a mass of smooth brown leather with two curved pommels jutting from it.

It wasn't an anvil Diana had been lugging around in her portmanteau after all. It was a sidesaddle.

Less surprising, of course, was that she'd brought extra clothes, as well, some of which she was sporting now: She'd changed into a plain black riding habit.

"I deduce that you intend to do some riding," I said to her.

Diana had acquired a riding crop along with her saddle and habit, and this she pointed at the pinto.

"I deduce the same of you," she said.

"Very astute. Only I intend to do mine alone. Till I catch up to my brother, anyhow."

"Well, now you'll have company all the way." Diana turned to Ernesto. "If you would be so good as to pick out an appropriate mount—"

"Hold on, Ernesto," I said, stopping the liveryman with a raised hand.

"If you're thinking of telling Ernesto here not to rent me a horse, I would point out that he is under no obligation to listen to you," Diana said. "I would also remind you that I could simply walk across the street and acquire a horse from his competition. And if that's what I have to do, not only would Ernesto lose my trade, I would lose my temper. You've never seen me lose my temper, Otto. So I'll give you some advice." She tightened her grip on her riding crop, the leather of her black gloves squeaking as she squeezed. "You don't want to."

Ernesto and Matthew turned to observe my reaction with "Ooo, I'm glad I'm not you" written across their faces.

"Miss Crowe, you know why my brother left you behind," I said. "This country obviously ain't safe right now. Especially where he's headed."

"Which is precisely why *we* shouldn't let him go there alone," Diana replied firmly.

It was plain she meant what she said: She was headed after

Old Red whether I approved or not. So the only thing to do was tag along and try to make sure this ride wasn't her last.

"Ernesto," I sighed, "would you pick out a horse for my friend here?"

The liveryman nodded and headed for the barn door. "I will bring a good pony for the lady. Nice and gentle."

"I would prefer fast," Diana told him. "And once it's saddled, you can tell us the way to Rancho Cañada de los Vaqueros."

She gave Matthew a nickel while we waited, and the boy bolted off in a way that suggested he was either desperate to reach the nearest outhouse or couldn't wait to start telling folks what he'd just seen. Even if it was the former, he'd get to the latter as soon as he was through.

A few minutes later, we were leaving DeBarge. We went the way Old Red had gone, heading south then curving off to the southeast to pick up the Pecos River, which we'd follow for the next five miles. There was a well-worn trail, so the riding was easy. Yet a lady riding sidesaddle—or any which way—wasn't something I'd seen often, and I half-expected Diana to go flying from her horse's haunches with every canter.

"Is something wrong?" she asked when she noticed me nervously eyeing her riding.

"You sure you wouldn't prefer a buggy? Ernesto could probably fix us up with one."

"I think you're the one who would prefer me to use a buggy," Diana said. "*I* would prefer to reach the Sweeney ranch before midnight."

She gave her horse a swat with her crop and sped up to a gallop.

I shook my head and snorted out a bitter laugh. My brother had ended many a conversation with me the same way—substituting spurs for the crop, of course. Why it is my lot in life to ever suffer such high-handedness and pig-headedness, I don't know. Maybe it's just because I'm good at it.

I gave my pinto my heels and matched the lady's pace.

Old Red should've known abandoning Diana in town wasn't

going to stop her. There was much we still didn't know about her, but more than once, she'd mentioned growing up on the frontier around soldiers and other rough-and-ready types. And though she was every inch the lady, you don't stay an agent of the Southern Pacific Railroad Police by getting the vapors and fainting every time things don't go your way. Watching her charge down the trail, body twisted to keep her seated sideways on the chestnut mare Ernesto had picked for her, I got the feeling she would've happily thrown her right leg over the horse's head so as to ride astride if convention—and her skirts—hadn't held her back.

Eventually, the Pecos curved east and we curved west, picking up a new, much smaller waterway to follow: a thin ribbon of muck called Eagle Creek. This we followed through scrub-covered hills that soon grew into tall walls of rock. We were entering the Canyon of the Cowboys.

It seemed to me it would make a great Canyon of the Bushwhacks, too. The Apache, like most Indians, pretty much leave the killing of white folks to white folks these days, but one still hears of the occasional nostalgic murder, especially down around Mexico as we were. The canyon was well stocked with shrubs and trees and rockfalls to hide behind, and Diana joined me in watching them warily as we snaked our way through the arroyo.

We made it with no arrows or bullets in our backs, and once the canyon was behind us we found ourselves in a broad valley with gently sloping sides. Hundreds of dark specks dotted the landscape—cattle—and a cluster of blocky yellow structures, the same shade as the arid soil thereabouts, was visible about half a mile ahead. I'm no tracker, but the trail leading toward the buildings was plain as day, as was the fact that it had been used recently.

We headed for the buildings, too.

As we made our way into the open, movement off to our right caught my eye. A lone rider was headed for us. I hoped it was Old Red charging up to tongue-lash me for letting Diana leave DeBarge. But the man changed course after a time, turning to head south, like us.

I heard Diana call my name, and when I looked her way, she jerked her head to our left.

Another figure on horseback was off thataway. Like the first rider, he was headed south and keeping his distance. And also like the first rider, I could see now, he gripped something long and gleaming in his right hand.

Both men were staying beyond the range of my Colt but well within reach for the rifles they each held, with the butts resting on their thighs and the barrels pointed—for the moment—up at God. They looked like cowhands, with heavy work saddles and coiled ropes cinched beside the horn, but the one to our left was sporting a broad hat, a sash, flappy chaps, and big *tapaderos* on his stirrups, *vaquero*-style.

"*Buenas tardes, amigo!*" I called to him.

He just stared at me. I guess he didn't consider himself my *amigo*.

I scanned the horizon for Old Red or his calico horse but saw neither.

A gunshot rang out, and I instinctively put a hand to my forty-five and whipped around toward the sound. The *vaquero* had fired his rifle. But the bullet wasn't going to bring down anything except, perhaps, a particularly unlucky buzzard, as the muzzle was still aimed skyward.

He wasn't shooting at me and Diana. It was a knock on the door—a signal to someone that they had company.

A moment later, that someone came to see who was on their doorstep. It was clear now that the yellow buildings ahead were adobe—the main house and assorted outbuildings of a *hacienda*—and two more men rode out through an opening in the waist-high stone wall ringing the place. They stopped about a hundred yards outside the wall, and Diana and I reined up to face them.

Our escorts drew close and stopped their horses, as well, staying behind and to each side of us. Diana and I wouldn't remain in our saddles—or upon this mortal coil—if they decided otherwise.

Our new acquaintances looked like a cross between the first

two. They were dressed in American fashion, like the one, but their coal-black hair and brown skin had more of Old Mexico about it, like the other. They were around the same age as me and Old Red and looked enough alike to be brothers, as well, though they swapped our sizing: It was the elder who was bigger and the younger who tended toward the scrawny.

I thought it perhaps brusque to greet them with what I really wanted to say: "Y'all shoot any impetuous big-nosed bastards out this way today? Cuz if you did, we're gonna have trouble." So I settled for "Howdy."

The younger fellow gave me a nod. The older, beefier man just squinted at me from beneath the flat brim of his drab brown campaign hat, which was identical to the one Marshal Hinkle wore. They shopped at the same store, it seemed.

"Would it be possible for us to speak with whoever is in charge here?" Diana said.

The bigger man kept his gaze locked on me.

"Take off your hat," he growled.

"Pardon?" I said.

"Take. Off. Your. Hat."

"You wanna trade?" I said. "Cuz if it's all the same to you I'd prefer to keep mine. That thing you're wearin' looks like a dented soup pot stuck to a dirty dinner plate."

The older man clenched his jaw. The smaller one smirked. I couldn't see what the two cowboys behind us were doing, but I assumed they were waiting patiently for the signal to put slugs through our spines.

"Take off your hat, Otto," Diana said.

"Oh, all right. It'll give me a chance to show these fellas how a man's supposed to greet a lady."

I swept off my Stetson and offered Diana a small bow.

"Madam," I said. I turned back to the two men before us. "See? That there's manners, goddammit."

The smaller, smirky fellow jutted his chin out at me and leaned over to whisper something to his compadre.

The older man grunted.

"Take off your gun belt," he told me.

"Listen, mister," I said, "we didn't come out here so I could strip nekkid for a bunch of punchers."

"Take. Off. Your. Gun. Belt."

"Otto," Diana said.

"Fine," I said, throwing in "But I don't like it" under my breath.

I slapped my hat back on and reached for my buckle.

The two men in front of us jerked their hands to their guns, and I heard the horses behind us nicker nervously as their riders brought their rifles to bear on my back.

"Slowly," the vaquero said, "*amigo.*"

"All right, all right...how's this?" I said, carefully working the buckle with small, measured movements. "Any slower and this thing won't be off till Christmas."

The gun belt came loose, and the vaquero rode up to take it from me. Before, Diana and I didn't stand much of a chance if any shooting started, but at least one of us could have shot back. Now all we'd be good for was target practice.

"What next?" I asked the man in the campaign hat. "If you want my trousers, you can't have 'em."

"Come on," he growled.

He wheeled his mount around and trotted off toward rancho HQ. The younger fellow followed. Diana and I followed *him*, and the two cowboys followed *us*. All we needed was a brass band and an elephant and we'd have had us a parade.

Nobody lined up to wave flags, but we did draw an audience. As we rode past the wall into the compound, I spotted two brown faces peeping at us around one of the adobe buildings. A black-haired boy of ten or eleven and a pretty girl of perhaps four more years were gaping at Diana and me. More Diana than me, naturally. They'd undoubtedly seen plenty of Stetson-sporting men on horseback before, and the guns pointed at me didn't seem to be any novelty, either.

The fellow in the campaign hat noticed the kids, as well.

"Maria!" he barked harshly. "Get back inside!"

The girl ducked back around the corner.

The boy, on the other hand, stepped boldly around it. He was wearing a black suit over a broad-collared white shirt that made him look like a Mexican Little Lord Fauntleroy.

I tipped my hat to him.

"And a good day to you, young master," I said.

He folded his arms across his chest.

"Go to hell," he said.

The men with the rifles laughed.

"I hope you'll forgive me if I don't oblige you," I told the boy. But I had to wonder, of course, how much say Diana and I had in the matter anymore.

"Run along, Miguel," the man in the campaign hat said, speaking with a mildness he hadn't shown the girl.

The boy just stood there, arms crossed, and glared at us as we passed.

A moment later, we were riding up to a yucca-studded court-yard before what was clearly the hacienda's main house. Another cowboy—this one lean, tall, and blond—was sitting in the shade of the porch, a shotgun propped up beside him.

"Fitz," the man in the campaign hat said, and he jerked his head back at Diana and me.

The cowboy rose and came toward us, leaving his shotgun by his chair.

I looked over at Diana. If we were going to try to ride hell-for-leather out of there, this was our last chance.

The lady looked back at me serenely.

"I think your passport has seen us through, Otto," she said.

Before I could ask what she meant, Fitz had taken both our horses by the bridle.

"Inside," the man in the campaign hat said to us.

He dismounted, and the smaller man beside him did the same. No one offered to help Diana down—this bunch was proving to be quite the disappointment etiquette-wise—yet by the time I had my feet on the ground she had hers planted, too.

The bigger, older man led us toward the house, and the

smaller fellow fell in behind us like he was riding drag on a herd of mavericks. The cowboys and their artillery we left outside, which was some small comfort. If we were to be shot, it probably wouldn't be indoors where the smoke and splatter might muss the lace curtains.

And there *were* lace curtains. And a foyer with patterned tile underfoot and beyond, smooth floorboards and family pictures upon the wall and large rooms with fine oak furnishings.

The man in the campaign hat led us down a long hallway, spurs jingling with every heavy footfall. We were about to meet Sweeney Numero Uno, I presumed, and I steeled myself for the confrontation to come. Lace curtains or no, he'd have to be a tough hombre indeed to inspire the hiring of Bartlett and his gang. If the man was aware that Old Red had ridden in through the Canyon of the Cowboys, he'd no doubt know where my brother was—or was buried—now, too. But if he *didn't* know—if Old Red had managed to sneak into the valley unobserved— Diana and I would have to learn what we could without giving him away…and hope that the Sweeneys would let us ride out alive when we were done.

I suddenly missed my long-ago days as a Kansas granary clerk. Life had been pretty boring before I hit the trail with my brother, but have you ever noticed how long boring lives seem to last?

There was a dark door at the end of the hallway, and the big man opened it and led us into the room beyond. We were entering the lair of the Boss Man, *El Jefe*, the Rustler Chief.

"We're back, Mom," the big man said.

A plump, fifty-ish, olive-skinned woman in a black dress looked up at us from a rocking chair and smiled. Old Red was seated across from her in a padded leather chair, his Stetson on his lap and an expression of smug comfort on his face—until he spotted Diana.

"And we brought more company than we were told to expect," the man in the campaign hat went on with a nod Diana's way.

"Mom" stood up.

"And what charming company it is," she said to Diana. "Welcome to Rancho Cañada de los Vaqueros, señorita."

Old Red, meanwhile, whipped his blazing gaze from Diana to me with an obvious, infuriated question.

What the hell is she *doing here?*

All I could do was shrug a quick apology, and then the woman turned from Diana to me.

"And you must be Otto Amlingmeyer," she said. "I'm Martina Sweeney…the person you were brought here to hang."

SIX

THE HANGING BUSINESS

OR, DIANA STICKS OUR COLLECTIVE NECKS OUT, AND OLD RED REACHES THE END OF HIS ROPE

"I AM PLEASED to make your acquaintance, ma'am," I said, swiping off my hat and offering the woman a little bow. "But you have my name right and my intentions wrong. I'm not here to hang anybody, least of all a lady as gracious as yourself."

Mrs. Sweeney's dark eyes crinkled with amusement.

"Gustav told you Otto might be coming?" Diana said to her.

The woman nodded. "We tend to be…cautious here, and Gustav wanted to make sure that Otto was escorted to the house safely should he follow his brother onto our land."

"So he told you to watch for a visitor with red hair," Diana said.

"And a big mouth," said the younger of the two men who'd walked us in. As I'd taken them for brothers and the older, larger fellow had called Mrs. Sweeney "Mom," I had to assume we were now surrounded by Sweeneys. It was reassuring that two of them —"Mom" and the younger of her sons—were smiling. But the big man in the campaign hat continued to glower at us dourly.

I took a quick look around to make sure I hadn't missed more members of the clan. The room we'd entered was a small study, with book shelves along two walls. Hanging upon another was a colorful Navajo rug beside a portrait of a lean, bearded, steely-eyed gent in a gray suit. The one window looked out onto a garden of desert flowers and cactus.

It was just the six of us there in the room, but I could see the boy we'd spoken to earlier strolling by outside, doing his best to look like he wasn't listening for shouts and gunfire.

Mrs. Sweeney turned back to Diana and gestured at an empty club chair identical to the one Old Red was in.

"Would you care to have a seat, Miss…"

"Crowe. Thank you."

Diana and Old Red locked eyes as she seated herself near him. My brother's anger and Diana's air of frosty defiance didn't go unnoticed.

"And what brings *you* here, Miss Crowe?" Mrs. Sweeney asked, eyebrow cocked as she eased herself back into her rocking chair.

"The same thing that brought the Amlingmeyers," Diana replied. "Business."

"The hanging business?" the man in the campaign hat spat.

I was growing tired of thinking of him as "the man in the campaign hat" and his brother as "the other one." If a fellow's going to hate me—and the man in the dumb hat sure seemed to —I at least wanted to know his name.

"Long as we're gettin' to know each other," I said to his mother, "your boys have been hostin' us without makin' proper introductions."

"Please allow me. This is my son Eduardo." Mrs. Sweeney held a hand out toward The Man in the Campaign Hat, then moved it toward The Other One. "And this is my son Juan."

"Most people around here call me Johnny," said Juan. He gestured at his brother. "And him Ed."

"Johnny. Ed," I said, giving each man a nod.

Johnny kept smiling. Ed kept *not*.

I turned back to their mother.

"Now, about all this hangin' talk," I said. "I don't know what gave anybody the idea that's along our line. My brother and I never put a noose around anyone's neck."

It was true, too. The folks we'd gone toe-to-toe with in our detectiving had ended up shot, crushed, drowned, or burned. There are two still awaiting trial who might yet be the guests of honor at a necktie party, but to include them in our tally would have been pure speculation.

"Well, hanging's not a rare thing around here," Johnny said, his smile finally fading. "Last year, three of our neighbors were strung up by vigilantes."

"'*Vigilantes*,'" Ed scoffed with the same tone my brother uses to bark out an incredulous "Feh!"

"It looked like they were going to come for us, too," Mrs. Sweeney said. "I even sent my youngest to live in town so they wouldn't see their mother and brothers strangled to death. But the 'vigilantes' never came. Picking off nesters…that was all they had the stomach for. At the time."

"Only now it's calving season again," Johnny said. "And Clayton Haney's been taking on a *lot* of new hands."

"A lot of new 'vigilantes,'" Ed added sourly.

My brother nodded. "We run across 'em in town. A dozen or so lowlifes makin' trouble with Haney's man Bartlett."

Mrs. Sweeney sat up a little straighter in her rocking chair. "Making trouble how?"

"Pushin' folks around. Baitin' the marshal," Old Red said. "Itchin' for a fight."

"They're gonna get one," Ed growled.

His mother and brother shot nervous looks at each other, then Mrs. Sweeney's gaze strayed to the window. The little boy, Miguel, was still out by the garden, practicing his balance by walking, arms outstretched, atop a low stone wall.

"Why would anyone want to hang your neighbors, Mrs. Sweeney? Or you?" Diana asked. "What possible justification could they have?"

The roly-poly woman leaned back in her rocking chair and regarded Diana soberly for a moment. She knew what she was really being asked—"Are you thieves?"—and she was considering her reply carefully.

"That's what Gustav and I were discussing when you arrived, actually," she said slowly. "Do you know how Clayton Haney got his start as a cattleman?"

"No," said Diana.

After his first glare the lady's way, Old Red had refused to look at her, and now he scooched around in his leather chair to direct his words at me.

"Had himself a little herd down El Paso way, apparently. Got it to be not-so-little by helpin' himself to steers over in Chihuahua."

I nodded. We'd heard the same story about a dozen other outfits. Stealing wasn't stealing if done south of the Rio Grande. It was merely seizing an opportunity.

"If Haney had been caught in Mexico, *he* would have been hung," Mrs. Sweeney said. "Instead, he became rich. And then, when he came here four years ago and began pushing out the old ranchos and the small-timers, slithering his slimy way along the Pecos until he was in this very valley that has belonged to my family for a hundred years, anyone who fought back...*they* were the criminals."

"And how exactly have you been fighting back?" Diana asked.

Mrs. Sweeney shrugged. "How does one fight a cattleman?"

"Through cattle?" Diana said.

"By fighting fire with fire," Ed said.

Diana cocked an eyebrow at him. "What does that mean?"

"Oh, for god's sake!" Old Red cried, throwing up his hands in exasperation. "I told the Sweeneys what brought me and Otto to DeBarge: thirty dollars a day from Clayton Haney with a bonus for 'stoppin' his losses.' So you don't have to keep askin' the same question ten different ways. We got all the answer someone on Haney's payroll's gonna get."

Diana's face flushed, and she stared daggers—and swords, spears, bullets, and cannonballs—at my brother. There was a moment of awkward silence while the rest of us looked back and forth between them. Then Mrs. Sweeney settled her gaze on Old Red.

"You also told us that you came here to Rancho Cañada de los Vaqueros because you wanted to hear our side of things," she said. "So now that you have, I would like to ask *you* something."

"Yes, ma'am?"

Mrs. Sweeney folded her hands in her lap and gave my brother a small smile.

"What do you think?" she said.

Old Red blinked at her. "What do I think?"

The woman nodded, then tilted her head toward the portrait on the wall.

"You remind me of Mr. Sweeney, my late husband," she said. "He was a forthright man, and I believe you are, too. So I'm wondering...what do you think about our situation? About us? About working for Clayton Haney?"

I could sense Ed and Johnny tense up beside me. Not that Ed had ever un-tensed much. Diana had basically asked their mother if they were rustlers, and now their mother was flat-out asking Old Red if we were to be their enemies.

My brother stared at the painting a moment as if waiting for Mr. Sweeney to start throwing out questions, too.

"Well..." he said, "I think the situation ain't one I find very inviting. And I reckon you're just doin' what you think you gotta to protect what's yours. As for workin' for Clayton Haney..."

Old Red looked from Mr. Sweeney to Mrs. Sweeney to, finally, Diana.

"It's not something I care to do," he said. "We'll be leaving DeBarge first thing tomorrow."

SEVEN
THE END OF AN EXTREMELY BRIEF ERA?
OR, OLD RED IS SINGULARLY INSUFFERABLE, AND THE DOUBLE-A SPLITS IN TWO

I HAVE SEEN some strange sights in my twenty-one years upon this earth. Steers' horns glowing green as an electrical storm draws near. A box full of dried scorpions—fixings for medicinal tea—in a Chinatown apothecary shop. A squirrel in a tuxedo.

Yet none of these things filled me with dismay quite like seeing Gustav Amlingmeyer, the would-be Holmes of the Range, riding away from both the Sweeneys' hacienda and our first paying job as professional detectives with a smug smile of satisfaction upon his face.

"So you're quitting," said Diana, who was riding between us looking very, very unsatisfied indeed. "Just like that."

"It ain't exactly quittin'," Old Red replied lightly. Him "replying lightly" to something qualifies as a rare occurrence, as well, though perhaps not squirrel-in-a-tuxedo rare. "I never formally started workin' for Haney at all."

"Exactly," Diana said. "Because you never even gave the man a chance to state his case."

"He don't need to. Bartlett and his boys made it plain right quick. Thugs and bullies—that's all that lot is."

"Oh? So what are *they*?"

Diana nodded first to the left, then the right. The vaquero and cowboy who'd escorted her and me onto Rancho Cañada de los Vaqueros were now escorting us out, trotting along fifty yards to either side of us with their Winchesters pointed at the clouds.

"My men are gonna see to it you find your way off our land," Ed Sweeney had told us as we'd mounted up. "And that you don't come back."

His mother and brother had seemed pleased by Old Red's announcement that we'd be leaving. Ed, on the other hand, couldn't have looked less convinced if my brother had announced that he was Santa Claus.

Watching those two fellows with the rifles riding alongside us, I couldn't help but wonder what Ed had meant when he said they were going to see to it we didn't come back. Had he been giving us a warning or them an order...to be carried out as soon as we were a decent distance from the hacienda?

Old Red swiped a hand at them dismissively.

"Them two? They're just a precaution. And a wise one, given the mess your father sent us into," he told Diana. "Believe me, miss—you oughta be thankin' me for doin' what I've done."

Diana reared back as if she'd been slapped.

"Let me see if I understand you," she said. "I cajole and wheedle and browbeat the colonel into partnering with you. After much effort and expense, he finds a client for us and makes all the arrangements for us to begin our work together. You then try to cut me out of the investigation, abandon me in town while you ride off to pay a social call on the chief suspects, and finally *quit* without consulting me. And for all that you want my thanks?"

Old Red's little smile wilted.

"Umm...well..."

"Yes'm," I told the lady. "You summed it up real nice."

Diana glared at Old Red.

"Feh, Mr. Amlingmeyer," she said. "Feh!"

It was the first time I'd seen anyone *Feh* my brother rather than vice versa. He didn't care for it.

"Now look here," he shot back, his hatchet face darkening. "Ain't you ever heard of a range war?"

"Of course, I—"

"The Lincoln County War? The Pleasant Valley War? The Johnson County War?" my brother kept on ranting. "Well, your father put us smack dab in the middle of the DeBarge War. One buncha ranchers tryin' to wipe out another. Or more like one big rancher tryin' to wipe out *everybody*."

"Of course, I'm familiar with range wars, Mr. Amlingmeyer," Diana managed to cut in. "And, yes—it's been clear from the moment we arrived that we've stepped into a tense situation."

"'A tense situation'!" Old Red scoffed.

"*But what truly surprises and disappoints me*," Diana forged on, "is that you would simply turn tail and run because our first assignment has proved too challenging."

"Too challenging? You think that's why I'm leavin'? Well, a 'Feh!' to you, Miss Crowe, if you don't know me better than that!"

I'd been riding along silent, stiff, and still in my saddle, doing my best to just blend into the scenery. But my brother now leaned forward to gaze around the lady and pin me with an angry, affronted look that told me I wasn't going to stay out of the fray.

"You think I'm fixin' to go cuz this case is so damned challenging?" he asked me.

"Nope."

"Good. At least one of ya understands." Old Red jerked his head at Diana. "Explain it to the lady."

"Well…"

I cleared my throat and offered Diana a wary smile.

She stared back at me with eyes filled with quiet, barely contained fury.

"Gustav would probably say this case offers no challenge at all, beyond stayin' out of the crossfire," I told her. "Mr. Haney faces no puzzle and requires no deducifyin'. He's hirin' guns. And a hired gun Gustav is not." I shifted my gaze to my brother. "How am I doin'?"

"*And,*" he prompted me.

"And," I said, "the Sweeneys might be slappin' their brand on some of Haney's mavericks, but that's how the game is played when ranchers ain't neighborly. What's more, by bringin' in the likes of Bartlett and his gang and sendin' 'em off into the countryside to string people up outside the law, our would-be client Mr. Haney has proved himself to be—"

"An asshole," Old Red broke in. "And I'm through workin' for assholes."

I cleared my throat again. "I was going to say 'unworthy of our services,'" I told Diana.

"Same thing," my brother grumbled.

Diana shifted her glare from me back to him.

"So...you think that the AA Western Detective Agency can succeed accepting work only from saints," she said. "And by limiting itself to 'puzzles' and 'deducifying.'"

Old Red squirmed in his saddle. "I didn't say that."

"Well, I'm glad...because it would be an extremely foolish thing to say."

"No more foolish than your father sendin' you out to hunt 'rustlers' in the middle of a damn range war," my brother snapped. "Or you gettin' your head shot off for the likes of Clayton Haney."

Diana jabbed a pointed finger at him.

"A ha!" she said.

"A ha?" said Old Red.

"You resent my presence here. You refuse to work with me."

"What? No! I...I'm...I'd be...I just..."

My brother cut off his stammering with a frustrated "*Aw, hell,*" then took a breath and tried again.

"I just don't see the sense in you taggin' along this time," he said.

He should've kept on stammering.

The lady's expression shifted, her anger cooling and hardening into icy disdain.

"My father wanted me to 'tag along' because, believe it or not, this..." Diana waved a hand at the dry, yellow landscape dotted with tufts of green yucca and prickly pear cactus. "…is nothing new to me. In addition, running a professional investigation is a game *I* know how to play and you and your brother do not. You two have gotten as far as you have through a combination of natural talent, luck, and bluster. That's not going to be enough anymore. If you want the AA to survive, you'll need to accept help and learn. And not only will you have to work for 'assholes' from time to time, you'll have to stop acting like one yourself."

She swatted her mare with her riding crop, giving us a puff of dust to eat as she galloped away.

"See how it feels when someone rides off on you like that?" I said. "Ain't pleasant, is it?"

"Feh," Old Red growled, and he dug in his heels and gave me another puff of dust to chew on.

"Asshole," I coughed.

We stayed strung out like that as we kept heading north: Diana a hundred yards ahead of me, Old Red fifty yards behind her, and the two Sweeney hands off to the sides no doubt wondering what the hell we were doing. As to what *they* were doing, I got my answer when we reached the canyon. My brother had been right—they were there to watch us, not shoot us—and they peeled off as, one by one, we followed Eagle Creek into the rocky gorge.

The three of us tightened up a bit as we wound our way through the ravine. It was too inviting a place for an ambush for us to lose sight of each other. But once we were on open range again, the gaps between us grew wider than ever. By the time we reached town, night was falling, and Diana was so far ahead she was nothing but a little gray blob in the gloom.

I caught up to Old Red at the DeBarge Arms after one by one we'd returned our mounts to Ernesto at the livery.

"My, my—got all the modern conveniences, don't they?" I said as I walked into our small, drab room. "Four walls, a floor, a ceiling. What more could a person ask for?"

"Quiet," Old Red said. He was already stretched out on our rickety-looking bed with his boots off and his gaze aimed at the ceiling.

"Quiet? I don't know if they have that here…especially when I'm a guest," I said. "But I'll ask the manager for some in the morning."

My carpetbag was on the floor at the foot of the bed where either Matthew the bellboy had left it or my brother had kicked it. I unbuckled my gun belt and plopped it atop it.

"So," I said, as I got undressed, "when are you gonna apologize to Miss Crowe?"

Old Red moved his Stetson from the bed beside him to his face.

"Cuz I think you're right about Haney," I went on, "but she's right about the Double-A. And us. And, to be more specific, *you.*"

My brother just lay there silently, looking like an empty set of clothes left out for someone else.

"We're supposed to be part of a professional outfit now. We gotta act like it," I said. "That means not quittin' on a whim without no 'by-your-leave' from your partners."

I was stripped to my union suit by now, and I turned down the gas light and slipped under the thin, threadbare sheets trying not to think about the bedbugs the clerk from the other hotel claimed would be waiting for me.

"Now, I know Miss Crowe gave you a fright jumpin' in between all them guns like she did today," I said. "But ya gotta set aside your feelin's and—"

A stifled sound came from beneath my brother's hat.

"What was that?" I asked.

"Tomorrow!" Old Red barked.

"Meanin' you'll apologize to the lady tomorrow?"

"Yes! So there's no need to keep yappin' about it!"

"Well, good."

I let a moment go by in silence.

"I just hope Miss Crowe's feelin' forgivin'," I went on. "I would hate for our partnership to get wrecked cuz you're so worried about her you can't stick to the work. What do you think Mr. Holmes would say about a detective who's so besotted with a colleague he can't—?"

I was interrupted by another muffled exclamation from under Old Red's Stetson. I couldn't hear it clearly, but my keen powers of deduction allowed me to work out what my brother had said.

Shut up.

I closed both my mouth and my eyes, and despite my fears about the Double-A's future, sleep was soon upon me.

It was ripped away again by a shove from my brother.

"Sorry," I muttered, assuming I'd been snoring.

I started to roll onto my side, then heard what had really awakened Old Red: a low rapping sound.

Someone was knocking on our door.

Our room wasn't graced with either window or wall clock, but I've nighthawked on enough cattle drives to build up my own internal timepiece that keeps ticking even when I'm asleep. And it told me, in a general sort of way, the time: too damned early for anything but trouble.

"Maybe Miss Crowe decided not to wait till morning for your apology," I whispered. I didn't mean it, though.

I slid out of bed as silently as I could and fumbled in the dark for my gun belt. Old Red did the same.

Perhaps Ed Sweeney had changed his mind about trusting us to leave and had come with his brother Johnny and their friends to pack our bags for us. Or our coffins.

Or maybe Bartlett had discovered where we were staying—it wouldn't have been hard in a town as small as DeBarge—and was dropping by to let us know how he felt about our interference and ensure that we never interfered with him again.

Whichever it was, the upshot was the same: Without a window to slip through, Old Red and I were trapped.

I groped for my Peacemaker in the dark and, when I found it, slipped it from its holster. I could hear my brother doing likewise on the other side of the bed. Then we both crept toward the door.

The knocking had stopped for a moment, but now it began again, soft yet insistent.

"How do we do this?" I whispered.

"Can't unlock the door without bein' heard and maybe gettin' shot," Old Red whispered back. "So we ain't catchin' whoever's out there off guard."

"Yeah. I know. So *how do we do this?*"

"Ain't but one thing to do. We ask who it is…and we duck."

I thought that over and could only come up with one alternative: get back in bed and pull the sheets over my head.

I didn't bother proposing this to Old Red. Instead, I stopped just shy of the door, my back to the wall, and waited until I'd heard my brother position himself a few feet off.

"Who isssssssss it?" I sang out sweetly, feeling like Little Red Riding Hood's grandma when the Big Bad Wolf pays a call.

I waited for the wolf or wolves outside to start blowing holes in the door.

"Big Red?" a man said instead. "Is that you?"

"What the hell?" I said under my breath.

No one in town should have known my nickname other than Diana and my brother.

"I need to talk to you and Old Red," the man went on in a hushed, husky voice. "Please. It's an emergency."

I was about to let loose another "What the hell?"—no one should have known my brother's nickname either—when I heard footsteps and the turning of the key in the lock.

Old Red was opening the door.

I slid over to back him up, forty-five at the ready, and found myself facing Deputy Flip Compton. The young man already looked spooked even before he noticed me popping out in my skivvies with a scowl on my face and a Colt in my hand.

"It's just me!" he blurted out. "Deputy Compton!"

"Thanks for clearin' that up," I said, lowering the gun.

"What can we do for you, Deputy?" Old Red said. "The marshal send you?"

Compton shook his head. "I wish he had."

He stepped forward, moving past my brother to give me something with a quivering hand.

It was a note scribbled on a piece of creamy white writing paper. I took it with my free hand. Compton watched me expectantly, as if he knew exactly what would happen next: I would read the message aloud for Old Red's benefit.

I began to do just that, turning and holding the note up to catch the dim light from the hallway. But the words quickly caught in my throat, and all I could manage at first was a strangled, "Urk."

I swallowed and started over.

"'Come at once. There is going to be trouble,'" I read out. "'Marshal Hinkle is dead.'"

EIGHT
THE FAN
OR, WE MEET AN ADMIRER AND SET OUT TO LEARN HOW HINKLE MET HIS MAKER

THE NOTE WAS SIGNED, "Mrs. Liam Sweeney."

"How'd that get to you?" Old Red asked as I handed the paper back to Compton.

The young lawman stuffed the note into a pocket in his heavy corded jacket.

"Johnny Sweeney brought it to the boarding house I room at," he said, voice hoarse. "My landlady wouldn't let him in, so he gave it to her and told her I needed to see it immediately. By the time I read it and came down to talk to him, he was gone."

I walked to the wall and turned up the gas on our light so we wouldn't have to keep talking in the dark. As the room brightened, I could see how puffy and red Compton's eyes were.

"Well, I am truly sorry, Deputy," my brother said. "I didn't really know the marshal, of course, but I liked what I saw of him."

Compton nodded. "Alf was a good man. A very good man."

"I'm sorry, too, Flip," I said. "But I'm afraid I gotta ask: Why bring this to us?"

"I'm hoping you'll come with me to see the Sweeneys."

Two questions leapt immediately to mind: another, "Why us?" and "Why in god's name would we go with you?"

Old Red, for once, found a more tactful way to phrase things.

"Ain't there anyone else in town to help you?"

"No one who'd be happy about it," Compton said. "And no one with your experience...if you are who I think you are."

That's when the realization hit me, and from the glare my brother sent my way, I knew it had hit him, too.

"You've read my stories," I said.

The deputy nodded, a small, sad smile managing to curl one corner of his mouth.

"So it is you. I knew it," he said. "I told Alf if you've got a grumpy, scrawny cowboy with red hair and a beefy one with a big mouth and a lady named Diana who doesn't give a fig about impropriety and they're poking their noses into other people's business, why, that's gotta be Old Red and Big Red Amlingmeyer and Diana Crowe. He said those magazines are full of bullshit, yet here you are right out of *Smythe's Frontier Detective*."

"He wasn't entirely wrong about the bullshit," my "grumpy, scrawny" brother mumbled.

I cleared my throat.

"Always a pleasure to meet a reader," I told the deputy. "But—"

"We'll need a few minutes to get ready," my brother cut in.

Compton perked up even more. "You mean you'll come?"

"Ain't doin' nothin' but sleepin'. May as well make ourselves useful," Old Red said. "You mind gettin' horses for us from Ernesto at Carrera's Livery? I liked the calico mare he put me on yesterday."

"Sure! Of course!" Compton said eagerly, backing toward the door. "Thank you! Thank you so much!"

He spun around and darted off up the hall.

"Yes, Brother. Thank you," I said as I closed the door. "Thank you so much *for volunteerin' us to get shot*."

Old Red shrugged. "We don't know Hinkle was shot. Maybe the man had a stroke. Maybe a rattler bit him."

"Yeah, yeah. And maybe a piano fell on him, but the odds don't favor it. And they won't be so good for us, either, when Ed Sweeney sees us back on his family's land."

"Aw, he's all bark and no bite. Anyhow, we gotta help. That poor kid's in over his head."

"Clearly. But that ain't why you want us to jump in with him. Now that someone's dead, you're curious, simple as that."

"No, not quite *that* simple. Not entirely. I'm thinkin' there might be some work for us down here, after all."

"Oh ho, I see. And that'd help you smooth things over with Diana, am I right?"

"Well, it wouldn't hurt." Old Red walked over to the bed, snatched his gun belt up off the floor, and jammed his Colt into the holster. "Enough jawin'. Get some britches on so we can go."

A few minutes later, I was dressed for a cool desert morning—wearing not just britches and shirt but a sheepskin coat—and my brother and I were stepping out into the hall.

I started to head for the stairs, then stopped.

"Say…don't you think we oughta tell Diana what's goin' on?"

Old Red sighed. He'd obviously been hoping to escape the hotel before that thought occurred to me.

"I didn't like her stickin' her neck out for Clayton Haney. I don't guess I'd like it much better if she was to do it for free," he said. "Anyway, I already owe her an apology for one thing. Won't be much extra effort to apologize to her for two."

It made sense, in a self-serving "If I'm gonna get yelled at, it may as well be later" sort of way. There would be a key difference now, though, no doubt Diana would be mad at me, too. But, well…as the wise man once said, if I was going to get yelled at, it may as well be later.

I started for the stairs again.

Compton was waiting in front of the DeBarge Arms with three horses, two of them the ones Old Red and I had ridden the day before.

"When did you last see the marshal?" my brother asked as we rode out of town.

The deputy didn't reply straight off. He looked unsteady in the saddle, and I got the feeling it wasn't just because he'd had a shock that morning. He was more townsman than horseman.

"Last night," he said, clinging to his reins with white knuckles. "I finished my rounds at ten and dropped by his office to say goodnight, like always."

"He say he was goin' out to see the Sweeneys?" Old Red asked.

"No. It seemed like a normal night. He'd do one more walk through town, and if everything was quiet, he'd go to bed."

"Callin' on the Sweeneys at night a regular thing for him?"

Compton shook his head without looking over at my brother. Instead, he kept staring down at his horse as if he was afraid it was going to rear back and bite him.

"He didn't ever visit the Sweeneys that I can recall, day or night."

Old Red gave that a thoughtful "Hmmm" and then lapsed into silence, letting the deputy concentrate on his riding.

As we neared the spot where we'd peel off from the Pecos River and swing west toward Cañada de los Vaqueros, I wondered what we'd find on the other side of the gorge. I'd assumed that Marshal Hinkle had met with what the newspapers like to call "foul play," but maybe my brother was right: It didn't have to be foul to be fatal. Could be a piano did fall on him. If so, though, why did Mrs. Sweeney's note say there was going to be trouble? Folks were fixing to lynch the keyboard?

We'd find out when we reached the hacienda, I figured. Wrongly. We got our answer sooner than that.

As we rode through the arroyo, I noticed Old Red squinting up at something. I followed his gaze and saw three black shapes pinwheeling through the orange-pink early morning sky.

As ominous sights go, circling vultures aren't quite a graveyard at midnight or a funnel cloud on the horizon, but they're up there toward the top of the list. When we rode out of the canyon, we saw what had drawn them.

Two clumps of riders were facing each other on nervous, nickering horses. On one side was Bartlett and his whole bunch, each man with a hand over his holster. Across from them were Ed and Johnny Sweeney and the three cowhands we'd seen the day before, reinforced by Mrs. Sweeney herself in an open-topped surrey. The men had their hands near their irons just as Bartlett's boys did—while the widow Sweeney, again clad in black, gripped a shotgun in her plump fingers like she meant to use it.

Everyone there seemed to be shouting but for one exception: the man face down on the ground between the two groups, his horse cropping grass not far away and the dirt around him dark with dried blood.

NINE
DETECTIVE STUFF

OR, WE WIND UP IN THE MIDDLE OF ANOTHER NEW MEXICAN STANDOFF WITH A CORPSE TO KEEP US COMPANY

"ALF," Deputy Compton groaned.

Indeed, the dead man did seem to be Marshal Hinkle even though we couldn't see his face. The height and weight were right, and the silvery gray hair, too. A light brown, flat-brimmed hat lay on the ground near him, the crown crushed, no doubt by a horse's hoof.

As we rode closer, I could count the holes in Hinkle's back.

There were four: two up high in each shoulder blade, one a little lower dead center through the spine, and another lower still and to the left in just the right spot to pop out a kidney.

Both Bartlett's men and the Sweeneys were too busy hollering from atop their horses to notice us, and there was such an all-around uproar it was hard to sort out who exactly was saying what.

"...murderer...backshootin' thief...string him up!" I could pick out from one side.

"...liars...sons of bitches...just you try it!" I heard from the other.

Then there was a softer, surprised, "Well, well...would you look at this?"

The clamor died down as both sides turned to watch us ride up.

The "Well, well" had come from a man mixed in with Bartlett's bunch—one we hadn't seen in Mr. Martinez's store the day before. He was older than the rest, perhaps sixty, with big shoulders and a bulky build. He sized us up with steely blue eyes and a stern expression on his broad, weathered face.

He looked like a dour man. A hard man. And I knew his name before he said a word.

We were about to meet Mr. Clayton Haney.

"You're the…A.A. men, aren't you?" he said. "The…stock detectives from…Ogden."

There was a slow, drawling, stop-start cadence to his speech. Not like he couldn't think of the right words. More like he didn't give a damn if he was making you wait for them.

"That's right, sir," I said.

He gave me a curt nod. "I figured from what…Bartlett here told me about yesterday. Can't say I'm…impressed by a coupla detectives who can't detect who the hell they work for."

"You haven't told him yet?" Ed Sweeney snarled at us, jabbing a pointed finger at Haney. "What you told us yesterday?"

He scoffed and looked over at his mother and brother, obviously thinking Old Red had lied when he'd said we'd quit and leave town.

Haney cocked his head.

"What exactly did you tell…*them?*" he asked us.

"That ain't the business at hand," my brother said. He nodded at the body stretched out on the ground nearby. "He is."

Haney leaned back in his saddle, the leather creaking beneath his bulk.

"Alright. Let's…deal with that," he said. He shifted his gaze to Deputy Compton. "Only what are *you* doing here?"

"I got a n-note from Mrs. S-Sweeney," Compton stammered with a shaky gesture toward the lady—whose shotgun, I noted, was still pointed squarely at Clayton Haney. "Said Alf…M-Marshal Hinkle was dead."

"Naw, he's just napping," said Bartlett's chubby, bearded buddy Jody. He looked even grubbier than he had the day before —an accomplishment I wouldn't have thought possible without a roll in a pig pen. He dropped his voice to a stage whisper. "Why don't you turn around and head back to town 'fore you wake him up?"

The rest of Haney's men snickered.

The deputy's face went from chalk white to beet red, but he said nothing.

"Please, boys...a little respect for the dead," Bartlett said mildly, an indulgent half-smile on his bland face.

Haney didn't look amused, though. He didn't look capable of amusement, actually. He seemed about as likely to crack a smile as a cigar store Indian.

"You don't have any authority out here...*Flip*," he said. "Go back to DeBarge and send a wire to the sheriff."

"Who'll be here in two days. If we're lucky," Mrs. Sweeney snorted from her buggy.

Haney ignored her.

"Go on. Everyone'll understand," he told Compton. "This isn't your job. *Go*."

The color drained from the young man's face again. As he lost his angry blush, I could see him losing his nerve, too.

"Deputy Compton's got him a star under that coat of his," Old Red said. "That gives him more authority here than you, Haney."

Haney looked over at him again. Amusement might have been beyond him, but you couldn't say the same for rage. It was right there on his face.

"What did you say?" he growled with the seething fury of a powerful man who's heard a lesser one say something he doesn't like. It wasn't so much a "What did you say?" as a "Who do you think you are?"

Of course, Old Red's pretty good at whipping up a seething fury himself. But he managed to keep his tamped down for the moment.

"Deputy Compton might be town law, not county law, but he's still law," he said. "I reckon that puts him in charge."

"You shut your mouth," Haney said, "before you're out of a job."

I looked over at Ed Sweeney.

"Get ready," I said to him.

Old Red still had his gaze locked on Haney.

"*No*," he said.

"Get out of here," Haney snapped back. "You're fired."

"That work for you?" I asked Sweeney.

Old Red hadn't formally quit, but getting us fired two minutes after meeting our client was the next best thing.

Sweeney just glared back at me.

"Told you we should've gone to the Pinkertons," Bartlett said to Haney with a smirk.

"Yeah," said one of the lanky, long-haired twins who'd yipped at us like coyotes the day before. "These two are more like Stinkertons!"

His brother burst out laughing, but the rest of the bunch winced or rolled their eyes. Haney shot the twins a look that suggested he was in the mood to keep on firing men with big mouths.

"Shut up, Konrad," Jody said.

The jokester twin looked hurt.

"I'm Knute," he said. He jerked his head at his brother. "He's Konrad."

Old Red used this commotion as cover to shoot a quick whisper at Compton.

"Say you deputized us."

"Huh?" Compton said.

"Say you deputized us," my brother repeated under his breath. "So we got reason to stay."

"Oh. Right." Compton sat up a little straighter, trying to look like a lawman rather than a scared boy. "For your information, this is Old Red and Big Red Amlingmeyer, the famous frontier sleuths. And I've...I've deputized them."

This pronouncement stirred up murmurs from both sides of the standoff.

"You've *what?*" Ed Sweeney said.

"Can a deputy deputize more deputies?" Bartlett asked Haney.

Haney cocked his head and nodded in a way that said, "Good point."

"Get the story, Flip," Old Red said, voice low.

"What?"

"Get to askin' questions 'fore they can ask more of you."

"Right."

Compton swiveled to face Mrs. Sweeney, and out popped the question that was foremost on his mind.

"Ma'am...what is happening here?" he said.

Mrs. Sweeney settled her shotgun across her lap and picked up the reins to her carriage horse before answering.

"This morning one of our hands spotted Alf's horse and rode out to investigate. When he saw the body—and realized it was the marshal and that he'd been murdered on our land—he rode to the house to let us know. I sent Johnny into town with that note for you, and the rest of us came out here to have a look for ourselves. Then *they* showed up..." The lady threw Haney and Bartlett the kind of look one usually reserves for something particularly putrid stuck to the bottom of one's boot. "...and it didn't take them ten seconds to decide Ed had done it and needed to be dealt with here and now. I told them it would be a cold day in hell before they lay hands on one of my boys."

"You left out a thing or two...Martina," Haney said. "Like *why* we wanted that...'boy' of yours."

"Did you know he came into town last night?" Bartlett said to the deputy. He pointed at Ed Sweeney, who scowled back at him with his usual air of barely contained anger. "Folks saw him going to Hinkle's office...and heard an awful argument after he went inside."

"I already told you," Ed grated out. "It wasn't an argument. It was a discussion."

"Sure," Jody said. "And the Battle of the Little Bighorn was an ice cream social."

The Haney men chuckled, and Knute opened his mouth to add another funny of his own.

Jody silenced him with a stare.

"What was this discussion with the marshal about?" Old Red asked Ed.

The man glowered at him a moment, seemingly weighing whether a question from my brother was worth answering.

"Politics," he finally said.

The chuckles turned into outright guffaws.

"And let me guess!" Jody roared. "When you followed Hinkle out of town later, you just wanted to chat about the weather!"

"I didn't follow Alf out of town," Ed protested over the laughter. "I headed back to the ranch, that's all."

"Not twenty minutes after Hinkle started this way, I hear," Haney said. He hadn't joined in the hilarity with his men, of course, and his sober, stern tone settled them back into silence. "So if you didn't shoot him, how is it you missed his body? And his horse?"

"It was dark," Ed said with a shrug.

Bartlett snorted and shook his head.

"Hinkle's lying right in the middle of the trail, Sweeney," he said. "You would've ridden right over him."

I glanced over at Compton. The deputy looked tortured and torn. Haney and his men were making a good case—if not for Ed's lynching, at least for his guilt. But what was the junior lawman from DeBarge supposed to do about it...especially with the senior lawman dead?

"How do you know so much about what was happenin' in town last night?" my brother asked Haney and Bartlett.

"Some of the boys were still there," Bartlett said. "Enjoying themselves before they had to come back to the Pecos Bend."

Old Red nodded and gave that a skeptical, "Mm hmm."

"And how is it you come to be here now?" he asked.

"We had riders on the...eastern rim of the valley. We always do," Haney said. He threw a scornful glance at the Sweeneys. "Looking for strays—or anyone collecting ours. They saw the commotion down here, and the body, so we...came to see what was what."

My brother '*Mm hmm*ed' again. Then he swung down from his saddle, handed me his reins, and started walking toward Hinkle.

"Only one set of footprints," he said, looking down at the ground. "Your man who found the body, Mrs. Sweeney...he touch it?"

"He did," she said.

"Just to see who it was," said the fair-haired Sweeney hand Ed had called "Fitz" the day before. "I didn't take anything off him, if that's what you're wondering."

"It ain't." Old Red squatted beside the body. "I was thinkin' of the killers...and the fact that they kept their distance."

"'They'?" Johnny Sweeney said. The more calm and quiet of Mrs. Sweeney's two grown sons was on a horse beside his big brother, quite literally in his shadow.

Old Red pointed at the bloody holes in Hinkle's back. "The marshal was hit four times. By rifle fire, I'd wager. Maybe one man could get off four good shots at night before Hinkle keeled over, but I doubt it." My brother lifted his head to peer back at the rocky foothills leading up to Cañada de los Vaqueros. "They was back there somewhere. Waitin' for him to ride out of the canyon."

"Aww, he's just guessing," Jody said.

My brother shot him both a glare and a Holmes quote. "I never guess. It is destructive to the logical faculty."

"What the hell does that mean?" Knute stage whispered.

"Beats me," Konrad whispered back. "Little runt sure likes big words, don't he?"

"Must be why he's a 'famous detective'!"

The brothers laughed.

Haney looked at Bartlett who looked at Jody who looked at the twins.

"That's enough of that," the fat man snapped.

"Yessir," Konrad and Knute said in unison. But they went on

making faces at each other and giggling like naughty boys at the back of the schoolroom.

"Look," Bartlett said to Old Red, "it doesn't matter if Eduardo there shot the marshal himself or just lured him out here into an ambush. It adds up to the same thing." He moved his cold, steady, snake-ish gaze to Deputy Compton. "Hinkle is dead on Sweeney land. And it's obvious who's responsible."

My brother opened his mouth to answer, but I beat him to it.

"There is nothing more deceptive than an obvious fact," I said, tossing out another of Old Red's favorite Holmes quotes. "Isn't that what you were about to say, Brother?"

"Somethin' like that," Old Red grumbled.

"Bullshit," Haney spat. "There's nothing 'deceptive' about the sky being blue or water wet. Or a dead man on Sweeney land meaning the Sweeneys killed him."

"Killed him and then just left the body on their doorstep when they had all night to move it without bein' seen?" Old Red shot back. "Now *that's* bullshit...beggin' the lady's pardon."

He tipped his hat to Mrs. Sweeney.

She acknowledged him with a grim nod.

"The word fits," she said.

"I don't agree," Bartlett said coolly. "Just because it's stupid doesn't mean the Sweeneys wouldn't do it. They're arrogant."

"Or maybe, in this case, just plain innocent," said my brother.

He turned back to the body and rolled it over.

Deputy Compton gasped and looked away as Hinkle's bloated, discolored face came into view. The frigid chill of the desert night had kept the flies from doing their worst, but there was already some buzzing, and I was glad to be spared the up-close view Old Red was getting.

"What the hell do you think you're doing?" Haney said.

"It's...detective stuff," Compton said weakly, head still turned to the side.

My brother looked Hinkle over a moment, then reached across the body to pull the marshal's Peacemaker from its holster.

Bartlett and the other Haney men jerked their hands to their own guns.

Old Red flicked open the Colt's loading gate, pulled back the hammer, and gave the cylinder a spin. Then he brought the gun up to his prodigious nose, the barrel angled down toward the ground, and sucked in a deep sniff.

"Five rounds, empty chamber under the hammer. Ain't been fired," he said. "The marshal never saw it comin'."

He closed the loading gate, gently lowered the hammer down, and returned the Peacemaker to Hinkle's holster. Then he started going through the pockets of Hinkle's coat.

"Now, what kind of 'detective stuff' is this?" Bartlett said.

"The marshal left his warm office to ride out here where he ain't got no jurisdiction in the middle of a cold winter night," my brother said. "Ain't you curious as to…hel-lo."

He pulled a small box from one of the pockets. He frowned down at it, looking annoyed, then got up and walked it over to me.

As he handed it to me, I saw what was vexing him: The box was covered with writing, and he needed me to tell him what it said.

"'Dr. Faraday's Female Remedy,'" I read out.

Konrad and Knute began to hoot.

"'Restorer of blood health to sufferers of feminine complaints and complications,'" I went on.

Konrad and Knute began to howl.

"'Rebuilds the womanly constitution in wives and mothers suffering from headache, stomachache, backache, toothache, morning sickness, and ovarian dropsy.'"

Konrad and Knute were pounding their thighs and wiping tears from their eyes, and some of Haney's other men began to join in.

"Alright, alright," Old Red snapped. "We get the idea."

He snatched the box back and opened one end.

"You need a dose?" Konrad taunted.

"I suspected he wasn't all man!" said Knute.

My brother answered them sourly—"I'm just seein' if the

bottle's still there"—but I doubt they heard him over their belly laughs. Maybe because it so clearly irritated Old Red, Haney and Bartlett and Jody let the men keep on guffawing as long as they liked.

"Hinkle have a wife? A daughter?" my brother asked Compton over the laughter. He closed the box and returned it to the pocket he'd produced it from.

"No. Not anymore," the deputy said. "His wife died two years ago. They never had any kids."

Old Red turned toward Mrs. Sweeney, his face going red.

"Quiet," Haney said. "I want to hear this."

The gunmen went instantly silent.

"Ma'am," my brother said, "is there any chance Marshal Hinkle was bringin' this for you?"

The twins snickered.

Jody silenced them again with a scowling shush.

"No," Mrs. Sweeney said.

"Or for someone else at your place?" said Old Red.

Mrs. Sweeney just frowned at him.

"Forgive us the indelicacy, ma'am," I said. I gave the woman a shrug. "It's detective stuff."

Mrs. Sweeney shifted her frown to me for a moment, then answered Old Red slowly and firmly.

"Alfred Hinkle was our friend, not our errand boy."

"Right. Fine. Thank you," my brother said.

He walked quickly back to the body, eager to put that particular line of investigation behind him.

"This has gone on long enough," Ed Sweeney growled. "Get off our land. *All of you.*"

"Ain't quite done, Ed," Old Red said, kneeling beside Hinkle again. He still had two more pockets to check—the ones in the marshal's vest. My brother's eyes widened when he unbuttoned the dead man's coat to get at them, and a moment later, we could all see why.

Old Red was pulling out a tightly wound wad of cash.

"Not your...errand boy, huh?" Haney said to the Sweeneys.

"Well, the proof is in the pudding." He jabbed a meaty finger at the money while looking around at his men like they were a jury on horseback. "A payout from some…crooked cattle dealer. He's been in it with the rustlers all along."

"Don't be ridiculous," Mrs. Sweeney said. But Ed and Johnny exchanged a shifty, tight-lipped look that seemed to say the money on the marshal wasn't a surprise.

Old Red, meanwhile, was quickly counting out the bills. He might not be able to read "five dollars," but a "5" on a greenback, he knows by sight.

"If the marshal was in on something with the Sweeneys," he said, "why would they kill him?"

"They had a falling out," Bartlett said. "Over money, probably."

"Over money…which they don't even take off his body after they back-shoot him?" My brother looked up at Bartlett and gave him a dubious look and a shake of the head. "That don't fit at all."

He rolled the cash back up and returned it to Hinkle's vest.

"Fit?" said Haney. "He had a fight with a Sweeney, and then he was murdered on Sweeney land. That's all the fit I need." He turned a cold stare on Compton. "You want to stick your nose into this, Flip? Then do your duty and haul Ed Sweeney off to jail…or get the hell out of here and leave justice to me."

"I'll give you justice, you murderous bastard," Mrs. Sweeney said, lifting up her shotgun again.

All those hands hovering over all those holsters were finally filled with pistol grips as men on both sides drew their irons. Even Haney whipped out a Colt. In about a half-second, it seemed, Marshal Hinkle was going to have a lot of company down in the dirt. Someone needed to do some mighty fast talking before the first trigger got squeezed.

"Uhh…oh…umm," I heard Deputy Compton splutter.

There was now half a half-second left. Not even enough time for a sigh as I realized who was the man for the job when fast-talking was called for.

"Whoa there! Looks like the gunfight at the O.K. Corral all over again. And that ain't O.K.!" I said with a big, hearty, entirely fake laugh. To be on the safe side, I made sure my hands were well away from my sides—and my gun belt. "Mr. Haney, Bartlett...I do believe there's something important you two're overlookin'."

Haney and Bartlett didn't lower their guns, but they did at least take their eyes off whatever target they'd picked so they could look my way.

"What?" Haney said.

"Y'all claim Ed Sweeney threatened the marshal last night," I said. "Well, maybe he did, maybe he didn't. But what the deputy here knows for a fact—because he saw it with his own eyes—is that Bartlett and the rest of your boys there most definitely, publicly, no-ifs-ands-or-buts, *did* threaten the marshal. And the deputy himself, as a matter of fact. Yesterday. In Mr. Martinez's store. And that juicy little bit of gossip has had time to make its way from one end of DeBarge to the other and halfway to Denver to boot."

"So?" Bartlett said.

"*So*, if there was to be shootin' here and something was to happen to Deputy Compton and me and my brother...tragically hit by stray bullets, say, with no malice aforethought, of course... folks might not take your word for it when you say the Sweeneys murdered the marshal and then drew on you and in all the confusion everyone you've ever threatened around here suddenly ended up punched fulla holes. Might be greeted with skepticism. And warrants. And trials. And nooses."

Bartlett's eyes slid from me to Haney, and I thought maybe —*maybe*—I saw the business end of his gun angle down a mite.

Haney just kept staring at me.

"So you know what the deputy would advise you to do?" I went on with a nod toward Compton, who was watching me with wide eyes and a slack jaw. "Ease back and let things play out as they will. Flip here's gonna take the body to town and wire the sheriff about what's happened and set everything in motion for an inquest. At which, no doubt, Ed Sweeney will be called to testify.

And you and the deputy and probably even me. It'll be quite the heartwarming reunion, actually, and I'm sure we will look back on this troubled time and laugh. Because we will all still be alive."

As I spoke, Bartlett's gun seemed to angle down a bit more. Everyone's did except Haney's. I didn't know if I was getting through to anyone or not, but at least I'd blathered on so long that most of their hands were getting tired.

"I guess my little chat with Hinkle probably was the talk of the town yesterday," Bartlett said to Haney.

"That's right. It was," Compton said, voice quavering. "Everyone in town knows you threatened Alf."

"Now, now. There were no threats. Just a little conversation about where I do my shopping," Bartlett said. "I would never threaten a duly appointed lawman…though I suppose I can see how people might get the wrong idea."

He spoke slowly, soothingly, eyes shifting from Compton to Haney. His gun hand had dipped even lower by the time he was done.

He was sending a clear message to his boss.

Not now. It wouldn't look right.
  Just wait.

Haney took a deep breath, then jammed his Colt into its holster. Bartlett stowed his gun, too, and Jody and the rest of the men around him followed suit. Some seemed relieved. The twins looked disappointed.

I gave the Sweeneys and their men a pointed look, and they lowered their weapons, as well.

"'Blessed are the peacemakers,'" I said with satisfaction. I had to compliment myself because the odds of my brother doing it—even when I've just talked the Grim Reaper into swiping his scythe elsewhere—are usually pretty slim.

"Alright. We'll leave this to you…Flip. For now," Haney said. "But we know who's to blame…and who's to pay."

He threw a hate-filled squint at Ed Sweeney—then slid it first to me, then to my brother, holding it on each of us a moment to make sure we didn't miss it.

It was obvious that Old Red's first deduction about the man, made sight unseen, had been correct: He was an asshole. And now it was just obvious that he hated our guts for thwarting, however temporarily, his latest assholery.

He savagely jerked his horse toward Eagle Creek and the gently sloping valley wall beyond it. As Haney rode off, Bartlett doffed his hat to the Sweeneys with a sly "I'll see you later" smile. Then he followed his boss, Jody and the twins and the other gunmen right behind him.

"Thank you," Mrs. Sweeney said to me.

She looked over at my brother, who was still kneeling beside the marshal's body, and said it again.

"Thank you."

Old Red watched the drifting dust cloud that Haney and his bunch kicked up as they rode away, then finally stood.

"You can do more than thank us, ma'am," he said. "I'd say it's high time you hired us."

TEN
THE ROCKS AND THE HARD PLACE

OR, MY BROTHER FINDS CLUES IN SOME ROCKY SPOTS, AND THAT PUTS US IN A TOUGH ONE

"THIS IS your plan for making amends to Miss Crowe and the colonel?" I wanted to say to my brother. "You want us to go to work *for the rustlers we were sent to catch?*"

But I couldn't even get in a good scoff, because Ed Sweeney was beating me to it.

"How stupid do you think we are?" he said. "You show up and claim you're too high-minded to work for Clayton Haney, then he fires you right in front of us, and now out of the goodness of your hearts, you offer to help us?"

Old Red shrugged. "It ain't outta the goodness of our hearts if we're gettin' paid. As for how stupid I think you are, Ed...that remains to be seen."

Ed's already dark face flushed even darker.

"Ed," Mrs. Sweeney said from her surrey.

The one word was enough. Ed clenched his jaw and looked away.

"Old Red and Big Red aren't trying to spy for Haney, if that's what you're thinking, Ed," Deputy Compton said. "When Bartlett picked a fight with me and Alf yesterday, they really backed us."

Ed growled out something that sounded like "Playacting" but

left it at that. The men on horseback around him—his brother Johnny and the Sweeneys' cowhands—watched him warily. Like a lot of men with a temper, it seemed, Ed Sweeney was nitroglycerin: Shake him up, and he might explode.

"Why should we hire you?" Mrs. Sweeney said to my brother. She pointed her well-padded chin at Hinkle's sprawled body. "We didn't do that to poor Alf."

"Ma'am, I wouldn't be offerin' our services if I didn't believe that already," Old Red said. "But ain't everybody gonna see it that way...especially with Haney and Bartlett doin' everything they can to get your son there blamed for it. And you know what's liable to happen if he's taken into custody."

Mrs. Sweeney nodded grimly. "Another lynching by the 'vigilantes.'"

My brother nodded along. "You gotta make sure Ed's in the clear. And quick."

"And if we pay you, you'll put him in the clear?" Johnny asked.

"Well, we surely will try," Old Red said.

"They've done it before," Deputy Compton said. "Solved crimes, caught murderers. They've been in all the magazines for it."

Ed snorted and started to say something. All it took was a look from his mother to shut him up again.

"When we hire a hand, we always ask for a demonstration," she said, turning back to Old Red. "Show us what you can do."

"Ma'am, you already got yourself a free sample—when you saw me work out that there was more than one killer and they didn't bother searchin' the body."

"That's seeing you ride," Mrs. Sweeney replied. "Now I need to know if you can rope."

My brother eyed the woman silently a moment, then waved a hand at the buttes to the north. "The killers was back thataway hidin' in the rocks, I reckon. Shall we see what I can get a rope on there?"

Mrs. Sweeney nodded. "Yes. Let's."

At Old Red's request, the Sweeneys' hands were put to work gathering up Marshal Hinkle's remains and tying them to his horse for the return to town. Then the rest of us—my brother and me, Deputy Compton, Mrs. Sweeney, Johnny, and Ed—rode off toward Cañada de los Vaqueros.

"Your audience just got even bigger," I said to Old Red as we approached Eagle Creek and the big rocks at the base of the bluffs.

I jerked my head toward the east. A pair of riders were watching us from a rise about a quarter mile off—two of Haney's gunmen left behind to keep an eye on us.

"I saw 'em," my brother said without bothering to turn his head. His gaze was glued to the ground, searching the scrubby brush and dry, yellow-brown dirt for clues.

"I'm just glad Col. Crowe ain't here to see this, too," I said, dropping my voice low. "He hires us out to catch cattle thieves and you wanna put us on their payroll?"

"He'd say himself the Double-A needs customers," Old Red replied, eyes still pointed down. "Better they be thieves than murderers."

"Oh, I agree. But my real preference would be for neither."

Old Red had nothing to say to that. He had a puzzle to bust, and in the moment, I suspected, that trumped who he was doing it for.

"Hel-lo," he said a minute later. He stopped his horse and practically threw himself out of the saddle. "Don't let my mount wander off."

I reached over and gathered up the reins as Old Red went scurrying away. He was doubled over so far it looked like he wasn't just staring at the dirt now but on the verge of sniffing it, blood-hound style.

"Stay back!" he called out. "Can't have you mussin' anything up!"

Deputy Compton and the others stopped just behind me.

"So he really does that," the deputy marveled as my brother

went zigzagging toward an outcropping of elevated rock as broad and flat as a theater stage. "Just like in your stories."

"Oh, yes," I sighed. "It's all too true."

"There, there, there and there," my brother said, jabbing a finger downward. "And there. And there."

"There, there and there what?" Mrs. Sweeney asked, rising up from the seat of her surrey to peer Old Red's way.

"Somebody made water, ma'am," my brother told her. "Over the side of this here ledge, from the looks of it. Dried hours ago, of course, but you can still see the splatter in the soil."

Old Red started scrambling up the rough, gravel-strewn incline until he was atop the big rock.

"That's a lot of relief someone needed," I said.

"Sure was," my brother said. "Instructive, wouldn't you say?"

He began doing his bent-over scuttle around the rock's broad, flat top.

"It's 'instructive' that there were men here with small bladders?" Johnny Sweeney asked, incredulous.

"It's instructive that they kept fillin' 'em," Old Red said.

Ed Sweeney snorted with annoyance and moved his horse closer to his mother's buggy.

"Let's go," he said. "He's just making up a bunch of nonsense."

He'd dropped his voice low, for once, but not so low that my brother's big jug ears couldn't pick up his words.

"I ain't makin' up the spent shells up here. Nor the footprints, neither," Old Red said, pointing down. "Two men. In boots." He stood up to his full height to scowl at a far corner of the rock. "Drunk."

Ed rolled his eyes. "How could you possibly know they were drunk?"

"Cuz not only were they pissin' up a storm, one of 'em upchucked. Plus, there's this, if it ain't plain enough already."

Old Red scooped up a brown bottle that glinted in the morning sun. He waggled it in the air and said, "Heads up, Brother," then tossed it down to me.

I freed my hands of reins just in time to catch it.

I didn't have to ask why my brother was throwing bottles at me. This one had a label on it, with words in fancy scrollwork beneath a picture of a charging stallion.

"'Ballard's Best Extra Fine Rye Whiskey,'" I read out. "'Frank Ballard & Sons Distilling, Louisville, Kentucky.'"

"Not the usual two-bit rotgut," Old Red said. "Y'all ever hear of it?"

Compton, Mrs. Sweeney, and Johnny shook their heads.

"What difference does that make?" Ed said.

My brother shook his head, too—slowly and sadly, as if for the folly of Man.

"It's data, mister. Facts. A fella should be on friendly terms with 'em," he said. "Flip, I reckon you oughta take that bottle in. These shells, too. Plain ol' .44-40s, I'm thinkin'."

"Which means I can introduce you to another fact, Sweeney," I said to Ed. "The killers probably carry '73 Winchesters."

"Half the men in the saddle do." Ed reached down to pat the rifle butt jutting from a scabbard under his left leg. "Even I…"

He snapped his mouth shut.

Mrs. Sweeney heaved a sigh.

"Ma'am, I don't know if you should let your son ride around with rope," I said, pointing at the coiled lariat hanging beside Ed's saddle horn. "He seems bound and determined to get some wrapped around his neck."

"Shut up, Amilema…Amply…Ammel…"

"Amlingmeyer," Compton told Ed.

Ed didn't give the name another try, settling instead for a simple glare. Still, I obliged him by closing my mouth, though I was sorely tempted to ask Old Red why we should save a man I wouldn't half-mind hanging myself.

While Compton rode over to take the whiskey bottle from me, my brother gathered up the shells and clambered down off the big rock. He gave the shells to Compton, then walked off toward a thick cluster of sagebrush.

"They had their horses picketed over yonder," he said. "You

can see the turds when you get a little height. Their trail in and out, too. Came in through the canyon and left thataway. It's a wonder you didn't ride straight into 'em, Ed."

Ed had finally learned his lesson. He said nothing. To my surprise, though, it wasn't my brother he chose to throw a resentful glare at. It was Compton. And Mrs. Sweeney and Johnny were watching the deputy, as well.

Then it hit me: Old Red and I had lessons to learn ourselves. About handling clients, for instance—and the things they'd rather not discuss in front of a lawman.

"It's probably time you headed back to town, Flip," I said. "Folks are surely startin' to wonder what's become of you and Marshal Hinkle. And you'll wanna get the marshal squared away before the full heat of day sets in, if you follow me."

"Well..."

Compton looked over at my brother, who'd gone to his hands and knees about fifty feet away.

"Two horses. Average size. Shod. Healthy," he announced. "Nothin' special."

"See?" I said to the deputy. "I don't think there's anything more to learn here, and if there is, Gustav and I will tell you about it in a bit. You've got a long ride ahead that you'll wanna take slow so the marshal don't come loose. We'll catch up to you before you're halfway back to DeBarge."

Old Red stood and dusted off his hands. "Otto's right, Flip. You get started. We'll be along directly."

"Alright...I guess that makes sense," Compton said. He took his leave of Mrs. Sweeny with a touch of the hat brim and a mumbled, "Ma'am."

"Thank you for coming, Flip," she said. "And I'm sorry about Alf."

"Someone's gonna be even sorrier," he said. "That's a promise."

He rode off toward the Sweeney ranch hands, who had Hinkle's horse—and Hinkle—ready for him.

"So," I said to the Sweeneys, "what is it you didn't wanna say while the deputy was around?"

"What are you talking about?" said Ed.

But Johnny looked to his mother.

"There is something," she told me.

"*Mother*," Ed snapped.

She silenced him with a raised hand, then went on talking.

"Ed didn't come back through the canyon last night. There's another trail to the north, further from the Pecos Bend. A secret trail. He and Johnny and the boys take it if they're riding back from town after dark. We don't think anyone else knows about it…and we want to keep it that way."

"So none of us ends up like Alf Hinkle," Johnny added.

"You're sayin' that's why Ed didn't run across Hinkle's body or his horse?" I said. "He didn't come this way at all?"

Mrs. Sweeney nodded.

"And that's *all* you're sayin'?" I pressed.

Mrs. Sweeney nodded again.

"What else is she supposed to say?" Ed snarled at me.

"She's supposed to tell me the truth," I wanted to tell him. "And so are you if you wanna get out of this alive."

But Old Red replied first.

"You can forget about keepin' that secret trail secret. It's a good idea to have one with Haney's men out there gunnin' for ya, yeah. But it's more important at this point to be believed…especially when the sheriff shows up and there's an inquest. You can't hold back anything that could help clear Ed."

"Thank you for the free advice, Mr. Amlingmeyer," Mrs. Sweeney said. "Now tell me why I should pay for more."

"Well, ma'am…you've heard everything I've learned," my brother said. "Hinkle was shot from this spot by two drunk men in boots. They came here with a bottle of Kentucky rye, and most likely, Winchester rifles. When they was done, rather than go over Hinkle's body for valuables, they rode back into the canyon. So if a man wanted to track 'em down, that'd be the way to go. To the north. Toward town. Not toward your HQ. I will gladly place my hand upon a Bible and say all that at an inquest or a trial. And I might have more to say, too…like who the killers really are. Assumin' my brother and I are still in the county to testify, that is. Our detectivin' does tend to take us every which way."

"That worth payin' for, ma'am?" I threw in. I didn't even like the idea of working for the Sweeneys, but I couldn't resist placing the cherry atop such a perfect confection as Old Red's sales pitch.

While Mrs. Sweeney thought it over, she swiveled her head to watch Compton lead Hinkle's horse toward the canyon. The deputy—the only official law within a hundred miles now—rode with slumped shoulders and bowed head, looking as lifeless as the marshal tied over a saddle behind him.

"Remind me," Mrs. Sweeney said. "What rate did Haney hire you at?"

"Thirty dollars a day, with a bonus of five hundred if we got results," I told her.

"Alright…I can pay ten a day." The lady shrugged. "I'm not Clayton Haney."

"That's the whole reason we're here talkin'," my brother said. "As for your rate, we'll accept, with one provision: The bonus stands. If Ed's exeronted…" He looked over at me, a touch of blush coloring his sunken cheeks. "I get that right?"

"Exonerated," I said.

"Right, yeah. If that happens—no arrest after the inquest, the real killers in custody, whatever it happens to look like—you owe us five hundred dollars."

"That's too much," Mrs. Sweeney said with a shake of the head.

Old Red's pitch might have been perfect, yet she seemed perfectly happy to pass on it.

I sighed and fixed first her and then my brother with a forlorn look. What I was about to say, I wanted it clear, was for both of them.

"We are not the A.A. Western Detective Agency. We are here as its representatives. As such, we only have so much independence…which we have already pushed far, far past. There will be hell to pay when we get back to Ogden. A hell that can only be escaped one way: through a healthy fee. So, using what remains of my latitude, I am willing to accommodate a special, one-time-only, 'You Are Not Clayton Haney,' markdown. We will work for ten dollars a day...and if Ed is exonerated, the Sweeney family will owe the Double-A a discounted bounty of four hundred and ninety-nine dollars. I'll cover the extra dollar myself. If that is still too high a price to pay for saving Ed's neck, I will understand and shall wish the Sweeneys well as I return to Ogden and whatever paying work awaits me there."

Mrs. Sweeney looked at my brother, plainly gauging if his heels were dug in as deep as mine.

They were. He gave me a nod, then silently returned the lady's gaze.

"Fine," she said. "Deal."

My sense of satisfaction lasted about one second.

We'd managed to find a new client for the Double-A...by switching sides in the middle of a range war. And going to work for the rustlers. The *heavily outgunned* rustlers. Some of whom, judging by Ed's look of distrustful disgust, still preferred pointing their guns at us.

Old Red saw the chagrin on my face.

"Like you say, Brother: We need that fee. So let's get to earnin' it," he said. He walked back to his horse and swung up into the saddle. "Tell me, Ed...where is this 'secret trail' of yours?"

ELEVEN
THE SHUSHING
OR, OLD RED AIMS TO AVOID MY
QUESTIONS, WHILE SOMEONE ELSE
ENDS UP AIMING AT US

MY BROTHER and Ed Sweeney engaged in some spirited debate over the definition of "secret trail"—Ed arguing that if you point people to one, it's no longer secret—but Old Red prevailed, with the help of Mrs. Sweeney.

"Just spit it out, Ed, or I'll have *him* do it for you," she said. She nodded at Johnny Sweeney, who was sitting silently atop his horse between his mother's buggy and his big brother. "If Mr. Amlingmeyer didn't go see the trail for himself, he wouldn't be doing his job."

"That's it exactly, ma'am," Old Red said.

"Alright. Fine," Ed snarled. He jerked a hand at the mesas towering nearby like the tall walls of some great yellow castle. "There's a rockfall two miles west of the canyon. Steep. It doesn't look like it leads anywhere, but when you get to the top you'll see a trail that'll take you over the bluffs. It's slow going, but…you know. Secret. And safe." He shot a glare at his mother. "Till now."

"Thank you," my brother said.

He gave the lady a nod and a "Ma'am," then started his horse northward with a "Heyah!"

While "Ma'am…heyah!" and the pounding of galloping

hooves made for a nice, dramatic exit, it seemed to me that a little more in the way of parting was called for, these being—to my dismay—our new employers.

"You'll hear from us when we have something to report," I said. "In the meantime, Ed should stick to the rancho. All of ya oughta, probably."

"Sound advice," Mrs. Sweeney said.

Johnny nodded.

Ed opened his mouth to offer his own reply, but by the time he got it out, I couldn't hear it over the pounding of my own horse's hooves. This I did not consider a great loss.

Old Red stayed ahead of me as a couple of miles whipped past, the shrub-pocked desert grassland to our left and the sheer walls of the mesas to our right. He finally slowed to a trot as we approached a broad, jagged heap of sandstone shards along the cliff wall, yet I remained behind him. He was searching the ground for a trail sign, and I knew what he'd say if I got in his way.

"Ed wasn't happy about us checkin' his story," I said.

My brother leaned out so far from his saddle, it seemed to defy the law of gravity that he didn't fall straight to the yellow-brown ground he was eyeing so intently. The only reply I got from him was a grunt.

"And I'm bettin' there's even more he'll be unhappy about soon enough," I said.

Old Red stayed mum.

I didn't.

"The Sweeneys still ain't tellin' us everything. And I sure don't believe Ed when he says he went into Hinkle's office last night to talk politics."

Something in the rocks caught Old Red's eye, and he rode over for a closer look without saying a word.

"Makes a tricky job trickier," I said. "The Man himself would have a tough time findin' his way to the truth if even his client was pointin' him in the wrong direction."

It was the best bait I had for drawing out my brother's tongue:

Sherlock Holmes. Yet Old Red just sat up straight in his saddle
and looked to the south, then back to the rocks, then to the south
again.

He turned his horse and rode eastward—back toward where
we'd left the Sweeneys.

"Hey!"

I set off after him. I knew it was no use trying to ask what he
was up to, though: He kept his calico mare at a gallop so he'd
have an excuse not to answer. He didn't slow to a trot till we were
back near Eagle Creek and the canyon through which it flowed.
The Sweeneys and their men were gone.

Old Red swiveled in his saddle for one last, long look to the
south, then swung north into the ravine.

"You didn't wanna follow Ed's 'secret trail'?" I said as I trotted
along just behind him.

He was pointing his eyes down again, scanning the ground.

"Nope," he said.

"But it was there?"

"Yup."

"And you don't need a better look at it?"

"Nope."

"Why not?"

Old Red huffed out a gruff sigh but didn't look up.

"Cuz it was there but it was hard to spot—you know, *secret*—
and it'd been used recently," he said.

"Meaning Ed's story checked out. That part of it, at least."

"Yes."

"So you decided to come back here and follow the killers' trail
instead?"

"More or less."

"More or less? What's that mean?"

"I decided to *try* to follow the killers' trail, goddammit."

"Ah. I see. Would be tough, wouldn't it? A lotta people have
been back and forth along this creek the last day."

"Yeah, there's that. And then there's all the noise hereabouts.
So much damned racket a fella can't think."

"Noise?" I said. "Why, Brother, I don't hear a thing. If you weren't such a chatterbox, it'd be silent as the grave."

Old Red sighed again.

"But as long as you're feelin' so talkative," I went on, "maybe you'd like to tell me how you're gonna explain this to Diana and the colonel. You know there ain't a cattleman's association in the country that's gonna give a dime to the Double-A once it gets out how we switched sides here."

My brother stiffened in his saddle. His only reply to me was a startled "Oh."

We'd just burned our bridge to the most cash to be had for a "Western Detective Agency": working for stockmen to protect their herds. And Old Red hadn't even realized it. He'd been so intent on Holmesing that he forgot to worry about starving.

"Oh, well. I'm sure the Double-A will get by," I said. "There's always lost spectacles to find and stray dogs to return to their rightful owners. Gotta be plenty of money in that, right?"

"Is it possible for you to give me a single minute to work in peace?" my brother grumbled.

"Why, of course, it is."

I gave him two.

"You know, goin' to work for rustlers might actually be the smartest business decision we ever made," I said when time was up. "There's more thieves than ranches if you tally 'em up one by one. Once it gets around that we'll help 'em keep their necks unstretched for a mere four hundred and ninety-nine dollars apiece, every brand artist west of the Mississippi is gonna be linin' up to hire us."

Old Red opted for the direct approach this time.

"Shut up," he said.

He finally lifted his gaze and turned my way, but it wasn't me he was looking at. He was peering past me.

I turned for a look, too. I saw nothing but sheer rock walls, pockets of tall brush along the creek bed and just off the trail, the skull of some unlucky, long-dead longhorn. The canyon curved as it cut through the buttes, so the valley behind us was blocked from view. As would be anyone riding up behind us.

Old Red stopped his horse and cocked his head.

I did the same.

I heard the wind as it whistled through the ravine. The water as it rippled over the rocks. The distant cry of a hawk on the wing. The splatter of piss as my pinto relieved himself. And nothing else.

"You hear something?" I asked my brother.

"Maybe."

"How about you?" I asked the cow skull. "You hear anything?"

The skull just stared up at me with its black, empty eyes.

"He says no," I told Old Red.

"Well, I think I did," he muttered. "Idjit."

"Coulda been Flip. He's up ahead of us somewhere with the marshal's body."

Old Red shook his head. "It was from back there. Behind us."

I heaved a theatrical sigh. "Who do you think's trailin' us—the former client who hates us or the current client who hates us?"

"Could be someone else. Could be nobody."

"Well, at least we know it ain't both of 'em. They'd be shootin' at each other already. You know when it ain't a good idea to—?"

My brother shushed me.

We sat there atop our horses for a moment, listening. I heard the same thing as before, minus the horse piss. But Old Red's ears are sharper than mine—along with his eyes and his wits, he'd say —and he seemed to notice a sound he didn't like. He frowned, cocked his head even further, narrowed his eyes, and frowned harder. Then he straightened up and pointed at a large outcropping of rock a little further up the canyon. He started his horse toward it, and I followed.

The day just kept getting better and better.

The time had come to take cover.

We remained in the saddle once we were hidden behind the rock—the better for making a quick retreat if need be. I was all for making a quick retreat even if need weren't, actually. But I knew my brother's curiosity would keep him rooted there till it was satisfied. So there I stayed, as silent and still as Old Red. For a while.

"You know when it ain't a good idea to play both sides off against the middle?" I finally said.

My brother replied with another shush.

"When you're *in* the middle," I continued, "and both sides have guns."

That got me shushed again. Which didn't stop me from talking. Or Old Red from shushing.

What finally broke the cycle—and momentarily closed my mouth—was a sound that came echoing around the bend, low, slow, and steady.

Hooves.

Someone was riding up behind us after all.

My brother was already peering over the big boulder we were hiding behind, so I pushed myself up for a peek, as well. What I saw had been the stuff of nightmares for me in my youngest years, when the Cheyenne were still known to go on the warpath from time to time, not far from our Kansas farm.

An Indian was riding slowly around the bend on a spotted white pony, a rifle butt jutting up by his left thigh. He wasn't a Cheyenne, that was clear—not this far south, and not with his high-topped moccasin boots and the red handkerchief tied around his head.

I shrunk down behind the rock again.

"An Apache," I whispered to Old Red. "Damn. You reckon he's one of the men who killed—?"

"Shhh."

I hushed up, but my horse didn't: He shook his head and blew out an exasperated snort. We'd been bunched up behind that rock long enough for his tastes. I sympathized but shot him a "Shhh" nevertheless. Old Red shot one right back at *me*—as he reached down for his forty-five.

"What are you aimin' to do?" I whispered.

For the fiftieth time that day, I got shushed.

For the first time, the shushing came from someone other than my brother. Someone behind us.

Old Red widened his eyes, his hand mere inches from his Colt, while by sheer reflex, I started to look back over my shoulder.

"*No*," a man said.

The word came out soft, but what followed amplified it a thousandfold.

The man was cocking a gun.

It was unclear who he was speaking to or aiming at: me or Old Red. And it didn't matter. We both froze.

The hoofbeats of the approaching pony grew louder. Another half a minute, and the man atop it would be passing right by. White folks like to give Indians credit for a near-supernatural ability to read the landscape, but that Apache wouldn't need any such thing to spot us. A blind Dutchman in need of an ear trumpet couldn't have missed us. So the question was: What did the fellow with the drop on us intend to do about it?

"Just sit tight, gentlemen," he told us, voice low. "We don't wanna startle him."

It was some relief to realize he wasn't an Apache himself—not unless the tribe had spread to Alabama and picked up accents to match. Why he was holding a gun on us when an Indian brave was on his way remained a mystery...one that had my heart thumping and a cold sweat trickling down my back.

The Apache's pony came closer and closer, yet the man behind us said no more and did nothing I could hear.

At last, the horse drew even with us, then ambled past. *Just* the horse. The Apache—and his rifle—were gone.

But not for long. Suddenly he was popping up on the big rock before us with both a scowl and a Winchester pointed our way.

The man behind us finally spoke again...to say something in Apache. Maybe the tribe had spread to Alabama after all. Whoever he was and whatever he said, the Indian with the rifle sure liked it.

He squinted at me and Old Red a moment, then threw back his head and laughed.

TWELVE
THE INDIAN FIGHTER
OR, OLD RED AND OUR CAPTORS TRADE QUESTIONS, WHILE I'M FORCED TO TRADE BLOWS

THE APACHE on the rock went on guffawing for what seemed like a week, the muzzle of his rifle never wavering. When he was finally done, he looked at the man who'd got the drop on me and Old Red, and said something in what I assumed was his native tongue.

I don't speak a lick of any Indian language nor does my brother, though Old Red had picked up some of the hand signs different tribes once used to parley on the Plains. That might have helped us ask an Arapaho, "Which way to the Red River?" but it wasn't going to do us any good here. It felt like *nothing* would do us any good—especially when the man with the gun on us spoke again.

"Take off your gun belts," he ordered in his Southern drawl. "Slow."

I glanced over at Old Red. Two men with Winchesters had killed Marshal Hinkle, he'd said. Now here we were up against two men, one of whom—the one we could see—had a Winchester he seemed all too ready to use. Were we really going to put ourselves at the mercy of what was most likely the killers?

Yes, as it happened. We were.

Old Red looked over at me and gave a reluctant nod.

We both brought our hands to our buckles and started to unfasten them.

"Careful with your irons, fellas," I said. "If one were to go off —you know, accidental-like—there're folks at both ends of this canyon liable to hear and come runnin'."

"Oh, yeah?" the man behind us said. "And just who are these 'folks'?"

"Assorted friends and associates."

"They'll be quicker on the trigger than I was," Old Red said. "I was just curious. Feller's got a right to know who's comin' up the trail behind him, don't he? Speakin' of which, who are you two?"

He held his gun belt out to the side as if expecting the South-erner to step up and take it. Which might have given Old Red the opportunity to trample him with his horse or clonk him on the head or *something*.

"Just drop it. Both of you," the man said. He could have been anywhere in age between twenty-five and fifty—not young but not yet old—and he sounded tolerantly amused by my brother's attempt at treachery, as if he'd seen it a thousand times before and had seen it fail every time.

I let my gun belt fall to the ground beside my animal. Old Red did the same.

"Thank you," the man said. "As for me and my associate… well, you can think of me as Señor Noddy, and that's Geronimo."

The Indian tapped his chest and said something in Apache.

"My mistake," "Señor Noddy" said. "He's Cochise."

"Cochise" nodded happily.

My brother locked eyes with the Apache and contorted his fingers into a series of shapes. It looked like he was trying to make shadow puppets without the benefit of a wall and candle. I figured it was Indian sign language, probably for, "We're just a couple harmless cowboys passin' through. Why not wish us good day and let us go on our way?"

The Apache lifted his left hand—the one that was keeping the barrel of his Winchester steady—and began fluttering it spastically before his face. He was making fun of my brother's attempt to communicate, and just to make sure we got the point, he ended his hand-flapping with his middle finger upraised in a salute one needed no knowledge of sign language to interpret.

The Apache laughed again, then said something to us in his own language.

"'Tell it to the buffalo people,' he says," Señor Noddy interpreted. "'If you can find any anymore.'"

"'The buffalo people'?" I said.

"The Kiowa. The Comanche. The Pawnee," Old Red explained. "Him, he's mountain people, I reckon. Mescalero."

The Apache had both hands back on his Winchester, and he jabbed the rifle out at my brother and spoke again.

"He's impressed," Noddy said.

The Apache swung his rifle toward me and said some more.

"But it's you he's really interested in," the man behind us went on.

"Me? Why?"

Instead of answering, Noddy said some more in Apache. His Indian friend's lopsided grin grew wider.

"Alright, cowboys," Noddy said. "That body in the valley... who was it?"

If he wanted to play dumb about the marshal, I was more than happy to play along. He and the Apache would feel less inclined to raise their tally to three murders if they thought they could get away with the one.

"It's Marshal Hinkle. From DeBarge," I said. "It's a real shame. Looks like he got caught up in a feud between a couple of cattle outfits. I bet they never even figure out which side shot him."

Noddy grunted out a dry chortle. "Oh, yeah. Pretty dangerous, stickin' your nose into a range war. Especially if you don't have any 'friends and associates' around."

"Yup. There's a reason they don't call it a 'range picnic,'" I said cheerfully. "Well, now that we've straightened all that out, my brother and I will be on our way. Hinkle's deputy is expectin' us to be along shortly, and I'm sure none of us want the man to be kept waitin'."

I started to lift my reins. But before I could head my horse back out to the trail, the Apache snapped something at me that needed no translation.

Noddy translated anyway.

"Hold it," he said. "We're not done here."

I lowered my reins.

"He's right, Otto. We ain't done," Old Red said. "I still got some questions."

"*You've* got some questions?" Noddy chuckled.

"Yessir. Like who you two really are. It's clear you been watchin' us for a while—wouldn't know about the body if you hadn't. But you don't seem to be with the Sweeneys and don't seem to be from the Pecos Bend. So who are you?"

"Well, there's a simple answer for that, ain't there?" Noddy said. "How do you know we're not *bandidos* who killed the marshal and are now about to kill you?"

I stiffened in my saddle and got set to dig in my spurs.

"It's pretty obvious that's what your brother thinks," Noddy said.

"Yeah, well…my brother's been known to be wrong. Often," Old Red said. "And I know he is again because *bandidos* go through a man's pockets after they kill him. Hinkle wasn't robbed. And your partner up there on the rock might have the right rifle for the job, but what he's got on his feet is all wrong. The men who shot the marshal were wearin' white man's boots, with heels, not flat-bottom moccasins. So I ask again: Who are you?"

"Well, well, well," Noddy said. "The man can track. And think."

He and the Apache exchanged a few words, and the Indian nodded, still grinning.

"Tell you what," Noddy said. "You tell us who you're workin' for and I'll tell you who we really are."

Old Red cocked his head, mulling it over.

"It's gonna get around all over the county soon enough anyhow," I told him. "I don't see the harm in tellin' these gents now."

Whereas I did, of course, see the harm in *not* giving them what they wanted. I make a fairly large target, and the Apache's rifle was still pointed where it couldn't help but hit it.

"Alright," Old Red said. "We are Otto and Gustav Amlingmeyer and we work for the A.A. Western Detective Agency."

"And who does the A.A. Western Detective Agency work for?" Noddy pressed.

"At the moment? The Sweeney family of Rancho Cañada de los Vaqueros. But ask me again tomorrow," I said. "Uhh…better yet, *don't*."

The man behind us gave that a long, drawn-out "Umm hmm," then lapsed into silence.

"Well?" Old Red said. "Your turn."

"Oh, don't worry," Noddy said. "I always keep my word… sooner or later."

The Apache jabbed his Winchester at me and said something to his partner.

"Sure. Why not?" Noddy said. "Boys, we've got another bargain for you. We will let you go…if Otto can beat my friend here in a fight."

The Apache beamed at me. He seemed maybe thirty-five or forty, with rough, sun-baked skin that made him look as tough and taut as a bullwhip. It would probably hurt just to shake his hand.

"Why the hell does he want to fight *me*?" I asked.

"Because you're the big one," Noddy said.

"Allow me to rephrase that. Why the hell does he want to *fight* me?"

"Curiosity."

The Apache spoke again.

"Plus, he's gettin' bored," Noddy told us. "Too much talkin'."

The Apache hopped off the rock and jogged over to his horse, which had ambled off to Eagle Creek for a drink. He slid his

Winchester into its scabbard, then turned around and gleefully waved for me to join him by the stream.

"Hold on, Otto," Old Red said.

"Oh, I'm holdin'," I replied.

My brother started to turn to look behind us.

"Don't do it, cowboy," Noddy snapped.

Old Red froze.

"I was just gonna ask how we know you'll hold to the bargain," he said.

"Well, I'd just ask *you* what choice you have."

My brother grunted, then pointed at the Apache. "I was also gonna say it ain't a fair fight. He's got him a knife."

Indeed, there was a large sheath on the belt the Apache was wearing around his loose blue tunic. Judging by its size and that of the hickory handle that protruded from it, he was carrying a Bowie knife only slightly smaller than a cavalryman's saber.

Noddy and the Apache exchanged a few words, and the Indian drew out his knife, tossed it about thirty feet away, then gestured again for me to dismount.

"Well, thanks a lot, Brother. He got rid of the knife," I whispered. "Now he'll have to kill me with his bare hands."

"You're bigger and younger than him, and you've been in enough scraps to pick up a trick or two. You can beat him," Old Red whispered back. "Try to get a look at the talker while you're at it."

"No more chitchat," "the talker" drawled. "If you want us to let you go, Otto, you'll get down and fight."

I took in a deep breath. For all I knew, it was one of my last, so I savored it.

"Alright," I sighed. "I'm comin'."

I swung down off my horse, settling my feet just inches from my abandoned gun belt on the rocky ground. If I dropped down to grab it, I'd have to hope Señor Noddy was a terrible shot, for he'd have several seconds to put holes in me before I could draw my gun and get a bead on him.

I decided to stick to the plan and take my chances with the Apache.

I started to pivot to the left, moving my face Noddy's way as I turned toward the creek.

"Uh-uh. The other way," Noddy said. "It's my friend you need to keep your eyes on."

So I did my pivot to the right instead. I found the Apache waiting for me with a happy grin on his face. He, for one, expected to enjoy himself.

"Be careful, Otto," Old Red said as I took off my hat and coat and dropped them to the ground.

"If I were careful, I wouldn't be followin' you around," I said. "And I wouldn't be here."

I started toward the Apache. When I was about twenty feet from him, I stopped.

"Uhh…*en garde?*" I said.

The Apache gestured for me to come at him.

I shook my head. "Oh, no. I wouldn't dream of it. You first, by all means."

The Apache shrugged—then charged at me with a bloodcurdling scream.

I was so startled that I instinctively jumped back with a shriek of my own—more "Whoa!" than a warrior's battle cry—but I managed to recover my wits when the man was still two steps away. I darted to the left, letting my right leg drag behind me. I was going to use my attacker's momentum against him, simultaneously shoving him past me and tripping him over my outstretched leg.

The shove I almost managed, but not the rest of it. The Apache anticipated my move, grabbing my right wrist and swinging around behind me with the whole arm in tow. A bolt of agony shot up my shoulder and exploded in my brain, obliterating the world around me.

By the time the pain faded enough for me to get a grip on my surroundings again, I found the Apache with a death grip on me. His right hand had my arm twisted against my back. His left arm was wrapped around my neck as tight as a hangman's noose.

"Otto!" I heard my brother shout.

I couldn't shout anything back. I couldn't breathe.

The world started to slip away again. More slowly this time. Not replaced with blackness in a blink but fading away to gray with each fruitless gasp for air.

The Apache leaned in so close I felt his dry lips brush against my left ear.

"Very," he whispered, "disappointing."

The son of a bitch spoke English after all.

"*You're* disappointed?" I wanted to tell him. "How do you think I feel?"

My knees began to wobble. I was about to fall fully into the grayness and the void beyond.

I let my head sag forward—then whipped it back and to the left as hard as I could.

The Apache was no fool, though. He jerked his own head away just in time, and the back of mine delivered a hard but harmless thump on the cheek instead of the crushing blow to the nose I'd hoped for.

The pressure around my throat eased for a moment, though, and I was able to suck in a quick breath before the Apache— muttering in Spanish now—got a firm grip again and went back to choking me. That little bit of air was enough to fuel my next desperate move. I began stomping down hard with my boot heel, hoping to catch the top of the Indian's soft moccasins and squash his toes. I could feel him dancing a jig behind me when he realized what I was up to, but that didn't last long. He only needed a moment to reposition his feet well out of range of my heel.

"Nice," he hissed at me, "try."

But with all the jostling, I'd managed to draw in another couple breaths, and I used what little extra energy that gave me to press my biggest advantage: my very bigness. I locked my knees, straightened my spine, and threw myself back on the Apache. He bent a bit under the weight of me, and I dug in my heels and pushed. That forced him to take a step back, and the second I felt him resetting his stance, leaving himself momentarily off balance, I began pumping with my legs, ramming all my bulk backwards. The Apache had to move back again and again, searching for purchase, and after the fourth or fifth step, I finally got the lucky break I'd been looking for.

His heels caught against a rock. He stumbled and began to fall. And me—I fell right on top of him. The only thing missing was a lumberjack shouting, "Timmmmmmmmm-ber!"

As we hit the ground together, the Apache grunted out a bit of Spanish even I knew.

"Don't bring my mother into this," I could've said.

"How was that try?" I wheezed instead. "Nice?"

I threw back my head again, and this time the Apache had no way to escape. It felt like I caught him in the forehead this time, and I heard a dull *thunk* as his skull bounced off stone beneath him.

He brought my mother into it again—in English this time, lest I misunderstand—and began to rewrap his arm around my neck. I gave him the back of my head again, then pushed myself up and tried to scramble away. I heard him getting to his feet and starting after me, so I grabbed a fistful of dirt and pebbles— I'd been hoping for a nice, brick-like chunk of rock, but there was no time to be choosy—whirled around, and hurled it into his face.

He staggered back, wiping his eyes. By the time he was done, I was facing him from fifteen feet away.

We were right back where we'd started.

I put a hand on my knee and took in as many deep breaths as I could, trying to get my wind before round two kicked off.

"Still…disappointed?" I panted at the Apache.

He looked past me and waggled a hand.

"*Así así,*" he told his partner. Spanish for so-so. He grinned and continued in English. "But he fights dirty."

Clearly, coming from him, this was a compliment.

Noddy said something to him in what I assumed was Apache.

Now that I'd seen how many languages they both spoke, it could've been Russian for all I knew.

The Apache's grin wilted. Whatever he'd just been told, he didn't like.

As the two men dickered in one tongue or another, I remembered that I was supposed to be getting a peek at the Southerner. I'd been too distracted to try for it before—remaining alive requiring all my concentration—but now was my chance.

I turned my head, peeked over my shoulder, and learned this: Old Red and I were being held prisoner by a bear.

Or so it looked, at least. Señor Noddy was keeping to the shadows of the looming bluffs while I was under a near-noon sun, so I had to squint to make any of him out. What I saw looked like a mass of black, bushy hair gripping a strip of silver-gray—the gun he had pointed at my brother's back. All I could see of his face was a dark oval topped with another tuft of fur. If it wasn't a bear who got the drop on us, it appeared to be a particularly shaggy rug.

"You're really going to take your eyes off an Apache in the middle of a fight?" the bear/rug said when he/it noticed me peeping his/its way.

As if to illustrate my folly, Cochise let loose with another war cry, and when I turned toward him again, he was charging at me with arms out wide. There was no time for anything fancy—and I was out of tricks anyway—so I opted for simplicity.

I stepped forward and aimed a punch at his nose.

The Apache had time to see it coming and jerked his head to the side at the last second. But to my infinite surprise and satisfaction, the blow caught him under the right eye. The man spun around, stumbled backward, and fell flat on his ass, his legs splayed out in a V.

So astounded was I by my own success, I just stood there gawping at him for a moment. When the logical next step finally occurred to me—kick the shit out of the man and end the damn fight—I moved toward and drew back my right boot.

The Apache raised his hands.

"You win," he said.

A part of me wanted to get to kicking anyway. I'm a peaceable, easygoing, live-and-let-live sort of fellow, but even I hold a grudge if you try to choke me to death.

I'd had enough tussling and bloodshed for one day, though, and I stepped back.

"Well, I hope I've taught you a little something about fisticuffs, friend," I said. "Like don't pick fights with bigger, younger men. And if one tries to sock you in the face, don't let him."

The Apache grimaced with disgust then pushed himself up, shook his long, black hair, and began dusting himself off.

"So does this mean we're free to go?" I threw back over my shoulder without completely looking around.

Noddy said nothing.

"What do you say, mister? I won fair and square," I said.

Noddy remained silent.

I couldn't resist any longer: I looked back at him again. Or back where he'd been, more like.

There was no shaggy shape in the canyon shadows. The bear/rug was gone.

"You're the one with things to learn," the Apache said.

When I looked at him again, he was picking up the big knife he'd tossed aside before the fight. He gripped it firmly in his right hand, with the tip pointed toward me. Five quick steps, and he could bury it in my belly.

I braced for another charge.

"Twice now you turned your back on me. With this close by," the Apache said, thrusting out the knife and twisting it in the air. "'Fair and square'? What does that even mean?"

There was a creak of leather and a thud behind me. My brother was finally jumping down and going for his gun.

"That's more like it!" the Apache hooted with delight.

He jammed the knife back into its sheath and raced away. His pony had wandered a little further up creek during all the hubbub, and he swung himself up into the saddle and dug in his heels.

"I'm glad I decided to talk to you!" he shouted as the horse bolted away. "You've got potential! Try to stay alive a little longer and maybe you'll actually..."

His words faded into distant, echo-y gibberish before I could make out the rest of it.

Old Red stepped up beside me, forty-five in hand, as the Apache disappeared around the bend in the canyon he'd ridden from a quarter-hour before.

"You alright?" my brother said.

"Throat's a bit sore. Back's a bit sore. Hand's a bit sore. Hell, I'm a bit sore all over. But yeah...I'm alright."

I turned and scanned the rockfalls and crevices and shrubby clusters of foliage in the other direction, hunting for Noddy. There was no sign he'd ever been there at all.

"My brain's sorest of all," I said. "Who the hell were those two?"

Old Red walked over to where the señor had been standing.

"We'll find out sooner or later, I reckon," he said. He squatted down to examine the ground, then pushed his hat back and gazed up at the sky as if thinking maybe Noddy had simply soared off like a big, hairy buzzard. "But I don't know if we're gonna like the answer."

THIRTEEN
A TOUCH OF THE DRAMATIC
OR, DEBARGE GETS AN IMPROMPTU PARADE AS OUR SEARCH FOR ANSWERS LEADS US STRAIGHT TO HALE

I WAS anxious to move on out of the canyon, quick. No use letting Haney's bunch jump us and pick up where "Cochise" had left off. But Old Red was intent on finding Señor Noddy's tracks first.

"You manage to get a look at the man?" he asked as he zigzagged near the high ravine wall doubled over like he was following a line of ants.

"As a matter of fact, I did. For all the good it'll do us."

My brother stopped and looked back at me without straightening up. "What's that mean?"

"All I saw was fur."

"And what's *that* mean?"

"It ain't a riddle, Brother. It means *all I saw was fur*. Didn't see a face, didn't see clothes, didn't see a library card with his name and address written on it. Just fur. Thick, black fur."

"So you're sayin' we was jumped by a dog?"

"Don't be ridiculous," I said. "Looked more like a bear."

Old Red squinted at me a moment, then shook his head and went back to tracking ants.

"That Apache must've shook something loose in your skull,"

he said. "Though it wasn't exactly screwed down tight to begin with."

"Got my head on straight enough to beat the bastard."

"No, you don't."

"Oh? Case you didn't notice, he was the one knocked flat in the end, not me."

"That don't mean you beat him."

Old Red stopped near a mound of shattered shale.

"Your bear walks awful light. Ain't hardly a full footprint to be found. But there..." He pointed down at the ground. "Square toes, thick heels."

I raised my hands and gave my brother a round of polite applause.

"'There is no branch of detective science which is so important and so much neglected as the art of tracing footsteps,'" I said, quoting 'You Know Who.' "Bravo. We now know what kind of boots Noddy prefers. It'll make Christmas shopping for him oh so much easier."

Old Red looked like he wanted to snatch up the closest chunk of shale and chuck it at me.

"The men who shot Alf Hinkle in the back weren't near so careful," he said. "And they had smaller feet *in different boots*. Ain't neither of 'em was wearin' moccasins either, remember."

"Ah." I applauded again. "So the Indian and the bear didn't kill the marshal."

"No, they did not. These two today was good. Professionals. The ones last night..."

My brother waggled his hand.

"If 'Noddy' and 'Cochise' are so professional," I said, "why would they make me fight? What was the point of that?"

Old Red straightened up and shrugged. "What Noddy said, probably. The Apache was curious. Once they knew what they wanted to know—who'd been killed, who we're workin' for, and whether or not you can throw a punch—Noddy called off the fight and they left."

I ran my fingers gently over my sore throat. The scrap with the

Apache had sure felt real to me. Up until the end, anyway. I didn't want to believe Cochise had let me win, but I couldn't deny how miraculous it seemed that one wild haymaker had laid out such a wily fighter.

"But *why* would the Apache be so interested in me?" I said. "I know I'm a naturally fascinating fellow, but it don't usually draw Indian braves out of the woodwork."

"If you wanna know the answer to that, you oughta be chewin' on this: How is it they knew who we are?"

"Uhh…maybe cuz you told 'em?"

Old Red shook his head. "I just said we were Otto and Gustav Amlingmeyer of the A.A. Western Detective Agency. Then Noddy proceeded to say his friend wanted to fight Otto. You. 'The big one.' He knew which of us was which without bein' told."

"Lucky guess?"

My brother gave me the same look our dear departed *Vater* used to when he caught one of us kids taking the Lord's name in vain. What our father objected to was "Jesus Christ" or "god damn" or the like, but for Old Red it's "lucky guess" that's blasphemous.

"Well, I doubt Clayton Haney's got an Apache on the payroll," I said. "And them two didn't strike me as vaqueros either. So whose side are they on?" I took an aching breath that reminded me again—as if I could've forgotten so soon—of all my fresh bruises and contusions. "It sure as hell don't seem to be ours."

My brother threw a quick, forlorn look down at the ground again, then started toward our horses. He obviously wanted to keep tracking Noddy, but we couldn't keep poking around in that arroyo waiting to get bushwhacked again.

"Maybe Flip Compton can tell us who they are," he said. "No way he's made it back to town already with what he's haulin'."

And Old Red was right: Not ten minutes after we rode out of the canyon, we spotted Compton ambling along beside the Pecos River, Marshal Hinkle's body draped over the horse behind him. I gave the deputy a "Yo, Flip!" and a broad wave of the Stetson so as not to startle him as we came galloping up the trail. He turned and waved back, then drew a red handkerchief from his coat and wiped it across his face. When we reached him, we reined up to match his pony's slow trot.

"Hey, fellas," Compton said, his voice so hoarse and tremulous I could barely make out the words. "I'm glad you caught up."

The young lawman's eyes were puffy and bloodshot, his cheeks moist. His nose was running, too.

My brother and I took a moment to study the horizon while he blew his nose and cleared his throat.

"You learn anything more about the killers?" he said.

When I looked at him again, he was stuffing his hankie away, and his face was dry.

I just shook my head. I wasn't sure how much Old Red would want me to say about the men we'd encountered in the canyon—oh, what a tangled web he can weave when he practices his Holmesifying—so I'd leave the talking to him for as long as possible. Sometimes, you might have noticed, there's nothing on earth that can keep my mouth shut another second.

"Didn't find out anything more about the men who shot the marshal," my brother said. "But we did run across another interestin' pair. Señor Noddy and his friend Cochise?"

"Cochise?" Compton said. "Like the Apache chief?"

Old Red nodded. "Was an Apache himself, this feller. Mescalero."

"Takes a lot of sand to go around this country calling yourself 'Cochise,'" Compton said. "Apaches aren't very popular."

"No, I don't reckon they would be. So you don't know the man? Or anyone named 'Noddy'?"

"No." Compton cocked his head and furrowed his brow. "A Mescalero called 'Cochise'? Near here? Are you sure he didn't kill Alf?"

My brother shook his head. "We're lookin' for two men who had store-bought boots, a bottle of Kentucky rye, and precious little trail smarts. That make you think of anyone in particular? Somebody in town I maybe ain't heard about yet?"

Compton shrugged. "There's no one obvious. Alf was well-liked. Trusted. People were always bringing him their problems and squabbles. He'd be a peacemaker. A go-between. Even the Haney crowd respected him."

"Oh?" Old Red said. "I didn't see a lot of respect in Martinez's store yesterday."

"I didn't mean Bartlett." Compton scowled at the thought of the man. "I meant the people on Haney's side of the street."

"How'd Clayton Haney come to have his own side of the street, anyhow?"

"It didn't happen overnight," Compton said. "The older families around here are a mix. Mexican, Indian, white, black. Used to be when new folks came, they'd...blend in."

My brother nodded thoughtfully. "Like Mr. Sweeney, maybe? Mrs. Sweeney told me her family's ranched out in the valley for a hundred years. But I saw a portrait of her husband and I'd guess his kin wasn't even on this side of the Atlantic before the potato famine."

"Yeah. He'd be a good example," Compton said. "He came here, started his own little ranch, made friends, and married into the Martinez family. Eased in, you know? But that's not Haney's way. He's been throwing his money around ever since he got here. Crowding out the small ranchers, bankrolling new businesses right across from the old ones. A lot of Texans have come in with him, and they tend to stick together. It's like there's two DeBarges now. The one I grew up in and Clayton Haney's."

"Did you say Mrs. Sweeney was a Martinez?" Old Red asked. "Same family as the storekeeper?"

"That's right. She and Mr. Martinez are cousins, I think."

My brother found that food for thought, for some reason, lapsing into silence while he chewed on it. So I finally felt free to unclamp my mouth and ask the deputy some questions myself.

"Speakin' of the Sweeneys, you got any idea what Ed and the marshal were really arguin' about last night?"

"No. But if I had to guess I'd say it had something to do with

Haney's men. Some of them were still in town, and Alf wouldn't have wanted Ed going anywhere near 'em."

"What about that roll of greenbacks the marshal had on him? Why would he be takin' it out to the Sweeney place?"

Compton stiffened in the saddle. "I have no idea. But it's not like Haney and Bartlett said. Alf didn't have anything to do with any rustling."

"Alright, O.K. So he wasn't involved," I said. "But he wasn't stoppin' it, either."

"That wasn't his job."

"Do you think a different marshal would make it his job?"

"Alf wasn't some 'do-nothing,' if that's what you're saying," the deputy snapped. "He was a good man. A brave man. He did his best to uphold the law for everybody, whichever side of the street they were on, and anyone who says otherwise is full of—"

"Flip, Flip, Flip," I cut in, voice mild, hands up. "I ain't speakin' ill of your friend. I'm wonderin' if someone might have reason to want a new man wearin' his badge. Somebody more of his mind when it comes to the limits—or lack of limits—of local law enforcement."

Compton gave me a long, slack-jawed stare that reminded me how the marshal had described his deputy to us the day before: a good man, but thick as a brick.

"Who's the town council gonna appoint to take Hinkle's place?" I said.

Compton blinked.

"Oh. I hadn't even thought about that," he said. "I have no idea."

His look of bewilderment gradually gave way to something like dread.

Good lord, he was plainly thinking. *They might give the job to* me.

It seemed to take all his nerve to keep himself pointed toward town—which was now visible on the horizon.

"Alf always told me what to do," Compton said. "Without him...I can't do this."

"Yes, you can, Flip," Old Red said slowly, soothingly, like he was trying to calm a spooked horse. "It's like Otto told Haney and Bartlett back in the valley. You're gonna wire the sheriff and get ready for an inquest. Go to the town council. They'll help you get it all goin'."

"But what about the men who murdered Alf? What do I do about *them*?"

Old Red told the deputy exactly what he wanted to hear.

"You leave that to us."

Compton looked relieved. Quite understandably, too. Whoever the backshooters were, it wouldn't be him tempting them to ply their trade again. It would be me and Old Red.

There are times I wish my brother had gotten it into his head to be a dentist.

A group of kids playing on the outskirts of town spotted us soon after. Most ran up for a closer look, but a few turned and sprinted up the street, racing for the honor of shouting the news first: Deputy Compton and two strangers were riding in with a body.

"Who is it, Flip?" a boy asked.

A girl gasped. "It's Marshal Hinkle!"

More kids peeled off to run ahead of us.

"The marshal's dead! The marshal's dead!" they shouted.

"We should've ridden around and come in from the east," Compton muttered miserably. "Not gone straight up Main Street."

"No, this is the way to do it," Old Red said. "You never know what a touch of the dramatic might flush out."

It was Sherlock Holmes, of course, who'd originally advocated "a touch of the dramatic." "The Adventure of the Naval Treaty," chapter 2, verse 3. As we rode on into DeBarge, my brother eyed the crowd that came out to surround us as Holmes might have: coolly scanning for anything peculiar or telling.

I didn't see anything of the kind, myself. Just the shock and anger one would expect.

"What happened?" a white fellow in a bloody butcher's apron asked.

"Was he shot?" asked a dark-skinned man in a bloody apron of his own.

"Who found him?" asked a white woman in a brown dress.

"Where was he?" asked a brown woman in a white dress.

"I heard he and Ed Sweeney were arguing last night!" said Mr. Yadel, the manager of the DeBarge Arms Hotel.

"Everyone knows Bartlett threatened him yesterday!" shot back Julio, the manager of the DeBarge House Hotel.

Mr. Martinez appeared at the edge of the little throng following us up the street. He looked distraught, and the flesh around his left eye was puffy and bruised.

The man had a black eye.

After a fruitless moment trying to elbow his way in closer, he gave up.

"Flip—what are you going to do?" he called to us over his neighbors' heads.

The deputy had been ignoring everyone, his glassy gaze pointed straight forward. But now he finally looked over and spoke.

"First, I'm going to see Mr. Hale," he said.

"Mr. Hale" was waiting for us in front of his place of business directly across the street from the marshal's office. He was a tall, bearded man in his shirt sleeves gripping a bulb-handled awl in one big hand. Above him was a sign.

CORNELIUS HALE
UNDERTAKER * EMBALMER * CARPENTER
CABINETS AND FURNISHINGS MADE TO ORDER

For all his practice dealing with the dead, he sure looked unsettled at the sight of Marshal Hinkle folded over a horse.

"Stay calm," he said as we reined up before his storefront. "Stay calm."

It was unclear if he was talking to the milling, muttering mob or himself.

"Pete, Pablo," he said. "Bring the marshal in while I talk to Flip."

The two men he'd spoken to—one white-skinned, one brown, on opposite sides of the crowd—glared at each other a moment before worming their way toward the horse bearing Hinkle's body.

There were maybe forty people pressed in around us now, and Hale looked out over them like they were floodwaters about to rise up and sweep him off the roof.

"When there's more to know, you'll be told," he said, voice warbling. "For now, let's let a good man retain his dignity by not turning his misfortune into a spectacle. Flip—come with me, please."

He turned and fled inside.

For a moment, the townsfolk just stood there murmuring or shooting livid, accusatory looks at each other or gawking at Pete and Pablo as they inspected the ropes holding Hinkle to his horse. Then little clumps of two and three began breaking from the throng and drifting off. Martinez lingered longer than most, staring in mournful horror at the marshal's carcass. But eventually, he too, put Hinkle behind him and trudged away.

Compton had dismounted and tied his horse to the hitching post in front of Hale's place by now, and he started to follow the undertaker inside. He moved lifelessly, like a man walking in his sleep. But a couple steps from the door he seemed to wake up. He stopped and looked back at me and my brother.

"We're gonna catch them, right?" he said. "The men who… did that."

He nodded at the body without looking at it.

"We are, Flip," Old Red said. "I guarantee it."

Without another word, Compton turned and headed inside.

"So the A.A. Western Detective Agency offers guarantees, does it?" I said. "That go for the Sweeneys, too? Full refund if not completely satisfied? I doubt if the colonel'd like that." I pushed back my hat and scratched my head. "Come to think of it, have we done a single thing since gettin' here that he *would?*"

Old Red swiveled in his saddle, obviously about to remind me of that which I know so well: I am the world's biggest fool—in his opinion. Something behind me caught his eye and shut his mouth. I glanced over my shoulder to see what it was.

Diana Crowe was on the other side of the street, in front of the marshal's office, scowling our way. Beside her was a handsome, dapper gentleman wearing a double-breasted overcoat, a gray bowler, and spotless white spats over gleaming, pointy-toed Oxfords. As he looked us up and down, he crossed one foot over the other and leaned against a silver-handled walking stick, all jaunty haughtiness from head to toe.

"Speak of the devil—that reminds me," I said. "There *is* something you've done that would tickle Col. Crowe, Brother: You've turned his daughter against us. He'll be so pleased when he learns she hates us now."

"Oh, she don't hate us," Old Red said without the cocksure conviction he brings to his usual pronouncements. "Come on—I reckon we oughta tell her who we're workin' for now."

We swung down and hitched up our horses, staying as far as we could from Pete and Pablo as they untethered Hinkle's stiffening corpse. When I turned to cross the street, I found to my surprise that the dandy Diana had been speaking to was striding our way. The lady remained before the marshal's office, her glower replaced by a look of amused bemusement.

"Gentlemen," the dude said. "If I might have a word?"

"You can have as many as you like, sir," I said. "I have plenty to spare."

The man smiled and pointed his cane at the alley that separated Hale's building from the bakery next door.

"In private, if you don't mind?"

I glanced over at my brother.

He nodded.

"Why, certainly," I told the man. "Quite an audience here a moment ago. No need to put on another show."

The dude stopped a few feet off, still smiling.

"My thoughts exactly," he said. "After you."

I headed for the alleyway, Old Red and the stranger falling in behind me.

"You got some information for us?" my brother asked.

"Indeed," the man said. "And a question."

A little gaggle of kids was lurking in the alley, obviously plotting to get another look at the body. I shooed them off with a wave of the hands.

"Go on home, now," I said as they spun around and darted away. "Ain't nothin' to see here."

I turned to face the dude again just in time for his fist to smash into my jaw.

FOURTEEN
VARIATIONS OF "OOF"

OR, I GET IN ANOTHER BRAWL WITH A STRANGER, BUT STRANGER STILL IS MY BROTHER'S REACTION

"SON OF A BITCH!" someone yelled as I stumbled back a step, a murky curtain dropping down over everything around me.

As my vision returned, the world brightening from black to gray to noon-time bright, several surprising realizations came to me.

1. I had just been punched in the face.
2. I was in an alley in DeBarge, New Mexico Territory. You try getting punched in the face. You might forget for a moment where you are, too.
3. The fellow who'd punched me—the fancy pants we'd seen talking to Diana—was now punching my brother.
4. The punch I'd taken really, really hurt. I suppose this wasn't exactly surprising, but I was sure as hell realizing it.
5. My knees were wobbling and my head swimming, but I was still on my feet.
6. I recognized the voice that had called out, "Son of a bitch!" It was a fine, rich baritone infused with the salty seasoning of years spent in the saddle with Texas

cowhands. The kind of voice thespians and orators
envy and women find earthily alluring. Meaning, of
course, that it was my own.

Old Red was doing some speaking, too, though he only
managed to get out, "Otto?" and "Hey!" before all that escaped
his lips were variations of, "Oof!"

I took a lurching, woozy step forward, intending to yank the
dude away from him. But suddenly I didn't have to: The man
whirled around to take another swing at me.

I jerked my head back *almost* in time. The dude's kid glove-
covered fist clipped the tip of my already tender jaw, shooting pain
through me hot and blinding as lightning. I stumbled to the side,
emitting a variation of "Oof!" myself. I think it was more of an
"Uff!"

"That's enough!" my brother barked, yanking out his forty-
five.

The dude had been doing all his punching with his right hand
while his left stayed wrapped around his walking stick—which
now became his whacking stick as he slammed it down over Old
Red's wrist. My brother howled in pain and dropped his gun.

I went for my own Colt, but the dude was faster: He whipped
around and cracked the back of my hand with his cane before I
could get my fingers wrapped around the grip.

"Son of a bitch!" I said again as I instinctively snatched my
hand back.

"Sticks and stones..." the man replied with a smile.

"Mr. Burr!" someone shouted. "What are you doing?"

The voice was *not* a fine, rich baritone, being a woman's.
Diana's, to be exact. She'd appeared just beyond Old Red at the
entrance to the alleyway.

"Ahh...Miss Crowe. I'm merely teaching these louts a little
lesson," the dude said to her. "When school's out, perhaps you
and I could dine together. The restaurant beside the DeBarge
Arms serves a passable *soupe à l'oignon*, I'm told."

While this "Mr. Burr" was distracted, I made another grab for my Peacemaker.

The dude brought his walking stick up, and with a flick of the wrist, gave me a thump upside the head.

"Son of a *bitch*!" I blurted out as I staggered to the side.

Burr gave me a shake of the head and a "tsk-tsk."

"Language," he said, raising his cane again. "A lady is present."

"Stop it!" Diana snapped. "Now!"

Burr lowered his walking stick.

"You need to expand your vocabulary," he told me. "And learn to duck."

"Miss Crowe," my brother grated out between clenched teeth, "what *the hell* is goin' on here?"

The dude turned to face him.

"My, but you are an obstinate one," he marveled. "But…you all know each other? I mean…by name?"

"These are the business associates I mentioned to you," Diana said. "Gustav and Otto Amlingmeyer."

"Your business associates? These two? Oh, no!"

Burr began to laugh.

"You know, I like to think I've got me a decent sense of humor," I said. "Yet somehow I ain't tickled."

I pushed back my hat and gingerly put my fingers to the spot above my right ear where the man had thwacked me. There was no blood, but the lump there was already swollen up as big as a walnut.

"I apologize. I really do," Burr said, stifling his laughter. "It was a simple case of mistaken identity."

"Mistaken iden…" Old Red began.

His gaze drifted to the side and went glassy, as happens when some new thought hits him particularly hard.

"…ti…" he muttered, "…ty…"

Burr ogled my brother like he was a particularly peculiar creature at the zoo.

"So who'd you think we was to come at us like that?" I asked the man. "A couple of rabid dogs?"

"Yes, actually," he chuckled. "Something like that."

"Mr. Burr," Diana said firmly. "Explain."

"Yes. Of course."

Burr planted his cane in the ground, leaned against it, and took a moment to iron the smile off his face. Then he cleared his throat and spoke.

"I'd heard about a disturbance yesterday. A confrontation between the town marshal and a group of armed thugs that was only broken up through the intervention of a brave and beautiful lady. Naturally, Miss Crowe, when I realized you were in town, I knew exactly who that lady was. The ruffians, I'd been led to understand, had made threats after the incident, vowing to make the lady and her companions pay for their presumption and meddling, etc. etc. So then a few minutes ago when I observed the look you were giving these two…well, it was hardly collegial. And I assumed—"

"That my brother and I were two of the 'ruffians,'" I cut in.

Burr's smirk returned.

"It didn't occur to me that Miss Crowe's associates would be quite so…rustic."

"There's a lot you don't know about me, Mr. Burr," Diana said.

"He ain't alone there," Old Red murmured, still half hypnotized by whatever thoughts were running through his head.

Diana shot him a quizzical look, but he just kept gazing off at nothing.

I, meanwhile, was straightening my Stetson and dusting off my sheepskin coat and denim pants. "Rustic" it was, but I liked to think I wore it with a certain *savoir-faire*.

"Not everybody gets to be a fashion plate when they're workin'," I grumbled.

"No offense intended," Burr said.

I grunted to show I'd heard the apology without necessarily accepting it. Forgiveness is all well and good but it doesn't come easy when your head, jaw, and knuckles are still stinging from a thumping.

"How exactly do you two know each other, anyhow?" I asked.

"Oh. Well…" Diana began. Her anger at the man had evaporated, and she looked at him now with something almost like fondness. "We became acquainted through my work for the Southern Pacific. Mr. Burr and I often found ourselves on the same train."

Burr chuckled again.

"Your discretion is appreciated, Miss Crowe, but you can speak freely. My feelings won't be hurt."

"Alright," Diana said. "Mr. Burr is a gambler and a…dealer in unsound speculations. Because he plied his trade on S.P. trains, he came to the attention of my father, who asked me to keep an eye out for him."

"They banned me from the Southern Pacific," the dude translated. "Which truly broke my heart. The pickings were easier on other lines…" He tipped his bowler to Diana and offered her a small bow. "But the company wasn't nearly so pleasant."

Diana acknowledged the man's courtliness with a nod and a smile.

Old Red scowled as he looked back and forth between the two of them, finally fully in the here and now again.

"What brings you to DeBarge, Burr?" he said. "There ain't a train within a hundred miles of here."

"Oh, I've moved on to new endeavors, much as Miss Crowe has. Speaking of which, I have business to attend to." Burr turned back to Diana. "Although I could still make time to dine first, if you're free."

"The Amlingmeyers and I have business to attend to, as well," Diana said. "Perhaps another time."

Burr placed a hand over his heart.

"'Tis a consummation devoutly to be wished," he said. "Adieu, then."

I half-expected him to kiss Diana's hand, but instead, he just offered her another bow, gave me and my brother a nod and a "Gentlemen," and left.

"You and that swindler seem pretty chummy," Old Red said to Diana.

There was an air of wistfulness about her as she watched the man leave.

"Well," she said, "he is a *charming* swindler."

My brother's cheeks flushed red, and he shot a glare at Burr's back as sharp as an arrowhead. Were I an explorer or scientist, I'd have to dash off a report to National Geographic, for I was witnessing a wonder no mortal had laid eyes on before.

I was seeing Gustav "Old Red" Amlingmeyer jealous.

FIFTEEN
TEN-CENT WORDS AND ONE-CENT MANURE

OR, DIANA HAS TO EXPAND HER VOCABULARY TO EXPRESS HER DISGUST WITH US, AND OLD RED'S REACTION LEAVES ME MOMENTARILY SPEECHLESS

THE DUDE WENT STRIDING out of the alley and across the street, giving his cane a cheerful twirl before cutting right and disappearing from sight.

"I'd sure like to show him where he can stick that cane," Old Red muttered, rubbing his jaw. The skin on his chin was mottled pink where he'd taken a blow, but it already looked like the mark would fade fast rather than darken into a bruise.

The frown on his face wasn't going away, though. He swung it toward Diana as she turned our way again.

"Tell me why I shouldn't pick up the fisticuffs where Mr. Burr left off," she said, crossing her arms and glaring at us reproachfully.

"Uhh...cuz you *know* we ain't 'ruffians'?" I replied.

"Do I?" Diana said. "I told Burr we're business associates, but I'm not really sure we are at this point. First you unilaterally decide to quit on our one and only paying client."

"What-a-whatily decide?" my brother interrupted.

Diana didn't stop to offer definitions.

"Then you disappear without a word only to reappear *with the town marshal's body?* And before I can even ask for an explanation you begin brawling with a stranger?"

"Whoa, now!" Old Red protested. "*We* didn't pick that fight!"

Again, Diana talked over him.

"Is this how 'partners' comport themselves where you come from? Because to me it seems more like the behavior of rivals or enemies or at the very least, people I wouldn't choose to *associate* with if they were the last—"

"We have a new client," I said softly.

"—men on...excuse me?"

"We have a new client," I said again. "Pretty much the same terms as with Haney, only shootin' for a different outcome. We were gonna head straight to the hotel to tell you—and offer our sincere apologies for yesterday—once we were done helpin' Deputy Compton make his delivery. Which we were also going to tell you about. Only, as you saw, we got bushwhacked by your Mr. Burr first. Ain't that the way of it, Brother?"

Old Red bent down to pick up his forty-five, still scowling.

"Yeah, well," he said as he stood up and jammed the gun back in its holster. "The stuff about the new client and helpin' Flip and gettin' jumped by that dude, anyway."

He'd cut the apology out of the herd.

If I'd had a walking stick of my own, I would've clubbed him with it.

Diana noted the omission with a cocked eyebrow but chose to let it pass for the moment.

"And who is this new client?" she asked me.

"The Sweeneys," I said.

I braced myself for a cry of disbelief. A roar of rage. Another wallop upside the head.

Instead, I got a slow, thoughtful nod.

"Because of Marshal Hinkle," Diana said. "Half the town's already blaming them for his death."

"That's it precisely," I said. "Clayton Haney himself was out on the Sweeney spread this mornin' yellin' for Eduardo's hide. But

Gustav took a look at where the marshal was killed, and he's convinced Ed ain't to blame."

Diana looked over at Old Red. "Oh?"

"That's how the data stacks up," my brother said. "Ed didn't do it, and the Sweeneys' money is just as good as Clayton Haney's. Better, in my book. So I reckon the A.A. Western Detective Agency still has work to do…and oughta be gettin' to it."

Diana nodded again, firmly this time. "Fine. I agree. But it seems to me the first order of business is making sure every agency operative has the information they need to proceed, after which a strategy can be devised and labor divided."

Old Red squinted at her. "You want us to tell ya what's goin' on so we can figure out what to do?"

A look came over Diana's face of the sort you see on someone trying to decide if the milk they just sipped has soured.

"That *is* what I said."

"Yeah…in ten-cent words," Old Red growled.

I forced out a phony laugh and tried to shoo him away.

"Ho ho! You know who loves ten-cent words? Me! Makes me sad I'm not a rich man and can't buy 'em by the bushelful. Grandiloquence—that's what I need more of. Now, summarizin' tends to be my job, so allow me to get to it. Brother, why don't you step outta this little alley and clear your head with some fresh air, hmm?"

Old Red didn't move.

"Gotta make sure you don't get it all wrong," he said.

"How thoughtful of you," I replied. Then commence I did, filling Diana in on what we'd found at Rancho Cañada de los Vaqueros that morning: Marshal Hinkle with four bullets in his back, the wad of cash he had on him, the bottle of Dr. Faraday's Female Remedy in his pocket, and the tracks of two killers possessed of Winchester rifles and an inability to hold their liquor. My brother only had to correct me once when I said the men we were hunting had been swilling Ballard's Best Rye Whiskey.

"Ballard's Best Extra Fine Rye Whiskey," he said. "Frank Ballard and Sons Distilling, Louisville, Kentucky."

"Thanks," I said. "The 'Extra Fine' might make all the difference."

Old Red shrugged. "Might."

"Did you find anything else we can follow up on?" Diana asked.

I looked at my brother.

"Cochise and Señor Noddy," he prompted.

"Cochise and Senior Naughty?" said Diana.

"Señor Noddy," I said. "Though naughty he was, I suppose."

And back to summarizing I went, telling the lady about our strange encounter in the canyon.

"Is that a joke?" she asked when I got to the part about stealing a look at Noddy and seeing what seemed to be a bear.

"Miss, I like to think when I tell a joke that folks don't have to ask if they're supposed to laugh," I said. "No, I am not funnin'. What I saw of Noddy looked like it was covered in black fur. Mind you, it was only a little peek for a split second, and an Apache warrior was tryin' to throttle me at the time. But I saw what I saw."

"Maybe it was a…" Diana began.

She cut herself off, eyes widening slightly. Then she seemed to start over.

"A pair of drifters, it sounds like. Out in the desert too long. Looking for some amusement."

"They knew that I'm Gustav and him Otto," Old Red said with a jerk of the head my way. "Us crossin' paths with 'em wasn't happenstance. They're mixed up in all this one way or another."

"I see. Well, that gives us another solid lead to follow, doesn't it?" Diana said. "Along with the other two we had already."

My brother nodded. "The whiskey and the…female stuff."

"It's obvious which line I should pursue," Diana said. "I'll check with the general stores and druggists in town. In the meantime, you two can see who stocks Ballard's Extra Fine Best Rye around here."

"Ballard's Best Extra Fine Rye Whiskey," Old Red corrected.

"Yeah, yeah," I said to him. "Of Louisville, Kentucky."

Diana went on as if we hadn't spoken at all.

"You were rather indiscreet yesterday regarding the identity of our client. I would suggest that you apply more circumspection today. Working for Clayton Haney may have been problematic, but working for the Sweeneys is likely to prove outright perilous."

Old Red threw me a sour look.

"You ever notice that the madder she is at ya, the bigger her words get?" he said.

"Brother, if you don't shut up, she's gonna hit you with her thesaurus."

Diana cleared her throat.

"What's a thesaurus?" Old Red asked me.

Diana cleared her throat again.

"Shall we get to work?" she said. Her icy tone got across her real meaning.

Can I please *get the hell away from you two?*

"Just one more thing," my brother said.

"Yes?" Diana said. She glanced over at me. "See—I kept it to one syllable for him."

My jaw was still aching from the thump Burr had given me, so I decided it was a good time to give it a rest. I just looked back at the lady in a sympathetic, "Imagine having to put up with him your whole life" sort of way and kept my mouth shut.

"What's Burr doin' here?" Old Red said. "You musta asked him."

Diana regarded him coolly a moment before replying.

"I did, actually. And his answer was as evasive…as *vague*, if that's easier to digest…as the one he gave you. Fresh prospects, he said." The lady shrugged. "I'm sure a range war creates all kinds of opportunities for profit. He probably means to steer some into his own pockets."

"Makes sense, I suppose," Old Red said skeptically. "After all, that's the way your father looked at it, ain't it?"

I unlocked my jaw—*that* didn't last long—and stepped between him and Diana.

"Alrighty, then!" I boomed, clapping my hands together.

"Summarizin' concluded, plan of action complete! Let's get to it! Yeeehaaa! Evildoers beware! The Double-A Detective Agency is on the job!"

It felt like trying to stampede a herd that just stood there in the mud chewing its cud. Diana locked a long, livid look onto the middle of my chest—it would've been aimed straight at my brother if I hadn't been there—and though Old Red was now behind me, I knew he wasn't gathering up posies with which to make his apologies.

"Yeehaa," I said listlessly. "Gettin' back to work. Woo-hoo."

Neither Diana nor Old Red moved or spoke.

"Uhh...yippee?" I said.

Diana finally looked me in the eye again.

"Five o'clock. The hotel lobby."

And she turned and walked away.

"We'll see you then!" I almost called after her.

"See you then!" I said instead.

It felt safer without the "we."

Once the lady was gone, I whirled on Old Red.

"Dammit, Brother—I know you don't like feelin' the colonel's spurs, but he's the one you oughta be buckin', not her. That's Diana. Our partner. Our *friend*. What's gotten into you?"

It was, to use a phrase Old Red might have appraised at ten cents or even higher, a rhetorical question. I knew what had gotten into him and stirred up all the orneriness that was already there. Jealousy stoked by the dude's easy intimacy with Diana.

But did my brother know it?

"'Women are naturally secretive,'" he said, trotting out a Holmes quote from "A Scandal in Bohemia," "'and they like to do their own secreting.'"

"Oh, please—like you're an open book," I shot back. "You're so inclined toward 'secreting' you even got secrets from yourself."

"What's that supposed to mean?"

I opened my mouth to answer.

Old Red swiped a hand at me before I could speak.

"Aww, never mind," he said. "We got work to do."

He turned and headed up the alley.

It was far from subtle as changes of subject go, but I let him get away with it. A clue-hunting Gustav Amlingmeyer is a happy Gustav Amlingmeyer—or at least as happy as a Gustav Amling-meyer gets. And I'd had my fill of the unhappy one for a while.

When he reached the end of the alleyway, he paused to peek out cautiously at the street. I stepped up behind him and made a quick survey of my own. Having just been in two fracases in as many hours, I figured I was owed a break. So it was a relief not to see Bartlett or any of his fellow "ruffians" on the prowl for us.

"Tell you what," I said, stepping out of the alley. "Before we get to seein' who stocks Ballard's Best Extra Fine Rye Whiskey around here, I'd like to pop into the DeBarge Arms and wash off the trail dust." I brought up a hand and gingerly explored my still-stinging jaw for dried blood. "And whatever else we might've accu-mulated lately."

"Ain't got time to dandy ourselves up," Old Red said. "Come on."

He slipped around me, pivoted to the right, and walked off fast.

"Ten minutes to un-stink ourselves ain't gonna make any difference," I said as I headed after him.

Then I saw what he had his eyes locked on.

Diana was about thirty yards ahead of us, walking up the wooden sidewalk toward DeBarge Mercantile & Sundries, the business directly across the street from Mr. Martinez's DeBarge General Store.

She swept right past it without stopping. She didn't turn to go to Martinez's place, either.

Two young white men in chaps and Stetsons were riding down Main Street side by side, and when Diana paused to look at them, my brother spun on his heel and took a sudden interest in a hand-printed notice tacked to the nearest building. He grabbed me by the arm and yanked me to a stop beside him.

"What's this say?" he asked.

"'Manure for sale,'" I told him. "'Ten pounds per penny.

Inquire at Cameron's Livery and Sales Stable, B.L. Cameron, proprietor.'"

Old Red peeked over his shoulder. Diana had lost interest in the pair on horseback—it was obvious they were simply ranch hands or nesters, not gunmen—and the lady was moving swiftly up the boardwalk again.

My brother started after her.

"No need to call on B.L. Cameron for horseshit," I said as I caught up to him. "You got all you could need for free right between your ears."

Old Red just shot me a "Feh" and kept going.

We had a couple of murderers to catch, but he was more interested in bird-dogging our own partner.

SIXTEEN
SEÑOR NODDY

OR, WE LEARN WHO GOT THE JUMP ON
US IN THE CANYON: NOBODY

"WHERE DO you think she's goin'," I sighed, resigned, as Old Red and I followed Diana up the sidewalk.

"If I knew that I wouldn't be followin' her, would I?" my brother said.

I angled out toward the street to get a better look at what lay ahead. There wasn't much: half a dozen more stores and a smattering of houses, then DeBarge gave way to broad, flat, yellow plains and a line of telegraph poles that stretched all the way to the horizon.

"Wherever she's headed, she'd better get there soon. We're about to run out of town," I said. "Unless she's walkin' home to Ogden. Can't say I'd blame her, the way you been actin'."

Old Red reached out and pulled me in close to his side again.

"Careful," he said. "You want her to see you?"

I jerked my arm from his grip.

"Sure…why not?" I said. "That way I could just *ask her* where she's goin' instead of literally sneakin' around behind her back."

"We'll see who's sneakin' behind whose back," my brother muttered.

I looked over at him. There was a grim determination about

him of the sort you'd expect to see on a fireman fixing to rush into a burning building looking for babies. Here was a man who knew he was about to be barbecued but carried on regardless.

"You're worried she's…" I said.

Old Red cut me off before I could get out the rest.

…*runnin' off after the dude, ain't you?*

"Hel-lo," he said, stopping.

Diana had finally turned and headed inside one of the last buildings in DeBarge. There was a sign hanging over the door.

WESTERN UNION TELEGRAPH COMPANY

I glanced across the street to see what the competition might be on the western side of town, but, as is the case in so many places, Western Union had a monopoly in DeBarge. Facing it was an empty lot pocked with knots of prickly pear and random heaps of trash.

"She says she's gonna talk to the merchants and druggists," Old Red said, "and instead, she's off to the Western Union office."

"After which I'm sure she's gonna talk to the merchants and druggists," I replied. "You can't expect her to tell ya what she'll be doin' every minute. *I* don't need to know what time she's gonna take tea or visit the privy."

My brother shook his head. "This ain't sippin' tea or goin' to the privy. This is sendin' a telegram she didn't mention to us." He snorted in disgust. "The colonel sent her along to nursemaid and spy, and now she's tattlin' on us."

"Case you hadn't noticed, there've been a few surprises the last twenty-four hours." I waved a hand at the Western Union sign. "That's not tattling. It's reporting."

Old Red crossed his arms and glowered at the telegraph office. "It's runnin' to daddy…and we don't need him buttin' in. We always managed to get by on our own."

"Barely. And purely through the good graces of Lady Luck. Have you forgotten how many times you and I nearly cashed in

our chips since you dragged us into the deducifyin' business? I
have, actually—cuz the tally got so damn big I lost count. I reckon
it must be somewhere north of twenty and south of a thousand.
So if we're gonna keep detectivin', I for one am glad we ain't on
our own anymore. Huzzah for the Double-A, I say. And you
should be sayin' it yourself."

"Oh? So you think we oughta be sendin' us a telegram, too?"
my brother snapped back. "'To: Colonel C. Kermit Crowe,
Ogden, Utah. We have made a mess of things, stop. Please please
please tell us what to do, stop. While you're at it could you let us
know whether we need to blow our noses or wipe our butts, stop.'"

"*Stop*," I said. "I ain't sayin' we have to take orders from the
colonel. But you shouldn't be pissed at Miss Crowe if she does."

Sure he could, of course. This was Old Red Amlingmeyer. He
could get pissed about just about anything.

I didn't want to admit he was right—I am Big Red Amlingmeyer, after all—but I was a bit pissed at Diana myself. My jaw
still stung every time I worked it, and she'd been awful quick to
forgive the slicked-up swell I had to thank for that. "Charming,"
she'd called him. And the way she'd looked at him as he'd walked
away...

Aww, hell. Was *I* jealous?

"So...who done it?" someone said.

I blinked my way back into the moment and realized I'd been
just standing there glaring at the Western Union sign beside my
brother.

A passing man had stopped to talk to us. He was on the
smallish side, with white whiskers on his face, a tilted derby on his
head, and the nub of a dead cigar plugged into the side of his
mouth.

"The beaners, weren't it?" he said. "I always said Hinkle was
too cozy with 'em, and now look what it got him."

"We don't know who it was, mister," Old Red replied. "But I
sure would like to know where Señor Noddy was last night."

The little man scrunched his face up so much that it looked
like he was going to swallow his stogie.

"Who?"

"You don't know a Señor Noddy?" my brother asked.

"I sure as hell don't. 'Noddy,' you say? Don't sound like any beaner name I ever heard."

My brother didn't bother asking the man if he knew a "Cochise."

"Maybe I heard it wrong," Old Red said instead. "So who do *you* think done it?"

"The Sweeneys, of course," the man said. "Eduardo."

He stretched out "Eduardo" so that it sounded like "Ed-wahh-hhhhrrrrr-dough." He seemed disgusted that any man should have a name more than four letters long. I pegged him for a "Joe" or perhaps a "Bud" if his friends were particularly creative.

"The whole town's ready to string him up," he went on. "Well...half the town. The half that matters."

He threw a sneer at the other side of the street.

"You don't think it could've been somebody else?" Old Red said. "Clayton Haney's man Bartlett was ridin' the marshal pretty hard yesterday."

The little man smiled and swiped a hand in an "Aww, pshaw—boys will be boys" sort of way.

"Haney's hands may play a little rough, but that's what you gotta do when you're dealin' with beaners and nesters. They wouldn't actually kill Hinkle." The man's expression turned serious. "Not unless he or the Sweeneys started something."

"So they absolutely, positively didn't do it," I said. "Unless they did. In which case, it wasn't their fault."

The man shifted his cigar from one side of his mouth to the other.

"You bein' sarcalastic with me?" he said, squinting at me.

"I assure you, sir, I am never 'sarcalastic.' 'Sarcastic,' on the other hand—"

"Well, thanks for the chat, mister," Old Red said. He clapped me on the back so hard it felt like he was dusting me off with a carpet beater. "Come on, Otto. We gotta get our animals back to the livery."

I tipped my hat to the man as my brother stalked off.

"Have a wonderlicious day," I said.

I turned and followed Old Red back up the sidewalk the way we'd just come.

"Doesn't do us any good to goad folks," he said when I caught up.

"I know—ain't I usually the one tryin' to keep *you* from treadin' on toes? It's just that all that 'beaner' talk was gettin' on my nerves. And pigheadedness sticks in my craw." I threw my brother a sideways leer. "You of all people oughta know that."

"Alright, alright…that's enough 'sarcalasm' for one day."

"'Sarcalasm'? Brother, that came entirely from the heart."

Old Red angled off the sidewalk into the street, and for a moment, I thought his plan was to run from me screaming. It's bound to happen one of these days. Instead, I soon saw he was just stepping around to untie the horse he'd left hitched near the undertaker's place.

"So we really are returnin' our horses?" I said as I walked around to my own mount.

"Yup. Our business is in town for now," my brother said. "And I got me some questions for Ernesto."

The pot-bellied liveryman was cleaning out stalls when we walked into his stable a moment later. He turned and leaned against his push broom when he noticed us leading our horses in.

"I saw you ride into town with Flip and the marshal," he said sadly. "What happened?"

"We don't know all the particulars yet," my brother told him. "Just that Hinkle was shot in the back, probably by two men, out near the Sweeney place."

Ernesto winced at the words "near the Sweeney place."

"Does Flip think it was the Sweeneys?" he asked.

Old Red shook his head, and the liveryman seemed to relax a bit.

"The deputy knows it don't make no sense for the Sweeneys to murder the marshal," my brother said. "But the sheriff and whoever they scrape up to run the inquest…they might not be so reasonable." He nodded over his shoulder, toward the east. "Same goes for some of your neighbors here in DeBarge."

Ernesto's soft, round face hardened. "Have you seen Seor Haney's *sicarios* again? The trouble will start with them."

Old Red nodded. "Haney's gunmen? We saw 'em. They was with him this mornin' anglin' to get their hands on Ed, but we managed to put 'em off for the time bein'. That ain't gonna last long, though."

"*You* managed to put them off?" Ernesto said skeptically.

"That's right," my brother said. "And now I need to—"

The mare behind Old Red snorted and nudged him with her nose. That prompted my pinto to shake his head and stamp a hoof.

"Someone's anxious to get at the hay," I said. I put a hand to my stomach. "And I can't say as I blame 'em. Ain't none of us had breakfast."

"You can wait a little longer," my brother told me sourly. He threw a glare back at the horses. "And you can, too. There's a clock tickin'."

He turned back to Ernesto and picked up where he'd left off.

"I need to ask you some questions, quick, so you'll excuse me if I'm short with you."

"Alright," the liveryman said, still looking dubious.

"You got any notions as to who'd shoot Hinkle?"

Ernesto jutted his double-chin at the doorway behind us. "Ask the gring…"

He cut himself off and gave us a small, apologetic smile.

"Ask the *citizens* on the other side of the street," he said. "Everyone liked Hinkle over here."

It was my brother's turn to look doubtful.

"Hinkle was a good man, from what I can tell," he said. "But in my experience there ain't no such thing as a town marshal *everyone* likes, even if you're just lookin' at one side of the street."

Ernesto conceded the point with a nod and a shrug.

"Alright, yes—there were disagreements over this or that. Dumping garbage within city limits. Having too much to drink.

Fights over women. Fights over men. Fights *between* women and men. The marshal had to get in the middle of all kinds of things. But I'm telling you: No one over here held enough of a grudge to kill him. Not when we knew what would happen without him."

"And what's that?" Old Red asked.

Ernesto looked past us, out at the street, his expression grim.

"You'll see soon, I think," he said.

I knew what he was looking for: "Seor Haney's *sicarios*," he'd called them. Bartlett and Jody and the rest. Men who'd only minded their manners in town—barely—because there was someone with a badge who'd stand up to them.

The mare behind my brother gave him another shove.

"I'm almost done," he told her. "Hold your horses."

I opened my mouth to supply the obvious witticism. "Supplying the obvious witticism" being a large part of my job, as I see it.

"Oh, shut up," Old Red told me before I could get out the first word. He turned his attention to Ernesto again. "The marshal had a big ol' roll of money on him when he was shot. As Haney sees it, that's proof Hinkle was helpin' the Sweeneys sell stolen cattle. He was bringin' 'em their cut, he says."

Ernesto started shaking his head firmly the second he heard the words "sell stolen cattle."

"He might have been helping the Sweeneys somehow, but not like that. He wasn't crooked. He was…how do you say it?"

The liveryman shut his mouth tight and mimed locking it with an invisible key.

"Discreet?" I suggested.

Ernesto pointed at me. "That's it. He helped lots of people out that way. Quietly. Like when Señora Sweeney sent her two youngest children into town last year to be kept safe from *Bartlett*…"

The taste of the name made him scowl, and for a moment it looked like he was going to spit down at the hay and horse turds and dirt at his feet.

"…Marshal Hinkle helped look after them," he went on.

"Maria, the daughter, is very pretty, and…well, you know how men are. Sometimes there was the wrong kind of attention. The marshal made sure no trouble came of it. *Discreetly*, like you say. So no one had to be embarrassed. That's the kind of friend he was to the Sweeneys. Not the kind who helps sell stolen cows."

Old Red nodded slowly as Ernesto spoke, his eyelids growing so droopy it looked like he was about to fall asleep on his feet.

"One last thing," he said, dreamy and distant. Then he straightened up and snapped his eyes open wide. "You know of a 'Señor Noddy' around here? Or an Apache who likes to call himself 'Cochise'?"

Ernesto furrowed his brow and looked back and forth between my brother and me.

"Now you are joking with me?" he said.

I shook my head. "We run across two men out in the canyon who gave us those names."

"Then *they* were joking with *you*," Ernesto said. "There is only one Cochise, of course, and he has been dead for twenty years."

Old Red spun his hands in the air impatiently. "Yeah, yeah, we didn't think it was his ghost. Just wondered if someone you knew of had borrowed his name. What about Noddy?"

"*Nadie*," Ernesto said, giving the word a sharper sound and a little extra "eh" at the end. "It's a Spanish word. 'Señor Nadie' means Mr. Nobody."

I had to give that a laugh.

"Well, how about that?" I said to Old Red. "I've met plenty of nobodies over the years, but that's the first time one had it right there in his name."

"Hilarious," my brother muttered.

His mare nickered and gave him yet another push.

"Alright, fine…I'm about done here anyway," Old Red told her.

He handed her reins to Ernesto, and I did the same for my pinto.

"You liked them?" Ernesto asked, nodding at the animals.

"Fine horses," I said. "Gracias, Ernesto."

The liveryman grinned at me. "They will be here for you if you need them again. Free of charge." His smile faded fast. "I heard how you stood up to the *pistoleros* yesterday. Made Bartlett back down. That was good…but maybe not something you would want to try twice."

"Sounds like wise advice to me, amigo," I said.

I would've loved hearing "I couldn't agree more" from my brother. Him being him, of course, he had to say something that was more or less the opposite.

"Them pistoleros…they got a favorite place in town to drink?"

They did, Ernesto told us. It was called the Bull's Head. A better name would have been the Lion's Den, it seemed to me. Because that's what we were headed into next.

SEVENTEEN
"FRIENDS"

OR, WE SPREAD SOME B.S. IN THE BULL'S HEAD, AND SOON WE'RE UP TO OUR NECKS

"ANY CHANCE I could talk you into swingin' by a restaurant 'fore we go into that saloon?" I asked as Old Red and I left the livery stable.

"Nope," my brother said.

He turned right, steering us toward the south end of town—where we'd find the Bull's Head, Ernesto had told us.

"Any chance I could talk you into goin' to a saloon on the west side of the street instead of the one place in all DeBarge we're most likely to run into Bartlett and his bunch?" I asked.

"Nope."

"Didn't think so," I said. "Any chance I could talk you out of dousin' yourself in kerosene and lightin' yourself on fire if you got it in your head to do it?"

"Look," said Old Red, "neither Ernesto nor that mouthy feller with the cigar knew that we're workin' for the Sweeneys now. Word ain't made it back to town yet about that. But it will. Soon. And the second it does, there are folks 'round here who won't wanna talk to us...except maybe to tell us we oughta be strung up alongside Ed. So if we got questions to ask on the east side of the street—and we do—we gotta get 'em asked fast."

"Makes sense," I said. "Damn it."

There weren't many people on the street, but I could see what ones there were eyeing us or even, if in clumps of two or more, pointing and whispering. We were now local celebrities known to all.

Maybe it didn't matter that we were about to stroll into the Haney crowd's favorite watering hole: If Bartlett came looking for us, they'd find half the town gossiping about wherever we just went.

It was not a consoling thought.

"And nope," Old Red said. "You probably couldn't talk me outta lightin' myself on fire if I thought it needed doin'."

He stopped before an adobe-walled cantina from which drifted the sounds of low conversation and someone either learning how to play the guitar or attempting to peel one apart with his fingernails. Directly across the street was a clapboard building with the word BEER painted upon one grimy window and WHISKEY upon another. Between them, the broad head of a longhorn was mounted over an open door.

"The Bull's Head," I said, nodding at the saloon.

"Gee, ya think so?" Old Red said. "What do you base that deduction on, Mr. Holmes?"

He started toward the saloon.

I paused to imagine what it might look like if *I* doused him with kerosene and set him on fire. Then I followed him.

The Bull's Head turned out to be your standard shotgun-style affair: long and narrow, with a mahogany bar along the right side, half a dozen tables along the left, a single billiard table toward the back and a rear exit for whoever might need to step outside and make room for more liquor. No one was in the place save for a single barman in shirt sleeves and apron who looked up from a magazine to smile at us as we walked in.

"Afternoon, boys," he said.

His smile wilted as we stepped up to the bar.

"Oh," he said, straightening up and folding his arms over his chest. "It's you."

"Why, yes. It is us," Old Red replied, surprisingly cheerful. "But just who is it that you think we are?"

"You're the busybodies, that's who. The little one and the big one with red hair."

It's always a disappointment when I hear us described that way. I'd so much prefer "the homely one and the handsome one."

"You heard what happened in the general store yesterday?" my brother asked, still jovial.

"That's right," the barman said. He was a tall, long-faced fellow with slicked-back hair and a little black moustache perched atop his frown. "You two stuck up for Hinkle and a beaner when it was none of your business."

Old Red chuckled and threw me a little sidelong look that told me not to let any "beaner" talk get on my nerves until our work here was done. I showed him I understood by pasting a big, dumb grin to my face to match the one on his own.

"The boys was in here bitchin' about it later, I suppose," he said.

The barman nodded somberly. "They were talking about it, yeah. And what they were going to do to you two the next time you crossed paths."

My brother burst out laughing.

"That was Jody, wasn't it? That tub of lard *is* one to hold a grudge!" he said. "And them hayseed twins, Konrad and Knute. They love a laugh, but they're mean as mad dogs, too. I bet they was full of big talk about how they'd teach us a lesson!"

"They sure were," the barman said, confusion cracking through his hostility.

Old Red hooted and slapped a hand on the bar.

The barman looked over at me, brow furrowed.

"My oh my!" I said, laughing along with Old Red. "Why don't you tell the man why it's so funny, Brother?"

What the fellow behind the bar couldn't know was that "the man" I was referring to was *me*.

Old Red heaved a big, happy sigh and wiped laughter-tears from his eyes.

"Guess I should. Don't look like he's heard the punchline," he said. "Me and my brother here, we're stock detectives. We was sent here to work for Clayton Haney. Only when we run into Bartlett and the fellers, we had no idea they worked for Haney, too. We thought we was gettin' in good with the local law by helpin' the marshal run off some kinda gang!"

Old Red broke out in guffaws again. This time, the barman joined in.

"You're pulling my leg!" the man said.

I put one hand on the counter and raised the other up straight, as if swearing on a Bible.

"It's the god's honest truth," I said. "We work for the A.A. Western Detective Agency outta Ogden. Came down here to hunt rustlers for Mr. Haney."

All three of us laughed some more, suddenly chummy.

It sure helps when the lie you're trying to tell just happens to be the truth.

"Bartlett mentioned some detective agency was sending him more men," the bartender said as the belly laughs wound down into chortles. "So that was you?"

Old Red nodded.

"Well, that's quite a way to meet your new boss!" the man said. "How'd Bartlett take it when he found out who you are?"

"Oh, he got a little hot," I said. "Took some fancy talkin' for us to stay employed, I can tell you."

"I bet!" the barman said. "I'm Big Mike, by the way."

"Gustav," said my brother.

"Otto," I said. "Always pleased to be on first-name basis with a bartender."

Big Mike gave me a wink. "It does have its benefits. Speaking of which, first round's on the house. Any friend of Mr. Haney's is a friend of ours."

The barman's words echoed in my mind like he'd shouted them down a well—"Any friend of Mr. Haney's...Mr. Haney's... Mr. Haney's..."—and after a moment I realized why. Yadel, the manager of the DeBarge Arms Hotel, had said the exact same thing: "Any friend of Mr. Haney's is a friend of ours."

"Why, thank you, Big Mike," Old Red said. "What whiskies ya got?"

The barman's grin went a little stiff—he'd probably been hoping we'd settle for a couple of nice, cheap beers—and rather than answer, he pulled two shot glasses out from under the counter and slapped them down in front of us. He then turned to the shelves behind him and snatched up a nondescript brown bottle that didn't even have a label. He poured from it a liquid the color of muddy water.

We might be "friends" now, but a free round's not going to come from the best on the shelf. Or the second-best, third-best, or fourth, if they even had that many to choose from.

I braced myself, swept up the glass before me, and saluted Big Mike with it.

"To your health, sir," I said. "Brother?"

Old Red was warily eyeing his own glass. He reluctantly picked it up and raised it to the barman.

"Thanks," he said.

Then he threw back his head and tossed the shot down his throat like he was hoping it would miss his tongue entirely. I did likewise.

You don't spend years on the cattle trails without building up a tolerance—if not a taste—for rotgut, so neither my brother nor I coughed, retched, or heaved as the whatever-it-was burned its way down our gullets and settled in sizzling puddles in our stomachs. There were, however, watering eyes, suddenly sweaty faces, and silent prayers for mercy all around.

"Smooth," I wheezed.

"Another?" Big Mike said, moving the bottle my way.

Old Red spoke up before I could scream, "Hell, no!"

"You got anything with a little more…subtlety?"

"'Subtlety'?" the barman said, screwing up his face in wonderment and disgust as if my brother had just asked for a drink with a wee bit more horse piss in it.

"Yeah," Old Red said. "Little less fire, little more flavor. Like…" He turned to me. "What was the name of that Kentucky whiskey we got a taste of not long ago?"

"Uhh…Ballard's Extra Pure Rye?"

My brother allowed his irritation with me to peek through for less than a second.

"That's it," he said. "*Ballard's Best Extra Fine Rye Whiskey*. You got any of that in stock, Big Mike?"

The barman shook his head without hesitation. "Never heard of it, and we've got the best selection of booze in town. Mr. Haney himself bends an elbow here from time to time. He's a hard man, but when he wants to soften himself up a little, this is where he gets started."

"Can't think of a better place. Feller like him ain't gonna do it at some cantina on the west side of town, is he?" Old Red said. "He a friend-friend to you or more of a business-friend?"

Big Mike leaned toward us and dropped his voice to a whisper. "I don't know if Clayton Haney's the type to have 'friend-friends.'" He straightened up and waved his left hand in the air. "He's a silent partner in this place. Sharpest businessman I ever met. The second he pays his men, half of them stampede straight here and put their wages right back in his pocket. And by the time they're going out, the other half is coming in."

He chuckled appreciatively, and Old Red and I showed him what good new friend-friends we were by joining in.

"So when they came in yesterday, they was grousin' about what happened over at Martinez's store, huh?" my brother said. "Lotta noise about us and Hinkle?"

Big Mike nodded and chuckled some more. "Oh, yeah. That fat-ass Jody, he's always been a big talker. But some of the new boys make him seem like a Sunday school teacher. A real mixed herd Bartlett's got this year. Maybe you got off on the wrong foot with him, but he must be mighty glad Mr. Haney ponied up the cash to bring in professionals like you."

"'Glad' don't even begin to describe it," I said.

Old Red shot me another exasperated glower that was here-

and-gone so quick, only an expert on his various glares—such as myself—would've noticed it.

"Where'd he scrape up this mixed herd of his, anyway?" he said.

Big Mike gave him another shrug. "You'd have to ask him. He must've put out the word somehow, cuz they've been drifting in for days. Konrad and Knute were talking like they were on the run from trouble back east. Which seems about right for a couple squirrelly little…"

The barman cut himself off with a nervous glance toward the door.

"Don't worry—you can be honest," I assured him. "We're all friends here, ain't we?"

"Well, well. If it…isn't the…turncoats," someone said.

I recognized the deep, gravelly voice and the odd pauses before I even turned for a look. Yet it was still a shock to see who walked in.

Clayton Haney was making one of his occasional calls on the Bull's Head—and he had Bartlett and all the rest of his gunmen with him.

EIGHTEEN
MANIFEST DESTINY
OR, WE TRY TO MAKE HANEY LISTEN TO REASON, BUT HE DOESN'T THINK HE HAS A REASON TO LISTEN

HANEY AND BARTLETT stopped a few feet inside the saloon while their bunch crowded in around them.

"Jody," Bartlett said. When his pot-bellied buddy looked his way, he jerked his chin at the far end of the bar.

A grin appeared on Jody's round, grimy face. He scratched at his scraggly, patchy beard—which was either red caked with brown dust or brown caked with red dust, it was impossible to say —then led the two men nearest to him past me and my brother. They stopped beside the billiard table...which also just happened to be between us and the back exit.

Old Red and I were trapped.

"What do you mean 'turncoats'?" Big Mike said. He looked like he wanted to sweep our shot glasses off the bar and pretend he hadn't noticed us standing there till just then.

"That's a pretty emotional way to put it," I said. "I'd just say we disagree on a few things."

Bartlett shook his head. "You two have been working against us ever since you got to town."

"Traitors!" one of the twins piped up. I had no idea if it was Konrad or Knute. Whichever it was, he'd positioned himself to

Haney's left while his brother had stopped to Bartlett's right. Both of them snickered and caressed the holsters tied to their thighs with long, dirty, loving fingers.

"We ain't no 'traitors,'" Old Red said. "We're consulting detectives. And if you was wise, Mr. Haney, you'd consult with us again before things get outta hand."

"Oh, things are about to get out of hand, alright!" the other twin said.

"Shut up," Haney told him. He didn't snap it or snarl it or bark it. He just said it without even bothering to look over at the young man he was speaking to.

Clearly, telling people to shut up was nothing new to him.

"What were they doing in here?" he asked Big Mike.

"Asking a lot of questions," the barman said.

"About what?"

"You, Mr. Haney. And the fellas here. Where they come from and the like."

The gunmen murmured amongst themselves, keeping their voices low enough to avoid another "Shut up," yet loud enough for me to catch a stray phrase or two of the "Nosy bastards" variety. These men were tumbleweeds—prickly trash blown across the plains by the winds of fate—and it was a safe bet none of them felt kindly toward stock detectives or anyone else in the habit of inquiring about a fellow's past.

"Well, what else was we to do, Mr. Haney?" I said. "We came all this way to work for you, then got fired before we ever really talked man to man. Had to wonder if we were gettin' the whole story. Hearin' your side of things."

Haney looked over at the twin nearest to him.

"You need to hear my side of things?" he said. With his slow, stop-and-start rhythm and the seemingly random way he sprinkled in emphasis, it came out as "You need to...HEAR my... SIDE of things?"

"No, sir," either Konrad or Knute told him. "You're the boss. That's all I need to know."

"I don't work like that," Old Red said. "*I* decide what questions need to be asked. And I ask 'em."

"Which is what makes the A.A. Western Detective Agency such a unique and valuable service," I threw in. "You don't need men who just say 'Yes, sir' and 'No, sir' and 'May I take out my hankie and wipe the sweat from my brow, sir?' You need the truth. And that is our specialty."

"Bullshit," Bartlett sneered.

His men took that as a signal to snort and chortle.

"So," Haney said, and instantly the room around him fell quiet, "what exactly is the truth I need to hear?"

Or, to be more exact:

"SO…what EXACTLY is the…truth I need to…HEAR?"

I put on a smile and stretched an arm out toward one of the Bull's Head's empty tables—the one closest to the door.

"Why don't we sit down, have a nice, friendly drink and discuss it?"

Haney just stared at us. I think the realization was dawning on him that he was facing two men who *wouldn't* shut up if told to, and it had been a while since he'd laid eyes on such an exotic breed. For a second it almost looked like he might smile. His mouth dropped open, the edges curling, and his eyes crinkled and sparkled with amusement.

Then the light in his eyes went out.

"Alright," he said. "I'll give you five minutes to tell me why I shouldn't…throw you to the dogs."

He turned and pointed at one of the tables in the middle of the room with two jabs of his hand.

"Big Mike," he said. "The good stuff."

"Yes, sir, Mr. Haney! Coming up!"

Haney headed to the table with a halting, lumbering gait, his shoulders tilting and rolling as he walked. He was now what some call a "cattle baron," but plainly, he hadn't been royalty all his life. He'd worked hard, and paid the price for it with old injuries that made themselves felt with each step. He sat down slowly, and Bartlett took up position behind him on his right side.

As my brother and I walked over to join them, the rest of Haney's "dogs" backed up to let us pass, then closed in again to form a ring around us. I could hear Jody's heavy breathing just behind us as Old Red and I sat down across the table from Haney. The twins were at our backs, too. Them I could *smell*.

"Say…what happened to you?" Bartlett said, cocking his head and leering at us. "Looks like somebody beat us to the punch with you two. Literally."

His men chuckled again.

I rubbed my still-aching jaw. Between "Cochise" and the dude, the only part of my face that didn't hurt was an inch-long strip just above my right eye. My brother was only sporting a couple of welts—a matching set on each of his cheeks—but they were puffing up so red it was hard to tell where his mustache stopped and his skin began.

"We've been makin' new acquaintances," Old Red said. "Collectin' data."

"Doing *what?*" Bartlett said.

"Learnin' things," I explained. "It's what we do. This…" I waggled my fingers in front of my bruised and contused face. "… is what you might call a byproduct."

Bartlett leaned in over Haney's shoulder.

"They speak English," he said, "but I'll be damned if I can understand them."

Big Mike appeared, and two of Bartlett's bunch stepped aside to let him through. He put a bottle and shot glass down in front of Haney, then scurried off. The men who'd let him in stepped toward the table again, re-closing the corral around me and my brother like a gate swinging shut.

As Haney poured himself—and himself alone—a drink, I noted the label on the bottle.

"MILLER'S SPECIAL GAMECOCK RYE," it said.

Old Red glanced over at me, looking for a verdict, and I shook my head. Big Mike hadn't been Big Liar when he said he didn't stock Ballard's Best Extra Fine Rye Whiskey.

"What I don't understand," Haney said, "is what you two are

still doing here. Your Col. Crowe was supposed to send me men to stop rustlers. Instead I get you, and I hear, some woman, and not only haven't you helped, you've made a habit of getting in my way. Why? If your agency doesn't want the work, you should've gone back to Ogden."

"We never meant to get in your way, Mr. Haney," my brother said. "Yesterday, we was just tryin' to help the marshal, and this morning we was tryin' to help the deputy. That sidin' with the law set us against your man Bartlett from the get-go...well, I don't think that's anything you can blame *us* for."

Old Red shifted his gaze to Bartlett, making it plain who he thought *could* be blamed.

Bartlett just smirked back at him.

"You weren't sent here to help Alf Hinkle or Flip Compton," Haney said. "You were sent here to work for me. And for you, that means working for Bartlett...and doing what you're told without any lip. Since that's not something you seem capable of, fine. There's a stage out of here every day."

"You'd have us leave before you hear what we've learned about the marshal's murder?" my brother said.

"He's heard it already," Bartlett scoffed. "Hinkle has a fight with Eduardo Sweeney, gets shot on Sweeney land, and you say the Sweeneys had nothing to do with it." He looked down at Haney and jerked his chin at us. "Some 'detectives' they sent us. They couldn't find their asses with both hands."

The men around us laughed. This time, I joined in.

"Oh, I don't know, Bartlett. Seems to me I'm lookin' at an ass right now," I said. "And it ain't like we haven't dug up a thing or two on the murder."

I looked over at my brother.

"Marshal Hinkle was shot by two men armed with Winchesters and drunk on Kentucky rye," he said to Haney. "And when they was done, they headed into Cañada de los Vaqueros."

"Cowboy Canyon," Bartlett corrected coldly. All trace of amusement had drained off his face with the words "two men armed with Winchesters."

"Call it whatever you want, it don't change facts," Old Red said. "The killers didn't go home to the Sweeneys' *hacienda*. They headed for town…or something else in that general direction."

"Like the Pecos River," Haney said slowly. "And my land. Is that what you're trying to tell me?"

My brother shrugged. "I'm just tellin' you facts."

"You don't have to go through the canyon to get to the Pecos Bend Ranch from the Sweeney place," Bartlett said.

"No, you don't have to," I said. "But you can."

Bartlett grunted out a bitter laugh. This time I did *not* join in, nor did any of his men.

"This is how you talk your way out of trouble?" he said. "By pointing the finger at *us*?"

"I ain't pointin' any fingers. Ain't time for that yet. For any of us," Old Red said. "Speakin' of which—tell me, Mr. Haney, why'd you come into town?"

"To see justice done," Haney replied.

My brother gave him the kind of look my dear old Mutter pointed at me when I told her I didn't know what had become of the last slices of pie and maybe the dogs had got them.

"I think you're here," he said, "because you see an opportunity. And I'm tryin' to make you understand—again, just like this morning—that things ain't as clear cut as you think. You push too hard to 'see justice done,' and the facts ain't gonna back you up when the dust settles."

"So you're telling me to let Eduardo Sweeney get away with murder," Haney said, his words coming out as a long, low growl.

Old Red managed not to wince, but I'm not so sure I managed it, too.

"You see, but you do not observe," Mr. Holmes once told John Watson, and my brother had often told me. Haney, it seemed, had a similar bent. He could sit there listening and not *hear*.

"I'm suggestin' that you be patient, Mr. Haney," Old Red said. "Let the truth come to light, then see what oughta be done."

Haney grunted and shook his head.

"You think I got to be who I am today by being patient?

Waiting for things to happen?" he said. "I *make* things happen, Mr.…whatever your name is."

"Amlingmeyer," Old Red said.

Haney started talking over him before he got past the "ling."

"Like here in DeBarge. I've been making things happen for this town," he said. "It's starting to look like America here, not some mongrel Mexican mishmash. But you know who's slowed me down? Gotten in my way? Tried to keep everything just the way it was? Alfred Hinkle and the Sweeney family. So when I hear that Hinkle had a falling out with Eduardo Sweeney—"

"We don't know that," my brother said.

Haney's words had some momentum built up for once, and they didn't slow down.

"—and that greaser half-breed put some bullets in his back, I don't say, 'Golly, I wonder what will happen? Gee, I hope things work out for the best.' I say, 'Saddle up, boys. There's work to be done.' You think I see an opportunity? Well, let me tell you: I see a lot more than that. I see providence. I see manifest destiny. And by God, I'm not going to sit on my ass and let it slip away."

Haney's little speech must have made him thirsty, because he finally swept up his shot glass and tossed its contents down his throat.

"So what're you aimin' to do?" Old Red asked him. "Buffalo Flip Compton into arresting Ed Sweeney? Or just gather yourself a nice lynch mob and—?"

Haney slammed his glass back down.

"Your five minutes were up a long time ago," he said.

He pushed back his chair and stood up slowly, his knees practically squeaking like an old well windlass pulling up a bucket as they labored to lift his big frame away from the table.

"Get rid of 'em," he told Bartlett once he'd straightened to his full height.

And he turned his back on us and sauntered out of the saloon.

NINETEEN
A NOT-SO-FRIENDLY GAME
OR, WE TURN UP A WILD CARD, AND ALL BETS ARE OFF

"BY 'GET RID OF 'EM,'" I said as Haney walked out of the Bull's Head, "I believe he meant you fellas should show us to the door. Which would be mighty polite but not really necessary, as I see it right over there."

I nodded at the saloon's entrance. It was twenty yards off but may as well have been on the other side of the world, given what stood between it and me. Namely, nearly a dozen armed, ornery-looking men.

"Oh, I know what he meant," Bartlett said with a leering grin.

"Me, too," his slovenly pal Jody chortled behind us. He leaned in close enough for me to smell the rotten-gummed stink of his breath. "And this time you aren't gonna have your pretty little lady friend here to pull your ass outta the fire." He straightened up and cut loose with another wheezy chuckle. "We oughta look her up when we're done with these two. 'Show her to the door,' too…and show her a good time first."

The hick twins, Konrad and Knute, were also behind me, and they guffawed in unison. But the rest of the hired guns could barely muster up a few phony laughs. They were used to following Bartlett and Jody's lead—jumping at every jerk of the strings like puppets—but their expressions now were grim, strained, befitting men about to deal out—or be dealt—death.

Old Red tensed up beside me, and for a second, I was afraid he was going to go for his gun. Seeing as we were surrounded by men with their hands on their pistol grips already, that would have just got us shot a wee bit faster.

"Easy," I told him.

Slowly, carefully, I lifted my hands and put them on the table, the fingers spread wide. If I had to endure my third beating of the day, so be it. But I wasn't going to take the bait from Bartlett and Jody and turn it into an execution. Not if there was still a chance to talk our way off the gallows.

"Gonna look mighty suspicious if something were to happen to us while we were in here askin' questions," I said to Bartlett. "You'll just end up with the law in here askin' even more."

"Oh, yeah? Who's 'the law'?" Bartlett sneered back at me. "Flip Compton? Or the sheriff who's a hundred miles away… and comes here for a drink with Mr. Haney whenever he *is* in town?"

The twins snickered behind me, and I suddenly regretted moving my hand so far from my Colt.

"Uhh…you fellas wanna take this out back?" I heard Big Mike say from behind the bar.

He was right to be worried. Blood stains are oh-so-hard to get out of pinewood floorboards.

"No. We'll do this here," Bartlett told him. "You're our witness."

I felt a sharp shove between my shoulder blades—Jody jabbing at me with his grubby, stubby fingers.

"Yeah. They started it," he said. "And we finished it."

"Brother," Old Red said.

I had no idea what words were coming next. Maybe "Go for your iron!" We wouldn't have got off a shot. Maybe "Run for it!" We'd have been dead the second we were on our feet. Maybe "Sorry I got you into this." Well, miracles do happen.

Whatever it was to be, I didn't get to hear it.

A soft sound came from the other side of the room. Someone was clearing his throat.

Everyone turned toward the noise.

The dude Diana introduced us to, Burr, was sitting alone at a table near one of the windows, a gloved fist held daintily before his clean-shaven face.

He lowered his hand to reveal a cheerful smile.

"I think I should point out that I'm a witness, too," he said.

He raised his hand again, this time so he could lift his gray bowler an inch from his head and tip it to the men around us.

As he set his hat back in place and gave the crown a jaunty tap, Bartlett asked the question we were all thinking.

"Where the hell did *he* come from?"

"None of you idiots thought to watch the damn door?" Jody growled.

"We were watching them," either Konrad or Knute whined, flapping a hand at me and Old Red. "Why didn't *you* think of it?"

Jody muttered something under his breath that propriety forbids me to record, then turned toward the bar.

"You must've seen him come in," he snapped at Big Mike.

"Yeah, but I…I…I didn't think I should interrupt," the barman stammered.

Jody mumbled another phrase that'll get you jail time if you write it down and send it through the mail.

"That's enough of that," Bartlett said. "It doesn't matter. The gentleman is leaving anyway."

He gave Burr an unblinking glare.

"Yeah. Go pick a daisy to stick in your lapel," Jody added. "This ain't none of your business."

The dude kept smiling, unoffended. His legs were crossed casually, revealing the spotless white spats he wore over his pointy-toed Oxfords. Under normal circumstances, that would have been enough right there to get him in trouble in a place like the Bull's Head.

"A daisy? With gray wool?" he said. He shook his head and tsk-

tsked. "I should think only a white carnation would do. I may cut a fine figure, but I'm not Oscar Wilde. As for what is and isn't my business…well, I believe it's every man's business to see justice done."

There was a squeak beside me. Old Red was sitting up a little straighter in his rickety saloon chair. And I knew why.

The dude had quoted scripture. From "The Adventure of the Crooked Man," to be exact.

"And Sherlock Holmes descended from the mountaintop with a tablet. Upon one side was written, 'It is every man's business to see justice done.' And upon the other side was the fine print, saying, 'Thou shalt stick thy nose into other people's problems, and also the nose of thy younger, handsomer brother, until it doth get you both shot to death in a saloon.' And the people did cry out, saying, 'Why hast Thou forsaken the younger, handsomer brother, O Lord? For he is our favorite, and he really deserves better!'"

Or something like that.

"'It's every man's business to…'" Jody began.

That was as far as he got before the guffawing started.

"Fancy-pants thinks he's Deadwood Dick!" either Konrad or Knute hooted.

"Watch out, boys! He might spray you with his perfume!" either Knute or Konrad howled.

A few of the other gunmen joined in the cackling, looking grateful for a distraction from the bloody task at hand: doing something unspeakable to me and my brother. But the rest of them just stood there eyeing either Bartlett or us, unsure whether to laugh or kill.

Burr's walking stick was leaning against the table beside him, and he gripped the silver handle and pushed himself to his feet. He started toward us with smooth, measured steps, his affable smile never wavering.

"Ooooo!" one of the twins moaned in mock terror. "I think he's gonna challenge you to a duel, Jody!"

"Alright, alright…no more fooling around," Bartlett said,

clearly irritated by the interruption. "This is your last chance, mister. Butt out, or you'll regret it."

The dude stopped about three feet from our table.

"'To regret deeply is to live afresh,'" he said. "Henry David Thoreau." He turned to focus on Jody and the twins. "You should've left the lady out of it."

"Ooooo!" either Konrad or Knute said again. "I'm shiver…"

The dude whipped his walking stick up, and I heard a *thunk* and an *oof* behind me.

"Son of a——!" Jody managed to get out before Burr swung the cane his way.

There was a sharper crack, then another as the dude smacked Jody and the other twin upside the head. Burr went on hacking and slashing with his stick, but I didn't turn around to take in the show, much as I would've enjoyed it. I had things to do myself.

Bartlett was going for his gun. I didn't have time to reach under the table and make a grab for mine, so I threw the closest thing at hand at him: the table itself. I grabbed the edge in front of me and flipped the whole thing up into Bartlett's face.

As Bartlett stumbled backward and the men around him scattered, my brother popped to his feet and drew his Peacemaker.

"First bastard to go for a gun gets his head blowed off!" he roared.

"Yours truly excluded," I added, sliding out my forty-five. I took careful aim at Bartlett, who was still regaining his balance as the table smacked to the floor top-down and blood began to flow from his nose.

There were a few more thunks, thwacks, and cracks behind us, and first one twin, then the other, then Jody staggered past and hit the floor.

The dude stepped up between me and Old Red, his walking stick held out straight before him like a lance.

"The thing to say now is 'Hands up,'" he told us.

"I do believe you're right," I said. "Well, fellas—you heard the man. Hands up."

Bartlett's men were a weak-willed bunch, I'd come to see, and once again they followed their nature: They did as they were told. Bartlett himself just glared back at me, though, his arms firmly at his sides even as blood continued to dribble in twin streams from his already-swelling nose.

"Oh, for god's sake," I said to him. "If you're too stubborn to put your hands over your head, fine, but at least put them over your nose." I cocked my Colt. "I never could stand the sight of blood."

Bartlett finally started to lift his hands. Just before they reached his face, his eyes flicked to the side for a second, and what looked like a little smile curled the corners of his blood-streaked mouth.

"Behind us," the dude said.

I whipped around to find Big Mike pulling a rusty old shotgun out from under the counter.

I shook my head and pointed my forty-five at his broad chest.

"And here I thought you were a nice, old-fashioned coward," I said. "You know—the kind you don't have to shoot?"

"You weren't wrong," the barman said.

Slowly, gingerly, he put the scattergun back under the bar. Then he slid away from it sideways and straightened up with his hands held so high his fingertips could almost tickle the ceiling.

"What now?" I said over my shoulder.

"Isn't that obvious?" Burr replied.

"Yeah...I suppose it is," Old Red said. "Let's get."

He sounded a little reluctant, though. He probably had more questions he wanted to ask—he always has more questions—and he was wondering how long we could stick around trying to get answers before we got shot.

Which was a question I *didn't* want answered.

I started backing toward the door.

The dude did the same.

"Bartlett..." Old Red said.

Sweet Jesus, I thought. *He'd stand there asking more questions if there was a freight train coming at him.*

But my brother just said: "I'll be seein' ya," then began backing out with us.

"Yeah," Bartlett said. "You will."

The dude kept his cane up, tip pointed at Bartlett and his men, as we neared the open door.

"Uhh…that thing loaded?" I asked him.

"It might as well be," Burr told me cheerfully.

"Well, be that as it may, I think my forty-five'll give us better cover." I jerked my head at the doorway behind us. "After you."

The dude touched the tip of his gray bowler with his free hand. "Thank you, Otto. Most kind."

He picked up his pace and went gliding outside, backwards.

Old Red and I stopped shoulder to shoulder a few feet from the door. It wasn't wide enough for us to back out together. One of us would have to go first.

"You next," I said.

My brother didn't move.

"You go," he said. "You're the bigger target."

"And I'm the better shot. Go."

"Since when are you a better shot than me?"

"I don't know. Since the first time I picked up a gun?"

"Feh."

"'Feh' don't make it untrue. Now would you please just—?"

"Oh, for fun's sake," Jody spat, only he didn't say "fun" and what he did next he didn't do for the sake of it. He'd been watching us from the floor with his left hand pressed to a fresh welt on his forehead, and now he moved his right toward his holster.

"No!" Big Mike cried as Jody grabbed for his gun. "Don't do it!"

But it was too late, and Jody wasn't the type to listen anyhow. He was the type to shoot anyone who crossed him—which at that particular moment, of course, was us.

Several things happened simultaneously. Jody lifted a stubby arm to aim at us. The twins, beside him on the floor, went for their guns, too. Old Red did the sensible thing and finally ducked out the door. And I, startled and spooked, instinctively squeezed off a shot that plowed into the floorboard before Jody and blew a plume of gun smoke into the room.

"Get outta there, goddamn it!" I heard my brother shout, and for the next second the only sound—other than the ringing in my ears from the gunshot—was the pounding of my feet as I spun around and scurried through the doorway. Then the thunder came. A lot of it.

The gunshots blasted out so fast it was impossible to count them. There were other noises, too: bullets slamming into wood and plaster, glass shattering, and me screaming, "Whooooooaaaaaa!" as I ducked to the right to get myself clear of the door. Old Red and the dude were there waiting for me, and the three of us began moving away up the sidewalk at a pace just shy of a sprint.

People on both sides of the street screamed and scattered. Others either stopped to gawk or froze with fear, and we had to weave around a particularly horrified-looking woman clutching two young boys to her faded gingham dress.

"See? Your mother's right," Burr told the boys. "Stay away from saloons."

"Stop it! Stop it!" Bartlett roared back in the Bull's Head as the cacophonous volley wound down to a sputtering barrage of random shots. "I said *stop*! They're gone!"

The gunfire finally ended altogether.

Then the wailing started.

"My windows! My walls!" Big Mike cried. "My place!"

I looked back to see if Bartlett's men were following us or had shot up any poor unfortunate passersby. It was no on both counts. The doorway we'd just escaped through stayed empty, and there were no bodies sprawled in the dust beyond—though a man in a bartender's apron did step cautiously from the cantina across the street to shake his head at the fresh holes in his adobe.

As I turned my gaze away, I noticed that the townspeople who hadn't run for cover seemed particularly fixated on my right hand.

I was still clutching my gun.

"Has it started?" a cow-hand riding past asked me as he reined up his skittish, nickering horse.

I wasn't sure what he meant by "it," but I didn't like the way he moved his free hand to the rifle butt sticking from his saddle scabbard. If "it" had indeed started, it seemed, he was anxious to join in.

"Not yet," I told him. "That was just what you call an *aperitif.*"

The cowboy gaze me a puzzled look, then concentrated on settling down his spooked mount.

"That's an extremely apt metaphor," the dude said to me, seeming surprised, as he, Old Red, and I kept hurrying away from the Bull's Head.

"Yeah, well…I read a lot," I said.

I slid my Colt back into its holster. With the weight of it gone, my hand began to tremble.

I took a deep, shuddering breath.

"Thank you, Mr. Burr," I said. "That was as close as I've come to buyin' the farm in…"

I paused to think it over.

"Hours," I sighed. I shot a look at my brother. "Have I told you lately that we're in the wrong business?"

Old Red chose to let that pass. He glanced over his shoulder, then holstered his forty-five, too.

"Yeah, thanks, Mr. Burr. We're in your debt," he said. "Only I don't understand why you'd be whalin' on us one minute then savin' our bacon the next."

"It's as I explained earlier," the dude said. "Our little… exchange when we met grew out of a simple misunderstanding. After which, I felt obligated to make amends. So 'saving your bacon' seemed like the proper thing to do."

"Oh? And you're always careful to do the proper thing, are you?"

"Well," Burr said with a smile, "not always. But today, yes."

Old Red looked like he was holding in a "Feh!" of disbelief.

"Lucky for us," he said instead. "And lucky for us you slipped into that saloon. What brought you there, anyhow?"

"I was hoping to meet Mr. Haney. He's the richest man around here, I understand, so I thought I might talk a little business with him. Perhaps over a friendly game of cards."

"You ain't got much chance of a 'friendly game' now," I said.

Burr shrugged, his smile undimmed. "I'll manage."

Now that there'd been no gunfire for a good half minute, people on both sides of the street started coming out cautiously to see what had happened—some of them clutching guns of their own.

"Who got shot now?" asked a mustachioed man in a barber's white sack coat. "Eduardo Sweeney?"

I couldn't help but notice how hopeful he sounded.

"I heard it was Clayton Haney," I told him. "His own men turned on him when they found out he's bein' doin' unnatural things with the livestock."

A big man with a white cloth over his clothes and a face covered with shaving cream stepped up beside the barber and glowered at me. It took me a second to realize it was Clayton Haney.

"Maybe I heard wrong," I said.

Old Red returned the man's glare as we walked past. Burr tipped his hat.

"There's a cool customer for you," my brother muttered once the barber shop was behind us. "Leaves us to Bartlett while he gets himself a shave."

"I'm guessing Mr. Haney is the kind of man who makes it a point to be elsewhere when certain things are done on his behalf," the dude said.

Old Red gave him a sharp look, then nodded thoughtfully.

Up ahead, I saw a familiar figure trudging our way with slumped shoulders and a pained expression on his face.

"Poor Flip," I said. "I don't think he's happy bein' the only fella in town obliged to run toward gunshots instead of away from 'em."

Burr came to a sudden halt, and Old Red and I stopped beside him.

"I hope you don't mind if I leave you to provide the explanations. Badges tend to give me indigestion," the dude said. "Gustav. Otto…"

He touched the brim of his bowler as he nodded to each of us in turn, then pivoted sharply and went striding toward the nearest building—the DeBarge Arms Hotel.

"Interestin' gent," I said as my brother and I watched him go inside.

"Oh, yeah. I'd say he's already got him a 'friendly game' goin' here," Old Red replied. "Only damned if I know what it is."

TWENTY
DEBARGE HOSPITALITY
OR, WE ARE QUICKLY CHECKED OUT, CHECKED IN, AND FOULED UP

"DO you know what the gunfire's all about?" Flip Compton asked as he walked up to me and Old Red in front of the DeBarge Arms.

"Bartlett and his men were havin' a little target practice," I said. "And me and Gustav were the targets."

The deputy's eyes went wide.

"What?"

"Oh, don't beat around the bush," my brother grumbled at me. "Just tell him what happened."

So I did. It took about a minute to run through it, during which several townsfolk stopped nearby to eavesdrop. By the time I was done, there must have been twenty people scattered around waiting to see what Compton was going to do.

"Do you...do you think I ought to...arrest them?" he stammered.

"You get that telegram sent off to the sheriff?" Old Red asked him.

Compton nodded.

"Good," my brother said. "Wait and see what you hear back.

No need to rush things and spark off more shootin'. Otto and I ain't any the worse for wear."

"Speak for yourself," I said. "I need a drink after all that...but I'm sure as hell not walkin' back into the Bull's Head to get one."

"What's going on, Flip?" a man with a rifle in his hands called out.

"Yes, Deputy—are you going to do anything about that shooting?" asked another man holding a shotgun.

One was on the western side of the street, the other near us on the eastern. They each looked away from Compton to scowl at each other.

"Don't worry, Mr. Lopez...Mr. Baker...everybody," Compton said. "There's no danger." He threw an uncertain glance Old Red's way. "Uhh...right?"

My brother nodded.

"Just...go about your business, everyone," Compton went on. "It's over."

There was a long, awkward silence.

"Like hell it is," someone muttered.

Yet the crowd began to break up. As the townsmen slowly drifted off, two figures came weaving through them to join us on the sidewalk: Diana and Mr. Martinez the storekeeper.

"Are you alright?" Diana asked us.

Old Red held a hand out toward my chest.

"See any holes?" he said.

The concern on her face was instantly replaced with irritation.

"We're fine, aside from some jangled nerves. Thank you for askin', Miss," I said with a "Don't blame me" smile. I turned to Martinez. "We had another run-in with that bunch from your store yesterday. They remain as warm and sociable as ever."

"Ran into Clayton Haney again, too," Old Red added, gaze still locked on Diana. "Quite the stubborn S.O.B. your father sent us here to work for."

"Do you know the old saying 'Takes one to know one,' Mr. Amlingmeyer?" Diana replied.

Mortified, Flip and Martinez cleared their throats and shuffled their feet and generally looked like they wanted to climb up the nearest tree.

Rather than answer Diana, my brother shifted his attention to Martinez.

"Looks like me and Otto ain't the only ones gettin' in scrapes today," he said, nodding at the dark, swollen flesh around the storekeeper's left eye.

"Yeah—what happened, Mr. Martinez?" I said. "You weren't sportin' that shiner yesterday."

The way Martinez winced, you'd have thought we'd just blackened his other eye.

"Some of Haney's men caught me on the way home last night," he said. He pointed up at his bruised face. "They gave me this."

"You…you wanna press charges?" Compton asked.

Martinez gave the deputy the answer he plainly hoped to hear, and did it quick.

"No!" he said with an emphatic shake of the head. He winced again, then went on with less ardor. "I don't want to cause any more trouble. It was too dark to see which ones it was anyway."

"Alright," Compton said, looking relieved. "It's your decision."

Diana peeped over at my brother, and the two of them exchanged a look that, for the first time in a while, said something other than "I can't believe I used to like you." Instead, the message was along the lines of "Well, well…isn't that interesting?" Which, speaking personally, didn't come as an improvement, as I hadn't heard anything that seemed meaningful, and getting left behind when Old Red and the lady are deducifying is always an irritant.

There was a thump behind us, and I glanced back to find Matthew, the blue-capped bellboy from the DeBarge Arms Hotel, standing between a pair of carpetbags he'd just dropped onto the boardwalk.

"Sorry," he said to me.

He spun on his heel and marched back into the lobby.

I didn't understand the apology till I looked down at the bags.

They belonged to me and my brother.

Matthew came back through the door dragging Diana's portmanteau. When he had it outside next to the carpetbags, he let the end he was holding come down with a crash.

"Hey, kid," I said. "What's goin' on?"

"Mr. Haney came by a little while ago," he told me. "He said you were…"

The bellboy squinted with concentration as he tried to recall the exact words.

"…'a pack of useless, back-stabbing ass…'"

Yadel, the hotel manager, popped through the doorway and jerked the bellboy inside.

"There are no longer any vacancies at the DeBarge Arms," he said.

He looked around to see if any other potential customers had overheard him.

"For *you*, I mean," he said.

In a blink he disappeared, diving inside like a prairie dog ducking back into its hole.

"Well, that's just lovely," I said. "Looks like we need to find someplace around here where we're welcome."

"I believe it's already found *us*," Diana said.

She nodded toward the street.

The little balding fellow who'd approached us from the DeBarge House Hotel the day before—the man Yadel had called "Julio"—was coming toward us again, this time with a slender, dark-haired boy Matthew's age at his side.

"I see you're in need of lodging," he said. He held out his arms and grinned. "Our best rooms await you!"

Without waiting for a reply, he pointed at the luggage and snapped his fingers.

"Antonio," he said.

The skinny kid darted ahead and snatched up the carpetbags.

"Antonio," Julio said again, shaking his head.

The boy sighed, put down the bags, and turned to Diana's portmanteau.

"Thank you, sir," I said as Antonio lifted one end of the trunk and began dragging it toward the street. "We appreciate the hospitality. It's something we ain't seen a lot of around here."

The little man hopped up onto the boardwalk and picked up our bags.

"That won't be the case at the DeBarge House, I assure you," he said. "Any friends of the Sweeneys are friends of ours."

He pointedly turned his grin toward Martinez, and I recalled that the storekeeper was Mrs. Sweeney's cousin.

Martinez gave the man a smile in return, but it was so small and wobbly, it barely lasted a second.

"Shall we get you checked in?" Julio said, heading toward the DeBarge House.

Our little gaggle followed along. As we left the eastern side of the street, I noticed the hard stares we were getting from the folks we left behind us. Diana did, too.

"We're announcing to the whole town which side we're on, you know," she said under her breath.

My brother looked over his shoulder. The woman we'd spoken to after escaping the Bull's Head was passing by again with her two young sons, and even they looked like they were hoping a herd of buffalo would suddenly run through town and flatten us.

"Word was gettin' around anyway, but yeah. Now we're shoutin' it from the rooftop," Old Red said, keeping his voice low. "Which means that half of the town's about to get even more unfriendly."

"You can get *more* unfriendly than shootin' at somebody?" I said.

We'd caught up to Antonio now, and I reached down and picked up the end of the trunk he'd been dragging through the dirt just before it went through a clump of horse turds.

The boy looked back and smiled. "Gracias."

"Yes. Thanks," said Diana.

"Just don't forget to tip me," I told her.

Old Red rolled his eyes and turned to Compton. "You up for some detective work, Deputy?"

Compton blinked at my brother like he'd been asked to shove a gila monster down his pants. Still, he managed to get out a quivery "Of course."

"Good," Old Red said. "You know where folks go when they're lookin' for liquor on the east side of the street. Other than the Bull's Head, I mean. Check and see if any of them places stock Ballard's Best Extra Fine Rye Whiskey. I'd do it myself, but given what just happened I think me and my brother oughta stick to the west side."

"Sure," Compton said, though he sounded anything but. "That reminds me. I need to get that whiskey bottle and the shells you gave me put away. I guess it's all evidence, isn't it?"

My brother nodded. "The money and that bottle of medicine, too. Should still be in the marshal's coat."

Martinez had been tagging along silently at Diana's side—I could understand why a man would stick there even when he no longer had a reason—and now he piped up again.

"I have a safe in the back room of my store. You're free to make use of it, Flip. It's probably the safest place in town other than the vaults at the banks. You wouldn't want anyone making off with your evidence before the inquest."

"Thank you, Mr. Martinez. I might take you up on that," Compton said. "My main worry right now is keeping the peace until the sheriff or whoever he sends can get here." He sighed and threw a look back toward the Bull's Head. "It feels like one more spark and this whole town'll explode."

We were just outside the DeBarge House, but Compton didn't follow Julio inside. Instead, he came to a sudden stop, gaze fixed on something beyond the saloon down the street. The rest of us turned to see what he was staring at.

A little caravan was coming up the road from the south: a buggy and a chuck wagon flanked by six riders with rifles out and ready. They were still too far off to see faces, yet there was no mistaking the round, black-clad figure driving the buggy with a boy—her youngest son, Miguel—sitting beside her.

DeBarge was about to get its spark.

The Sweeneys were coming to town.

TWENTY-ONE
QUESTIONS INSTEAD OF ANSWERS
OR, WE GREET THE SWEENEYS' WAGON TRAIN, BUT THE CONVERSATION QUICKLY GOES OFF THE RAILS

THE SWEENEYS WERE STILL MORE than a hundred yards off, yet I recognized one of the lead riders from his light-brown campaign hat, ramrod-stiff spine, and all-around air of coiled rattlesnake intensity. Ed Sweeney, of course. His brother Johnny wasn't with him at the head of the column, though. That honor had fallen to the blond cowhand they'd called "Fitz." Johnny was driving the chuck wagon rattling along behind the buggy, if my eyes were seeing right.

Up and down DeBarge, people turned to watch the party approach. Some didn't do it for long, though. About half the townsfolk quickly scooted into the nearest building or hustled off toward the other end of town. The ones who remained—men mostly—stood their ground with grim expressions that dared their counterparts across the street to do something.

"I really should be going," Martinez said. "Deputy—remember what I said about my safe. Come by my store if you want to keep the evidence you've collected secure until the inquest."

As the shopkeeper hurried away, Julio stepped back out of the

DeBarge House to see why the rest of us hadn't followed him inside.

"Oh," he said when he saw the buggy and wagon and riders headed toward us. "Antonio?"

"*Sí?*" the bellboy said.

Julio pointed his chin at me and my brother and Diana. "*Doscientos seis y doscientos ocho.*"

Antonio nodded. "*Sí.*"

I don't *hablo* much *español*, but I know numbers when I hear them. Julio was changing where the boy was supposed to take Diana's trunk.

So much for getting the best rooms in the place.

Julio waved to the Sweeneys, who were almost even with the Bull's Head now, and Mrs. Sweeney lifted her buggy whip in response.

The hotel man threw a nervous peep at the opposite side of the street, then said something else in Spanish and headed back inside. Antonio started to follow him. I was still helping the kid with Diana's portmanteau, but now I put my end of it down.

"Hope you can manage from here, amigo," I said, moving my hand to my gun belt. "I think I oughta stick around to help greet your new guests."

And try to make sure they don't get shot, I could've added. Though there wouldn't be much I could do if Bartlett and his men started blazing away from the saloon.

"Sure. Thanks for the help, mister," the kid said, and he began dragging the trunk off again. Diana managed not to wince as it thunked up onto the boardwalk and scraped its way across the slats and into the lobby.

Ed Sweeney lifted an arm to point in our general direction, and Fitz went galloping ahead. He passed us without any acknowledgment, riding around into the broad alley beside the hotel.

The cowboy had been given the honor of scouting for an ambush. He wasn't met with a volley of gunfire—I could've told him where to look for those, but he didn't ask—so the rest of the group kept coming.

Compton tugged his hat brim lower, puffed out his chest, put his hands on his hips, and generally tried to look more 'lawmanly.'

"Hello, folks," he said. "What brings you into town?"

Ed reined up before the hotel, and the buggy, wagon and riders stopped in a line behind him.

"We need your permission?" he sneered.

Compton shrank in on himself.

"No, of course not, Ed," he said, seeming to lose three inches and twenty pounds in an instant. "It's just maybe not a good...I mean, it might be better if you stayed..." Compton took a breath and managed to get a little of his spine back. "There's already been some trouble today, that's all."

"So I see," Mrs. Sweeney said from her surrey.

She was looking at me and Old Red and our new-to-her bruises.

They were new to her youngest son, too, and, like many a boy, he wasn't the type to be coy.

"What happened to *you?*" Miguel asked me.

"Sherlock Holmes," I said, rubbing my sore jaw. I glanced over at my brother. "You know, I don't know what stings worse: all the places I got punched today or the fact that I have to keep talkin' about it."

The kid cocked his head and squinted at me. "Sherlock Holmes?"

"Just a little private joke, son," I said.

"Oh, is that why no one's laughin'?" said Old Red.

Mrs. Sweeney pointed at us with her whip looking extremely unamused. "Was it Bartlett?"

"Partially," my brother said. "We also ran into some strangers eager for a scrape, for some reason." He sighed, obviously about to ask a question he knew he wouldn't get answered. "Two men out near your spread? One a Mescalero Apache? Other calls himself 'Nadie'?"

Ed snorted but offered no further comment.

Miguel sat up straight beside his mother, eyes widening.

"A Mescalero?" he said, making it sound like "the Bogeyman."

He was wearing a little black suit with short pants, like the day before, and his mother put down her whip so she could place a reassuring hand on his bare knee.

"We don't know anyone like that," she told my brother.

"They must be more new Haney men," Johnny Sweeney said from the chuck wagon, which he'd stopped just behind his mother's buggy. He looked skeptical of his own words even as they left his mouth.

Old Red said what he seemed to be thinking.

"Clayton Haney ain't the type to have Apaches on the payroll."

"So you got in a fight with a couple of drifters," Ed said. "That's what we get for hiring the A-1 Detective Agency?"

"The A.A. Western Detective Agency," Diana reminded him. "And you've already gotten more than that, Mr. Sweeney."

Ed just snorted again.

"That medicine Mr. Amlingmeyer found in the marshal's pocket, for instance," Diana went on. "We know where it came from."

Old Red and I swiveled to stare at her but managed not to blurt out "We do?"

Diana, meanwhile, had moved her focus over to Mrs. Sweeney.

"Francisco Martinez told me that Marshal Hinkle got it from his store last night," she said. "And apparently, the marshal told Mr. Martinez it was for *you*."

The little boy turned to look at his mother. "Are you sick?"

"It's nothing, Miguel. Just some headache powder," she lied without looking at him. Tell him it was Dr. Faraday's Female Remedy and she might have to explain why females need their own remedies, and who wants to do that sitting in a buggy in the street with half the town gaping at you? She kept her gaze— which was now a glare—on Diana. "None of that matters. Alf

Hinkle wasn't killed because he had a bottle of patent medicine in his pocket."

"With all due respect, Mrs. Sweeney," Diana replied, "we don't know why Marshal Hinkle was killed. If we're going to figure that out—and who did it—we need to pursue every possible line of inquiry. Which is why, if the medicine was for you, it would have been good to know it earlier."

Mrs. Sweeney took a deep breath, and some of the anger seemed to seep out of her.

"I realize you're just trying to do your job," she said. "But it's not something a lady likes to talk about, is it?"

"I understand that, ma'am," Old Red said. "But still, I gotta ask: How did the marshal know that you needed…you know…a remedy of that sort?"

Mrs. Sweeney went back to glaring.

"*I* told him," Ed said.

"Oh?" Old Red said. "When?"

"Last night."

"When you two was 'arguin' about politics' in his office?'"

Ed made the glaring a family affair.

"Yes," he said. "I mentioned that my mother had been… uncomfortable lately, and I guess he took it upon himself to help."

"By bringing her medicine in the middle of the night?" Diana asked.

"With hundreds of dollars in his pocket?" Old Red added.

"*Yes*," Ed hissed between gritted teeth.

My brother opened his mouth. Mrs. Sweeney shut it with a clipped "*Mr.* Amlingmeyer."

Our employer slid her eyes to her right.

Miguel was taking in the conversation with a look of bewildered fright on his face.

"This is not the time or place for this conversation," Mrs. Sweeney said to us.

Diana nodded. "Yes, of course."

"Yeah, you're right. I do apologize," Old Red said. "We're just eager to see the job through for you, and that's hard to do without havin' all the facts."

"Well, you'll have to get them somewhere else," Mrs. Sweeney said. She glanced around at the townspeople watching us. Some of them looked like they were sizing up Ed's neck for a noose. "It's time I got my family to safety."

She lifted the buggy reins.

"Umm...ma'am?" Compton said before she could drive off.

"What is it, Flip?" Mrs. Sweeney said. She *almost* managed to sound like she wasn't tempted to pick up her whip and use it on him.

"Is this really the safest place for your family?" the deputy asked her. "I mean...Mr. Haney's here. And Bartlett. And all the rest. And...you know...folks are pretty upset about Alf."

"That's exactly why we're here," Ed said. "Jesús Luna rode out to tell us Haney was in town, and we knew what that meant: He'd be riling people up, spreading lies, throwing his weight around at the inquest."

"Ed," Mrs. Sweeney said.

But her son wasn't done.

"Well, we're not gonna just sit out there on the ranch and wait for the vigilantes to ride up with ropes or for the sheriff to come after me with some bullshit warrant. If Haney wants to stir up trouble, by god we'll give him some *now*."

"*Ed*," Mrs. Sweeney said again.

This time it worked. Ed not only shut up, he rode off, turning left to join Fitz behind the hotel.

"We won't be railroaded, Flip. We're here to make our stand," Mrs. Sweeney said. She graced me and Old Red and Diana with another glower. "You'll know where to find us when you don't have questions instead of answers."

She gave the reins a flick. Her horse set off at a trot, and she steered it down the alley beside the hotel. Two of the other cowhands who'd ridden in with the Sweeneys took off after her, their rifles still out of their scabbards. The last two hands stuck close to the chuck wagon, one on either side, as Johnny got it rolling after the rest of the group. It seemed to be their sworn duty to protect something that normally didn't carry anything more valuable than bacon, beans, and flour.

Johnny looked like he wanted to say something to us as he went by, but he turned away and gave his horses a "Heeya!" instead.

Once the wagon was past us, we had a clear view across the street again—and Haney and Bartlett, who were watching from in front of the DeBarge Arms, had a clear view of us.

TWENTY-TWO
ANTONIO

OR, SOME BIG SURPRISES COME IN A
SMALL PACKAGE

WE EYED EACH OTHER A MOMENT—HANEY
and Bartlett in front of the one hotel, and me, my brother, Diana,
and Deputy Compton in front of the other. Then Haney said
something to Bartlett, and the two men turned and walked off
down the sidewalk. They were headed toward the Bull's Head, I
noted. The deputy seemed to note it, too.

"I think I'll go check with the telegraph office," he said. "You
know…to see if anything's come in for me."

Like a message from the sheriff saying he was on his way to
take charge before DeBarge turned into Gettysburg.

"Don't forget to ask around about that whiskey," Old Red
reminded him. "Ballard's Best Extra Fine Rye."

"Right. I will," Compton said, though he looked like he could
think of something better to do with whiskey than ask about it. He
put a shaky hand to the brim of his hat. "Miss Crowe. Fellas."

He walked off briskly, as if he might break into a sprint any
second—and keep going straight on to the horizon.

At last we were alone with Diana. Or alone-ish, at least, as
there were still plenty of assorted citizens watching us on both
sides of the street. "It ain't polite to stare!" I wanted to shout at

them, but I didn't suppose that would bring us anything more in the way of privacy. I was about to suggest that we head inside the DeBarge House to consult—and hopefully patch things up between Diana and my brother—but Old Red got talking first.

"So…Hinkle bought that medicine from Martinez. Interestin'. Anything else you need to tell us?"

"Yes. In fact, there is," Diana said. "I could tell you were skeptical that Ed would discuss his mother's private health concerns with the marshal, but it might be true. I spoke to a Mr. Baker at another store in town, and he says Ed came in yesterday to ask if he stocked any medicine for female troubles."

The name Baker rang a bell, and I turned to look up the street. Directly across from Martinez's place was a store with: "DeBARGE MERCANTILE & SUNDRIES, M. BAKER, PROPRIETOR" over the door. I pointed at it for Old Red's benefit.

"*That* Mr. Baker?" I asked Diana.

She nodded. "That's right."

"On the east side of the street," my brother mused.

Diana nodded again.

"Interestin'," she said with a small, wary smile.

I smiled back. Old Red didn't.

"That all?" he asked.

Diana's smile faded.

"Well…there's nothing definitive to tell you," she said. "I was making more inquiries when the gunfire caught everyone's attention. Speaking of which, was there more to say about that? Something you didn't want to tell me in front of the—?"

"*We* ain't holdin' nothing back," Old Red cut in gruffly. "You go on and get checked in. Otto and me need to get back to the 'inquiries' while there's still daylight."

He turned away and started stomping down the street.

"I'm not done," Diana said.

Old Red spun around to face her again. "Not done with what? Goin' around askin' questions or gabbin' with us out here in the open? Cuz either one is likely to get you killed."

"Oh, I'm done talking to *you*," Diana snapped back. "I still have work to do."

"Much as I hate to admit it, Miss," I said, "my brother is right. He and I just came within an inch of the pearly gates, and there's two of us. Ain't no way you should be pokin' around this town on your own anymore."

Diana stared back at me through narrowed eyes, clearly taking my point without wanting to concede it. Then her gaze flicked away to the east for a second, and her little smile returned.

"Fortunately, I don't have to do it on my own," she said. "Happy hunting, gentlemen."

And off she went toward the other side of the street. And the DeBarge Arms Hotel. And a certain guest we'd seen head into the lobby fifteen minutes before.

"Burr," Old Red growled.

The dude had probably saved us from a meeting with Saint Peter, but my brother didn't sound particularly grateful to him just then.

"Yeah, well…you pretty much dropped her into his lap," I said.

Old Red shot me a scowl.

"Metaphorically speaking," I added. "By treatin' her the way you been, I mean."

My brother's scowl got 'scowlier.'

"What about the way she's been treatin' us?" He stabbed a pointed finger at the lady, who was at that moment stepping into the DeBarge Arms. "She had a chance to tell us she's reportin' everything we do to Col. Crowe, and she didn't take it."

I gave my brother a look of mournful disappointment and threw a line from "The Sign of Four" at him.

"One should never guess. It is a shocking habit—destructive to the logical faculty."

Old Red did not respond as per usual to a Holmes quote.

"Oh, blow it out your ass," he said.

"No. I will not blow it out my ass. I will continue to point out that you are talkn' through yours. You don't *know* Miss Crowe sent a telegram to the colonel about us."

"Why the hell else would she go to—?"

"*And even if she did,*" I forged on, "what does it matter if she ain't tryin' to boss us around on his behalf?"

"*It matters,*" Old Red declared, "cuz we're supposed to be partners and she's holdin' something back."

"The way you laid all your cards on the table with her just now?" I paused to stroke my chin thoughtfully. "Oh. Wait. You didn't. You just fussed at her again without comin' out and tellin' her *you followed her* and know she went to the telegraph office. No. You *held all that back.*"

"That's different," my brother grumbled.

I stroked my chin again. "Come to think of it, you're always holdin' things back…though I recollect you promisin' to stop that, once upon a time. Why, you keep me in the dark so much it's a wonder I ain't gone blind as a bat."

"Wouldn't be much of a change."

I didn't take the bait.

"You little hypocrite you," I scolded. "Gettin' mad at Miss Crowe for something you do every damn day."

Someone cleared his throat behind us, and we glanced back to find Antonio, the DeBarge House's skinny little bellboy, watching us from the sidewalk.

"Are you coming in?" he asked, stretching an arm out toward the hotel's front door.

"Why, thank you for askin', son," my brother said warmly, turning toward the boy with an agreeable eagerness that seemed unlike him—unless you realized it meant he was turning *away* from me. "We ain't ready to check in just yet. I reckon your boss Julio's busy helpin' the Sweeneys get settled anyhow. How come you ain't helpin'? Looks like they brought in so much luggage they need a chuck wagon for it."

Antonio shrugged his slight shoulders. "They wanted their own men to do the unloading, so Julio—Señor Diaz—told me to show you and the lady to your rooms." He looked this way and that, scanning the street for Diana. "Your friend is still staying here, isn't she?"

Old Red didn't answer. His gaze dropped to a spot just to the right of the boy's scuffed, faded shoes, his amiable expression suddenly stiff and distant.

"Doin' their own unloadin', huh?" he mumbled. "Around the back…"

"Yeah, the lady's still stayin' here…though when she'll be checkin' in, I don't know," I told Antonio. "But you may as well get us two squared away." I started toward the hotel. "I cannot wait to peel off these dusty clothes and get myself a proper—"

"Nope," Old Red said.

I stopped. I sagged. I sighed.

"Nope?" I said.

My brother looked over at me and shook his head. "We ain't done trackin' that whiskey."

"Oh," I said.

Then it hit me, and I straightened up and smiled.

"Oh! So we're off to the cantinas?"

"That's right."

I rubbed my hands together. "I approve."

"What whiskey are you looking for?" Antonio asked.

Old Red and I answered him at the same time.

"Oh, don't you worry about that," I said.

"Ballard's Best Extra Fine Rye Whiskey," said my brother.

Antonio focused on Old Red and shook his head.

"I don't know that one," he said.

"Well, why would you?" I chuckled. "It ain't like we're lookin' for Dr Pepper."

The boy shot me a frown, then pointed to the south.

"At El Culo del Toro they have rot-gut from a barrel and sometimes a bottle of Schenley Pure Rye under the bar." He swung his pointed finger to the north. "At Águila Dorada they have worse rut-got and something they pour from an Old Crow bottle that isn't Old Crow. Across the street from them is a place called the Bald Eagle where they actually have Old Crow and

Hermitage and even a bottle of Jameson's once every few months." He dropped his arm and jerked his head at the other end of town. "And the Bull's Head, I think you already know about. They've got grain alcohol with tea and pepper for the hands and Miller's Special Gamecock Rye for Mr. Haney. Every now and then a drummer comes through with a few bottles of a name brand—usually Thistle Dew or Old Forester—but they're never around for long. Ballard's Best Extra Fine Rye Whiskey I've never heard of."

The boy crossed his arms and smirked at me with his head tilted to the side.

I pulled out a nickel and flipped it to him.

"You have a fine future ahead of you in the hospitality industry," I said.

Antonio gave me a wink.

"I can tell you what women are available in DeBarge, too," he said.

"Umm...no thanks." I looked over at Old Red. "Guess we didn't need to send Flip out to ask around about that whiskey after all."

"Nope," my brother said. "No one carries it around here." His gaze started to go glassy again. "Which means we got us one of them 'dog in the night-time situations.'"

Antonio squinted at him. "You...need a dog?"

"Just an expression," I said. "No need to tell us what's on hand."

Old Red took in a deep breath and let it go slowly.

"You certainly seem to know your business, kid," he said. "Ain't no need for us to go to them cantinas now."

I held my hand out toward Antonio.

"I want my nickel back," I said.

The boy grinned and stuffed the coin in his pocket.

My brother tossed him another one, then turned to look out at the town. The light falling over the buildings to the east had gone golden-orange, while the shadows from the DeBarge House and its neighbors on the west side now stretched almost halfway across the street.

The sun was going down. We'd managed to survive an entire day in DeBarge.

"Well, we may as well go on up to our room and turn in," Old Red said. "Lead the way, Antonio."

The boy nodded and headed into the hotel.

"Hold on," I said, voice low, as my brother started to follow him. "I'm all for dustin' ourselves off, but goin' to bed? We're supposed to figure out who killed Hinkle before the sheriff shows up and holds an inquest and maybe gets one of our clients hung. I'd think there's more we oughta be doin' today."

"Oh, there is," Old Red said. He threw another look out at the street and the shadows there that seemed to grow longer and blacker by the second. "Only what we gotta do next we need to do after dark."

TWENTY-THREE
THE LAST SHOWDOWN
OR, MY BROTHER AND I WRANGLE OVER HIS HERO'S FATAL MISSTEP, THEN SET OFF TO MAKE OUR OWN

OUR ROOM on the second floor of the DeBarge House Hotel was identical to the one we'd had at the DeBarge Arms except that everything was a little mustier, a little dingier, a little dustier. Even the wallpaper seemed to be the same—beige diamonds of vines and fleur-de-lis—though here it was faded and peeling at the edges. The first time I spied a bedbug, I planned to ask him if he was related to the ones across the street.

Old Red took it all in with a grunt, then sent Antonio out to fetch us some food.

"We showed our faces around town too much today," he explained after the boy put our bags on the rickety bed and left. "Best if certain folks don't give us any thought for a while."

"I don't think they're likely to forget a couple of memorable fellows like us," I said. "And Miss Crowe's gonna remind 'em anyway if she's pokin' around with Burr."

"Yeah, well...nothin' I can do about where she chooses to 'poke around.'" My brother grimaced. "Or who she chooses to poke with."

"Not true. There is something you could do. You could talk to her about it."

Old Red just stomped over to the bed and jerked open his carpetbag. He rummaged roughly through his things until he found what he was looking for: the December issue of *McClure's Magazine*. The one with John Watson's last Sherlock Holmes story in it.

He tossed it into my hands.

"I'd like to do a little consultin' with Mr. Holmes," he said.

"And you want to stop consultin' with me. I get it." I dropped the magazine onto the bed. "Well, keep your shirt on. I need to get mine off."

By the time I'd cleaned up in the washroom down the hall and put on fresh clothes, Antonio was back with two pails—one filled with enchiladas, the other with the thick hominy stew called pozole. The four bits I gave the boy didn't get the smile one might expect for such a generous tip, just a distracted thanks. So I asked if anything was wrong.

"There are men walking the street with guns," he said. "Lots of them."

"Haney men?" Old Red asked. He'd been peering out the room's one window, but it faced north, offering a view of rooftops and distant desert and not much else. The way the light was fading it would soon show us nothing but stars.

Antonio nodded. "Yes, Haney men. And Sweeney men, townsmen, and nesters, too. It feels like a war is about to break out."

"Don't worry," I said. "Everyone's on edge cuz of what happened to the marshal, that's all. Things'll calm down overnight."

Antonio looked like he believed my words about as much as I did. Which wasn't much.

I pulled out another quarter.

"All the same, don't go out runnin' more errands tonight," I said as I handed over the coin. "In fact, maybe tell Señor Diaz you ain't feelin' too well and head on home."

The boy pocketed the quarter, then put his hand on his

stomach and began backing out of the room. "Thank you. Now that you mention it, I am feeling a little sick."

"Hold on," said Old Red. "I got a question for you."

Antonio stopped in the doorway. "Yes?"

"Do you know where Señor Diaz put the Sweeneys? Which rooms?"

"I'm not supposed to say."

"We ain't just anybody. We're workin' for the Sweeneys. Ain't no harm in us knowin' where our own employers are."

Antonio shook his head. "I was told not to talk about it."

My brother pulled out a dime and pitched it to the boy. At the rate Antonio was collecting coins from us, he'd soon have enough to build his own hotel.

"We're detectives," Old Red said. "We'd figure out where the Sweeneys are sooner or later. You're just sparin' us a little inconvenience by tellin' us now."

"And don't worry," I added. "We won't let on we heard it from you."

Antonio looked at the dime in his hand, then pointed up at the ceiling.

"They wanted the top floor. All of it," he said. "Señor Diaz had to move two guests down to other rooms himself, and they did not sound happy."

"You didn't get roped in to help with the luggage?" Old Red asked.

Antonio shook his head. "I was told to stay away from the third floor. No one is to go up there while the Sweeneys are here."

"Makes sense," I said to my brother. "I bet they've got Fitz up there watchin' the hallway with his scattergun. Anyone pokin' his head up for a look'll probably get some fresh holes in it."

"Yeah, maybe," Old Red said. "Or maybe…"

He didn't bother finishing his thought. Not out loud, anyway. He just turned back to the window without another word.

"That means good night," I interpreted for Antonio. "And thank you."

The boy nodded.

"Adios," he said.

I was about to point out the ominous air of finality of such a farewell—I would have preferred a "See you in the morning"—but the boy was already closing the door behind him. I could hear brisk footsteps as he hurried down the hall.

He wasn't wasting any time getting somewhere safer.

Smart kid.

I helped myself to half the pozole and enchiladas—I was so hungry I shoveled it down my gullet in less time than it takes to tell of it—then stretched out on the bed and picked up the *McClure's*.

"You really want to hear 'The Adventure of the Final Problem'?" I asked my brother. "Why not something a little more cheerful? 'The Adventure of the Blue Carbuncle,' maybe. Ain't nobody dies in that one but a goose."

"Read," Old Red said without turning away from the window.

I stared at him silently for half a minute until he spoke again.

"Please," he sighed.

I cleared my throat and began.

"'It is with a heavy heart that I take up my pen to write these, the last words in which I shall ever record the singular gifts by which my friend Mr. Sherlock Holmes was distinguished. In an incoherent, and as I deeply feel, an entirely inadequate fashion, I have endeavored to give some account of my strange experiences in his company...'"

I paused to give my brother a chance to say something. The third or fourth time I'd read "The Adventure of the Final Problem" for him, he'd interrupted to say that Holmes wasn't the only one to be burdened with an incoherent and entirely inadequate biographer. I'd put the magazine down and refused to pick it up again for the next three days.

Old Red held his tongue.

"'...from the chance which first brought us together at the period of the 'Study in Scarlet,' up to the time of his interference in the matter of the 'Naval Treaty'...'" I went on. And on. And on.

As I read, a powerful weariness came over me. It wasn't just the belly full of warm food weighing me down. It's a long day that starts not long after dawn with the discovery of a murder and goes on to include two fistfights and a narrow escape from a firing squad. Around the point in the story where Mr. Holmes and Doc Watson start their sightseeing stroll to the Reichenbach Falls, I found myself nodding off.

I jerked my head up and went on reading, telling of the messenger boy who comes after Holmes and Watson with a note about a sick Englishwoman and the doctor going back to see to her and Holmes carrying on by himself and the enchiladas he stopped to eat with Professor Moriarity when he reached the Falls and Clayton Haney and Bartlett hurling horse turds at them and Diana—who was suddenly with Holmes instead of Moriarity— picking them up and throwing them back while the dude and the Apache and a bear stood off to the side laughing and…

"Wake up," Old Red said. "It's time."

My eyes popped open, and the Falls and Holmes and Diana and the rest disappeared. I was flat on my back on the bed in the DeBarge House, the *McClure's* spread across my chest. I'd drifted off to sleep before I could finish the story.

The gas light on the wall nearby was putting out enough light for me to see my brother hovering over me, but just barely. He had it turned down so low that the flame was little more than a glowing cinder in the darkness. It was less important that we see each other than that we *not* be seen by anyone watching our window.

I sat up and swung my feet off the bed.

"I should've asked this earlier," I yawned, "but what exactly is it we gotta do in the middle of the damn night?"

"Snoop," Old Red said, voice low. He turned away from me and walked softly toward the door.

That was all I was going to get. Whatever the particulars were, I wouldn't know them till I was knee-deep *in* them.

"Oh, yeah," I said. "*That's* why I didn't ask earlier."

A thought occurred to me that I'd had many a time: that I

could just lie back down and go back to sleep and let my tight-lipped, high-handed brother do his detectiving alone. If he wouldn't explain why I should stick my neck out, maybe I should just keep it—and the rest of me—under a blanket instead.

The magazine had slid down into my lap, and as I picked it up and tossed it onto the bed, I knew I had my answer.

"Brother," I said, "has it occurred to you that Mr. Holmes didn't have to go off for that last showdown with Moriarity by his lonesome? He knew it was a trap. He could've brought Watson along or called for the local law and maybe not gone over that waterfall."

Old Red was standing by the door, head cocked, listening for movement in the hall, and in the dim light, I could see him look toward the bed and scowl.

"Sometimes a man's gotta do what he's gotta alone, that's all," he said. "Now come on."

I didn't get up.

"The only thing a man's *gotta* do alone is visit the privy," I said. "The rest of the time that's a lotta bunk...though I know you'd like to believe it. Why, if you didn't need me to be your readin' glasses, I bet you'd always be chargin' off alone like Holmes at the end there."

"You don't have to come with me," my brother growled.

I shook my head.

"Sometimes a man's gotta do what he's gotta with company. With *help*," I said. "Usually, in fact. That's something you need to accept, Brother...or you're gonna end up like Mr. Holmes."

My gun belt was on the bed beside the magazine, and I picked it up and got to my feet.

"Finally," Old Red muttered.

My Stetson was on the floor by the bed, and once I had my gun belt strapped on, I started to bend down and reach for it.

"Leave it," my brother said. "A man's hat can give away who he is when he ain't nothin' more than a shadow in the moonlight."

His white Boss of the Plains was on the floor, too, so he was practicing what he preached.

My sheepskin coat was on the bed, as well, and I picked it up and put it on.

"Alright. No hat," I said. "But if I catch my death of cold I'll never forgive you."

"It ain't the cold we need to worry about," Old Red said.

I didn't argue with him on that.

Seconds later we were tiptoeing down the hall toward the back stairs. My brother didn't pause as we passed room 208—or "*doscientos ocho*" as Señor Diaz had called it when assigning it to Diana—and neither did I. Yes, I did believe that Old Red needed to leave the "a man's gotta do what he's gotta alone" bullshit behind him. But another argument with our supposed partner when we were trying to be quiet wouldn't do us any good. And knowing her, she'd insist on tagging along for our late-night "snoop," and petticoats wouldn't do us any favors when attempting to slink around unseen. Best to leave the lady to her pleasant—or, if they were anything like mine, unnervingly peculiar—dreams.

Old Red led us down the rickety stairs, each squeaking step feeling like a telegram for Fitz and the other Sweeney hands guarding the third floor.

WAKE UP STOP YOU HAVE MEN TO SHOOT STOP

No one seemed to get the message, though: We made it to the bottom of the stairwell without any reaction from up above. It was so dark down there I had to feel my way along the wall so as not to walk into it, and in the utter blackness I could hear nothing but my brother's breathing and the low, slow, cautious rattle as he tried the knob on the back door.

The door opened slowly with a rusty-hinged squeal that put a shiver down my spine, and silver-gray moonlight and frigid night air spilled in upon us. Yet there was still no movement upstairs, and when the door was open just wide enough my brother turned sideways and slipped through it. I had to open the door a wee bit wider to do likewise—perhaps more than "a wee bit," actually, given the generous dimensions of my manly frame—but soon as I was standing alongside Old Red outside.

"Now what?" I whispered.

It wasn't my brother who supplied the answer. It was a noise. The double-*clack* of someone chambering a round in a Winchester —which was, I saw when I followed the sound, aimed squarely at a nice, big, unmissable target.

Me.

TWENTY-FOUR
SNEAKY BASTARDS
OR, WE FACE THE MAN WE'RE TRYING TO SAVE AND NEED SOMEONE TO SAVE US FROM HIM

MY BROTHER HAD BEEN RIGHT about a man's hat giving him away even in the dead of night. There was enough moon out for me to see the flat brim and dimpled peak of a campaign hat.

The man with the rifle was Ed Sweeney.

He was about thirty feet off, standing in an empty lot that gave way to desert behind him. Old Red and I may have set out for our prowl lidless, but he should've had no trouble recognizing us from our silhouettes alone: one little, one large, side-by-side behind the hotel. Yet the rifle didn't move. Ed was holding it at waist height, the barrel still pointed my way. All he had to do was pull the trigger to put a bullet right where my dinner was sitting.

"Just the man we wanted to see," I lied. "How goes it, Ed? Keepin' your eyes peeled for Bartlett and the other Haney boys?"

"I'm watching for anyone trying to make trouble," Ed said. "What are you two doing?"

"Like I said, lookin' for you, among other things. Wanted to check in and make sure y'all were takin' the proper precautions. It's pleasin' to see you are…though I think you can let your guard down a little now, if you know what I mean."

Ed gave no sign that he did. The Winchester still didn't waver —though I was sure starting to.

"How's your mother holdin' up?" Old Red said. "And the kids?"

Ed finally moved, although not in the way I'd wanted. He seemed to jerk up straight, as though startled, and the rifle rose up a little higher. If he fired now, he wouldn't blow a hole in my stomach. He'd put one through my heart.

"That's all you came out here for?" he snapped. "To ask me stupid questions?"

"Well..." I began. I didn't get any further. And not just because I had no idea what to say next.

Noises came from the scrub somewhere behind Ed. A shifting of sandy soil, a clattering of rocks, a rustling in the yucca.

Ed spun around, and the rifle spun with him. At long last I wasn't in his sights. The desert was.

"Who's there?" he said.

My brother gave me a gentle nudge with his elbow, and when I looked over, he jerked his head toward the wide alleyway running alongside the hotel.

Quick but quiet, we started to slip away.

There was the sound of more stirring in the brush, though there was no movement I could see.

"Show yourself or I start shooting!" Ed said.

A high, eerie, keening cry came out of the desert. As it faded, it was answered by three yips and another long wail.

Coyotes.

"Dammit," Ed spat, and I heard him spin our way again.

Heard rather than *saw* because Old Red and I were halfway up the alley by then. Another dozen strides and we could dodge left or right and take the targets off our backs.

A figure appeared at the end of the alleyway ahead of us, blocking our escape.

"What's going on? Who is that?"

It was Johnny Sweeney. He put a hand to his side—and the forty-five hanging there—but Old Red and I kept coming.

"It's us, Johnny—the Amlingmeyers," I said. "Your brother needs you out back. He thinks some sneaky bastards are creepin' around outside the hotel."

I didn't add, off course, that Ed was right, and we were the sneaky bastards.

"Oh. O.K.," Johnny said as we swept past him.

He took a step down the alley, then stopped and turned toward us.

"Hey…where are *you* going?"

"We got creepin' around to do elsewhere," I said, and Old Red and I swung left and hustled off up the sidewalk.

After we'd passed three or four darkened storefronts, I glanced back to see if the Sweeneys were behind us. They weren't—though I did spot a little orange pinprick of light across the street from the DeBarge House. Someone standing in the shadows by the DeBarge Arms was keeping himself awake with a smoke.

I looked up and down the street, wondering how many other men were out there watching us without advertising the fact.

"It's one thing knowin' Haney's bunch wanna see us dead," I said. "But when our own client wouldn't seem to mind it, I take it personally. Damn lucky for us that those coyotes happened by when they did."

"Was it?" Old Red said.

"What do you mean 'Was it?' You were there. Here we are tryin' to prove Ed ain't a murderer, and it looked like he had half a mind to murder *us*."

"I know that. I meant was it luck."

"What? How is it anything but? You think the coyotes was lookin' out for us? Big fans, maybe? Like Flip?"

"Maybe something like that."

I gave Old Red a long stare, then lifted my left arm and pinched my wrist.

"Nope," I said. "I ain't dreamin'. You sure you ain't sleepwalkin', Brother?"

Old Red rolled his eyes. "And you wonder why I don't tell you everything I'm thinkin'."

"Well, if it's along the lines of friendly coyotes gettin' us out of tight spots, you have my permission to go on keepin' it to yourself."

"I am *really* regrettin' wakin' you up," my brother sighed. "Come on."

We were passing another alleyway, and he turned sharply and darted into it. I did the same, following him into a darkness so complete, I could see nothing but a hazy gray sliver up ahead where the alley ended. When we reached it, Old Red paused for a quick look this way and that, then headed to the right.

Even without the dim light of the moon and stars to see by, I would've known where we were going. The familiar smell would've told me, as would a guttural groaning I also knew well.

Horses snore, you know.

We were slinking around to the back of Ernesto's livery stable.

"If you'd told me we were goin' for a ride I would've brought my spurs," I said, voice low.

"We *ain't* goin' for a ride," Old Red whispered back. "I figured the Sweeneys would leave their horses and tack and whatnot here for the night. And I was right."

He pointed at two large, boxy shapes in the gloom ahead: the Sweeneys' buggy and chuck wagon, which I saw as we drew closer. They were parked beside one of the corrals behind the stable.

My brother headed straight for them.

"What is it we're lookin' for back here?" I asked him.

"Same thing as always," he said. "Data."

I sighed. "Congratulations. That is the least helpful answer ever in your long history of unhelpful answers."

"Less helpful than 'Shut up'? Cuz that's the answer you're gettin' now."

"Well…at least 'Shut up' tells a man something."

"Yeah. It tells him to shut up. Which you need to do."

I shut up.

We reached the buggy, but Old Red carried on past it, not stopping till we were behind the wagon. My brother paused for a long look around, then pulled something from the pocket of his checked wool coat.

"Keep your eyes open," he whispered. "I'm about to tempt anyone out there who fancies himself a sharpshooter."

He turned away, and I heard the sharp flick and fizzle of a match being struck. White light flickered over the back of the wagon, revealing that the chuck box—the chest of drawers in which trail cooks kept their spices and other supplies—had been removed. Old Red hoisted himself up for a peek over the tailgate.

"Hel-lo" is his usual pronouncement upon coming across some new piece of "data," but whatever he saw now seemed to rate something a mite stronger.

"Holy shit," he said.

I stepped over and went up on my tiptoes to peer past him.

He was right. "Hel-lo" just wouldn't do.

"Goddamn," I said.

The little flame was about to reach Old Red's fingers, and he shook out the match and tossed it aside, bringing darkness back down upon the cargo lined up side-by-side in the wagon.

Two extremely bloody, extremely *dead* men.

TWENTY-FIVE
CALLING CARDS
OR, OLD RED INSPECTS THE KILLER'S HANDIWORK AND MAKES AN 'UNSOBERING' DISCOVERY

OLD RED STRUCK ANOTHER MATCH, and I made use of its wavering light just long enough to see who the bodies belonged to.

Konrad and Knute, the twin gunmen who worked for Haney and Bartlett, had entered the world in each other's company and had gone out the same way. They were trigger-happy assholes, to be sure, but I took no pleasure from their just deserts. As soon as I recognized their grimacing, blood-streaked faces, I turned away.

"You notice what they're laid out on?" my brother whispered.

I'm usually pretty quick on the draw with a smart-ass response, but just then, I only had the wherewithal for a shaky "No."

"Pillows and blankets," Old Red said. "Wagon bed's covered with 'em."

I steadied myself with a hand on the tailgate and took a deep breath.

"Well," I said, voice still quivering, "I'm glad to hear they've been made comfy."

My brother just grunted, tossed out a second dead match, then lit a third.

"How'd you know they'd be out here?" I asked him.

"I didn't. I was lookin' for somethin' else entirely."

Before I could ask what, the obvious thought finally hit me, and I let out a groan.

"Oh, no...the Sweeneys must've caught 'em and did 'em in. Probably figured on gettin' rid of the bodies later."

"Nope," said Old Red.

"Nope?"

"Yup. Nope."

He began rummaging around in the wagon with his free hand.

"You care to cut off more for me to chew on than 'Nope'?" I asked.

"They ain't shot, for one thing," Old Red said. "Their throats are cut, though they're both still wearin' their guns. That tells some of the story."

I heard a sniff.

"And you can smell whiskey on 'em," my brother went on. He paused for a stifled cough. "Once you get past the other smells."

Old Red leaned so far into the wagon I worried he was going to topple onto the bodies.

"Hel-lo," he said.

"What're you hel-loing?" I asked. I was in no mood to lean in beside him and look for myself.

"One of the twins...his fist is balled up. Looks like he got hold of something right before he died."

My brother pitched out yet another dead match, then bent over even further and wrestled with something in the darkness.

"Come on," he grunted. "Let go."

He was prying the dead man's hand open. Despite my little speech earlier about him needing to accept help, I prayed he wouldn't ask for any now. And my prayers were answered.

Old Red lit up another match, then said, "Well, well."

"And what are you well-welling?" I asked. I was pretending to keep a wary watch for anyone prowling around town, but I was really more interested in keeping my back to the bodies.

"There *was* something in that hand," my brother said. "Hair."

"Hair?"

Old Red went back to rooting around in the wagon bed.

"Yup," he said. "Not much of it. But hair."

"Well, hot damn. He must've pulled a clump offa the killer. All we gotta do is look for the feller with a bloody bald spot on his head and—"

"Wasn't that kind of hair," my brother said.

"What do you mean? What other kind is there?"

"The short bristly kind rather than the long straight kind."

"Short and bristly? Like he got a man by the…the short and bristlies?"

"Or grabbed him a handful of fur."

I thought of Señor Nadie out in the canyon—and his thick, dark pelt.

Was our friend the talking bear wandering around DeBarge slicing throats?

"Well, well, hel-lo," Old Red said.

Whatever he'd found now had to be good to rate both a "well, well" *and* a "hel-lo."

He handed something back to me. It was dark and smooth and about the size of a particularly generous biscuit.

"What the heck is this?" I said as I took it.

"I have no idea," my brother said. "It was in Konrad's pocket. Or maybe it was Knute's."

He pitched out his latest dead match and lit up another new one. I used the little light that reached me to inspect the 'whatever-it-was' in my hands. It was made of leather folded over upon itself, and when I flipped it open, I found flaps and pockets on the inside.

It was a boodle book—what some folks call a bill holder or flap book. There's another name for them, too, of course. One I've noticed becoming more popular of late.

"It's a wallet," I said. "A nice one."

"A wallet?" said Old Red. "Pretty classy for the likes of Konrad and Knute."

"Yeah. I'd figure those boys for the 'stuff-your-foldin'-money-in-your-boots' types."

I started going through the wallet's various compartments.

"Looks like whatever brother this come off of had five dollars and three rollin' papers to his name," I said.

I spread the main pocket wide and noticed a small, white sliver running along a seam on one side. I picked at it, and more white came sliding out.

It was the edge of a calling card tucked away in a slit in the leather. I pulled it out and squinted at it in the dim light.

"Well, well, hel-lo, to coin a phrase," I said.

My brother turned around. When he saw what I'd found, he held his match out toward me.

"What's it say?" he asked.

"Oh, I think you're gonna like it." I cleared my throat. "'Clyde Hartwell, Sales Representative, Branchwick and Fabermeister, Distributors of Fine Alcoholic Beverages, Colfax Avenue, Denver.'"

It had precisely the effect I'd expected. Old Red's eyes lost their focus, and his gaze drifted up and away from me.

"'Distributors of Fine Alcoholic Beverages,'" he mumbled. "Now *that's* worth a 'hot damn.'"

"Uhh...Brother?" I said. "You might wanna mind that match."

"Hot damn indeed," Old Red muttered, too lost in thought to hear me.

I leaned forward and blew out the little flame a second before it could scorch his fingers. Rather than thank me, my brother turned to scowl down at the bodies in the wagon bed.

"You little shits," he spat. Then he hopped off the tail-gate and flicked the dead match aside.

"What do we do now?" I asked him.

He rubbed his stubble-covered chin—the last couple of days being too overstuffed to allow for a shave—before answering.

"We go to Flip, I suppose. Tell him what we know. We're gonna need a badge behind us for what comes next."

"More like we'll need an army," I said. "When word gets around that two Haney men got their throats cut—even if it's these 'little shits'—this town's gonna go up like a powder keg."

Old Red nodded grimly. "That it is…so let's hope we can put the last pieces together before that happens. Come on."

He led the way toward the street. When we reached it, he turned right, heading for the marshal's office. If Flip wasn't spending the night there, we'd have to figure out how to find his boarding house.

I had no idea what time it was, but there was no hint of dawn yet. I eyed the east side of town warily though it was nothing but vague gray shapes and the dark outlines of rooftops cutting across a star-filled sky. Old Red had chosen to walk in the street rather than on the boardwalk, preferring, I supposed, to tread upon packed dirt rather than clomp along on planks. I appreciated the quiet but didn't like the thought of being even a couple of feet closer to anyone watching us—perhaps over a gunsight—from the darkness on the far side of the street.

"What the hell?" my brother blurted out.

When I looked over, I saw that he was gaping at something on the west side of town. A flickering yellow-orange light that flared up with a *whoosh* and a crackle. It was coming from the back of a small, squat building that lay directly ahead of us—because it was where we'd been going.

The marshal's office was on fire.

The powder keg was already going off.

TWENTY-SIX
BURNING QUESTIONS AND HOT TEMPERS
OR, EVEN WITH DEBARGE ABOUT TO GO UP IN SMOKE, CERTAIN FOLKS KEEP FANNING THE FLAMES

AS OLD RED and I charged forward for a better look at the fire, I heard someone else running up on our left. I looked over and saw Diana rushing into the wavering light with Burr, dapper as ever, even in the dead of night, by her side.

"What are you two doin' out here?" I asked them.

"What are you two doing out here?" the dude replied.

"I asked first," I said.

The four of us came together in a little clump in front of the marshal's office.

"There's something you need to know," Diana said.

She and Old Red locked eyes on each other.

"I reckon I know already, miss," my brother said. "And we got other things to worry about just now."

The flames were leaping up so high by this time they were visible over the roof, but the fire didn't seem to have spread any further than the back wall of the building. Yet. If it kept going, it would soon engulf the whole thing and most likely make the leap to the blacksmith's shop on one side and the bakery on the other. From there it could spread north and south till it reached the town limits.

"There's water in the troughs up and down the street," Old Red said. "But we need buckets."

"The liveries'll have some," I said.

"And the general stores," added Diana.

My brother nodded. "Alright. Me and Otto'll run to the liveries. Miss Crowe, you go to Martinez's store. And you..." He turned to Burr. "You got the most important job of all."

"What's that?" Burr asked. From the look on his face, he seemed to suspect that the answer would be "Go to hell."

"You stand here and shout 'Fire,'" Old Red told him.

"Ah. Of course," the dude said with a small smile. "And I suppose I'd better get to it."

He put his back to the glow of the flames and cupped his hands around his mouth.

"Fire! Fire!" he bellowed.

Old Red, Diana, and I darted away into the darkness. The lady peeled away from us quick, as Martinez's store was just a few doors down.

"I think someone's in there," she said. "I see a light."

She began hammering on the front door.

"Mr. Martinez? Is that you? Mr. Martinez! We need your help!"

My brother and I carried on up the street.

"You take Ernesto's livery," Old Red told me. "I'll go to the other one."

"Right."

I hustled over to the broad door of Ernesto's barn. Before I could start pounding on it, it creaked open and Ernesto leaned out to blink at me blearily.

"*Qué pasa?*" he said, lifting a hand to smooth down his dark, tousled hair.

"Fire! Fire!" Burr was still yelling.

"What *he* said!" I told Ernesto. "You got buckets?"

Ernesto's eyes went wide.

"Oh! Sí! Yes! Hold on!"

He ducked back into the barn, then reappeared a moment

later lugging three wooden buckets. He was wearing nothing but trousers—no shirt, no shoes—yet he paused only to push one of the buckets into my hands before hustling off toward the fire.

"Do you know how it started?" he asked as I caught up to him.

"Nope. But I'll be damned surprised if it was an accident."

The liveryman shot me a confused look, then grunted out a grim "Oh" when he realized which building was on fire.

"I see what you mean," he said.

He tossed a bucket to Burr, then dipped the one still in his hands into the trough in front of the marshal's office.

"Does DeBarge have a fire pump?" Burr asked him.

Ernesto gave him an emphatic, jowl-quavering shake of the head. "No. But there is a water wagon. It's kept behind my stable. I can hitch it up once we have more people here to help."

"Go do it," I said. "We should have enough folks here for a bucket brigade any second."

Ernesto nodded at something behind me.

"Maybe," he said. "Maybe not."

I turned to see what he was looking at.

Two dozen men and women lined the boardwalk on the opposite side of the street. None came forward to offer help. They just stood there watching the fire.

Some of them—the men with guns bunched up around Bartlett and Clayton Haney—were even smiling.

Finally, one man started toward us. As he moved into the light of the fire, I saw that it was Old Red. And he was empty-handed.

"Either that other liveryman does his sleepin' elsewhere or I ain't loud enough to wake him," he said.

"Ben Cameron spends his nights in his tack room, like me," Ernesto said with a scowl. "And he's a light sleeper."

He hurried off with his bucket.

Burr and I filled ours from the trough and followed him up the passageway—it was too narrow to call an alley—that separated the marshal's office from the blacksmith's shop. The fire still hadn't spread to the other building, but long tongues of flame were beginning to lick wooden walls that looked as brown and dry as kindling.

We got as close as we could, given the heat and smoke, and one-two-three we threw our water onto the fire. It didn't make any difference that I could see. The back quarter of the marshal's office was now ablaze.

"The three of us ain't gonna do no good like this," I said as we rushed back toward the street.

"I agree," said Burr. "We need more men and more buckets and that water wagon."

The men—and women—we found waiting for us out front. A few, anyway. Perhaps a dozen townspeople, freshly rousted from bed on the west side of the street from the look of them, were taking up leather fire buckets being handed out by Diana and Old Red. I assumed the buckets had just come off the shelves of Mr. Martinez's store, for Martinez was there, too. Though he was one of the few people there who wasn't dressed for bed, being in a full suit and shoes, he stood off to the side so stiff and still he could've been asleep on his feet.

"My god," a familiar voice said.

I turned to find Flip Compton stumbling up the street, shirt untucked, coatless, hatless. And close to senseless. Like Martinez, he seemed to be mesmerized by the sight of the fire.

"What's going on?" he said as he lurched to a stop by the trough.

My brother has often accused me of stating the obvious, but it truly seemed necessary now.

"It's a fire, Flip," I said. "And if we don't get organized about it, fast, it's gonna spread."

Compton nodded slowly. "Right...right..."

He gaped at the little smattering of townsfolk gathered before the burning building, then turned to look behind him.

The crowd on the opposite side of the street was bigger now— perhaps 30 strong—yet still no one left the sidewalk or doorways or alleys to offer help.

"Come on!" Compton shouted, waving an arm at them. "Get over here!"

A man started across the street…and didn't make it six steps before another moved out to block him. With his straight back and his cocked head and his balled fists on his slender hips, the second fellow radiated insolence and arrogance. Even looking at him from behind, the air around us full of smoke, I recognized him.

Bartlett.

There were more stirrings up and down the boardwalk. Yet no one else came forward, and at a single word from Bartlett— "Boys"—his flunkies spread out through the crowd to make sure everyone stayed in their place.

Over on the west side of DeBarge, meanwhile, the folks around me were milling around trying to organize themselves. But there was no clear leader and no clear plan, and people seemed distracted, almost dazed, by what was happening—and not happening—across the street.

"Come on!" Compton cried out again, his voice screechy, beseeching. "Help!"

"We're fine right where we are," Clayton Haney called back.

"Why, you…" my brother began, hurling the bucket in his hands to the ground.

It was obvious what was to follow "you." "Malicious son of a bitch," maybe. Or "nasty old bastard." Something other than "dear, darling sweetheart," that was for sure.

Diana cut him off before he could get there.

"No, Mr. Haney," she said. "You're not fine where you are."

She marched out to the middle of the street and lifted an arm to point back at the flames.

"Look at how that fire's moving," she said. "From the back of the marshal's office to the front. With the wind. *West to east.* You think the street's wide enough to protect you. To keep your side of DeBarge safe. But you're wrong. Wrong because when all these buildings over here go up, you're going to see a fire so big a few feet of dirt won't keep it from spreading. And wrong because this is part of your town. And when it's burning, *you do something.*"

Diana lowered her arm and just stood there a moment, smoke swirling around her in the fire- and moonlight. She hadn't just been talking to Haney, of course. She'd been talking to the east side of DeBarge. And it listened.

The man Bartlett had stopped slipped around the gunman, headed for the fire again. As he moved into the light, I saw that it was Cornelius Hale, the town's tall, bearded carpenter/undertaker.

"I'll take one of those buckets," he said, sounding scared but determined. He glanced back and spun a long arm in the air. "Matt, Pete—help Ernesto hitch up the water wagon and haul it around to the back of the marshal's office."

Two more men sidestepped Haney's gun-hands. They moved slowly at first, then sped up into a run as more people—both men and women—began streaming from the shadows.

"Deputy," Diana said, "I think we need to get the bucket brigade organized, don't you?"

"Right," the deputy said.

He just stood there blinking at her a moment before realizing *he* should do the organizing.

"Right," he said again, his voice a low croak. He swallowed and lifted a shaky hand toward the alley. "Uhh…form a line here. G-gentlemen closest to the fire. Umm. Please."

"Alright, you heard the man!" I hollered—because it was obvious most folks actually *hadn't.* "We need two lines from the street to the fire, one on each side of the building! Gents toward the front, and ladies at troughs to do the dippin'! Go!"

I pointed at a clump of kids in nightshirts getting underfoot as the adults started moving into position.

"You! We need runners! That's your job! The second a bucket's emptied onto the fire, you grab it and get it back to water! You understand?"

The kids nodded eagerly and rushed away as the adults started getting themselves in position.

I stepped close to Compton and lowered my voice.

"Hope you don't mind me helpin' out there, Flip," I said. "This ain't my first fire."

"It's not mine, either," the deputy said with disgust—not with me, but with himself. He straightened up from a slump and managed to put on a small smile. "Well...I did deputize you yesterday, didn't I?"

I smiled back. "That's right. You did."

"What are you two standin' around jawin' for?" my brother snapped at us. "There's work to be done."

He stalked off to join the men lining up in the alley.

"You heard the man," Diana said, throwing the phrase back at me with a smirk as she headed for the nearest trough.

"From him I could stand to hear less," I replied. But Compton and I were already falling in behind Old Red.

Within a minute we were passing overflowing buckets down as fast as we could. The smoke had grown heavier, yet I could see Burr at the front of our line, coat off, sleeves rolled up, fine white shirt turning as gray as his vest and trousers as he tossed water onto the flames.

After a while—perhaps around the time I'd handed off the fortieth or fiftieth bucket to my brother—the smoke let up a bit, and the blistering heat began to grow less intense. Compton peeled off out of the line to see how things were going elsewhere, and not long after that I heard his warbly voice calling out orders from the rear of the building.

"We need more buckets back here! And blankets! If you can't get at the water, throw sand!"

Old Red and I stayed where we were, handing off buckets, handing off buckets, handing off buckets as the sputtering yellow light of the fire was gradually replaced by the steady orange-tinged gray of dawn. With each splash, the heat and smoke tapered off just a bit more, until at long last, the dude and the other men at the end of our line had nothing to empty the buckets on any longer.

"We've stopped it over here," Burr announced after one final heave-ho. He looked at the blacksmith's shop behind us, its sides blackened but whole, and grinned triumphantly. "We should see if we're needed elsewhere."

Our line broke up then, Burr and my brother and me limping, exhausted toward the back, others heading out toward the street, and still others simply plopping down to the ground where they'd stood, utterly spent.

We found the men behind the marshal's office beating at smoldering wood rather than dousing flames. The water wagon was nearby, but no one was dipping into the huge barrel on the back. Instead, leather buckets lay scattered everywhere, discarded, and unneeded.

The fire was out. DeBarge was saved.

From burning, anyway.

Just to the south of the charred remnants of the building's back half stood the Sweeneys—Ed, Johnny, and dressed as always for mourning, their mother. Their various vaqueros and ranch hands were strung out on either side of them, hands filled not with buckets or blankets but rifles and shotguns.

Facing them from the north were Clayton Haney and Bartlett and that bunch, half of them toting rifles of their own, the other half with their palms hovering an inch from their holsters. They were missing about 200 pounds of rancid fat— Bartlett's bloated toady Jody wasn't with them—and Konrad and Knute weren't in any shape to report for duty, of course. But they still made an imposing sight. One not everyone noticed.

The two groups glared at each other like opposing armies lined up on the battlefield, with Compton and the other folks who'd been fighting the fire quite literally caught in the middle. But the deputy didn't see it.

"Can you tell what started the fire?" he asked the men smacking their blankets at the last little columns of smoke.

Hale, the bearded carpenter, turned to look at him. There were curving black lines behind him—the warped bars of a jail cell that was now roofless and unwalled.

"There's no way to know," he said. "But it's obvious it started in the back."

"I don't see no fireplace or stove there," Old Red said.

Hale nodded gravely.

"That's right," he said. "There wasn't one."

My brother rubbed his mustache, his gaze drifting slowly from the smoking ruins to the men and women gathered around them. The people of DeBarge weren't divided now. The fire had brought them together in one big, mixed mass—brown-skinned beside white, merchant beside workingman, and tradesman beside competitor from across the street.

Bartlett stepped forward and pointed at the marshal's office, and the cluster of townsmen before him parted warily as if he'd raised a pistol instead of a finger.

"I think that was a message," Bartlett said. "Someone telling the town its jail's not gonna get used no matter how obvious it is that there's a murderer strutting around."

He spoke loudly, obviously addressing himself to everyone present. But by the time he was done, he was staring at one man.

That man glared back at him and replied just as loudly.

"Someone was sending a message alright," Ed Sweeney said. "It was 'Forget the law. Clayton Haney's the law in DeBarge now.'"

"I didn't have…anything to do with that fire," Haney replied in his deep, halting drawl.

Ed barked out a scoff.

"Of course, you didn't, Haney," his mother said. "You always keep your hands clean. One of your hired killers set it for you."

"You're a dirty liar, Mrs. Sweeney," Haney shot back. "Among other things."

Ed started to swing up the rifle in his hands, but his brother Johnny grabbed the barrel and held it down.

"Ed! Don't!" Johnny said as Bartlett took a quick step to the side, putting himself between the Sweeneys and his boss.

Ed levered a round into the chamber.

"Why not?" he said. "We've finally got the son of a bitch right in front of us! It's either finish this now or wait for his neck-stretchers to come for us later!"

The crowd scattered, with ash-blackened men and women scurrying this way or that to keep themselves out of the crossfire.

Johnny looked over at his mother, his hands still wrapped around the rifle barrel.

"Mother! Tell him to stop!" he pleaded.

But Mrs. Sweeney didn't even look at him. Her eyes were locked on Haney. She was obviously thinking the same thing as Ed.

If they had to die fighting Haney, why not do it when they had a chance to take him with them?

"You and I finally agree on something, Ed," Bartlett said. "It's time to end this thing."

"Now w-wait," Flip Compton said. "J-just hold on."

The deputy was the only one still standing between the Sweeneys and Haney's men. Everyone else had fled to one side or the other—either to the back of the marshal's office to the east or out toward the empty desert to the west. Exhausted and panicked though they were, the townsfolk had still instinctively clustered up neighbor beside neighbor, I noticed. To the west, what faces were visible through the soot were every color a man could have, while to the east, every inch of skin was pure white.

Just like that, DeBarge had divided itself again.

I found myself on the edge of the white side by inaction rather than choice: I'd been so caught up in watching the confrontation play out that I hadn't thought to move. I looked around now for Diana, hoping she'd been herded to the back of one group or another.

But being swept along to safety wasn't the lady's way. I saw her pushing her way to the front of the west side crowd, the dude by her side. She was scanning the faces around me, searching for someone just as I'd been searching for her.

"What should we do, Brother?" I said. "Line up with the Sweeneys or try to get Miss Crowe outta here before the shootin' starts?"

I didn't get an answer. Because my brother, I saw when I glanced to the side, wasn't there.

"Lower that r-rifle, Ed," Compton said, voice wavering. "And, Mr. Haney—p-please tell your men not to do anything rash."

"I'll do no such thing...*Flip*," Haney sneered from behind Bartlett. "We're being threatened and we have a right to defend ourselves."

"*You're* being threatened?" Mrs. Sweeney said. "You've done nothing but threaten us since you came to the Territory. And *we* are going to defend ourselves."

"God damn it, Johnny," Ed snarled. "Let go!"

He jerked his rifle from his brother's hands.

Haney's men reached for their guns.

"Wait!" a voice boomed. "Don't start killin' each other yet!"

Old Red walked out to join Compton, arms raised so that his left palm faced the Sweeneys, the right Clayton Haney.

"Before all y'all get shot, you need to listen for a minute," he said.

"Shut up and get out of the way," Haney said.

"Yeah," said Ed. "The time for talk is done, Amlingmeyer."

Old Red stopped beside Compton and lowered his arms.

"So says you," he said. "But I reckon the deputy here and the rest of the good people of DeBarge might feel different...especially once they hear what I got to say."

"And what's that?" Compton asked.

The plain fear in his eyes was replaced by something new: hope. One kindled, I think, by the fact that he'd read my stories about Old Red and had a guess as to what he was going to say next.

I certainly did. And I was right, too.

"I know who set that fire, Deputy," he said. "And who killed Marshal Hinkle to boot."

TWENTY-SEVEN
THE INQUEST

OR, OLD RED ENDEAVORS TO PULL ANSWERS OUT OF A HAT AS THOSE AROUND HIM BLOW THEIR TOPS

A GASP WENT through the crowd. Or went through the crowds, I suppose I should say, for the townsfolk remained literally divided, with Old Red and Deputy Compton between them and the Sweeneys and the Haney bunch as bookends to the south and north.

"Ignore him!" Haney called from behind his makeshift rampart, Bartlett. "He's a...Sweeney man! He'll just try to... blame everything on me!"

"Whatever you've got to say, you can tell us in private later," Mrs. Sweeney told my brother.

She had to lean to be seen around her own fortifications, for the slim, blond cowhand called Fitz had sidled over to put himself —and his shotgun—-in front of her.

My brother looked from Mrs. Sweeney to the Haney gunmen lined up to face her like a firing squad.

"Ma'am," Old Red said, "I don't think there'll *be* a 'later' if I don't speak my piece now."

"Why not hear the man out?" someone said.

I was surprised to see that it was the dude, Burr. Even with his overcoat and bowler off and his shirt dirtied and his fancy walking stick nowhere in sight, he somehow projected an air of what the French call *savoir faire*. An American might call it "style" or "class" or perhaps, if he knew me and Old Red, "everything the Amling-meyers ain't got."

"I understand he's a consulting detective of some renown," Burr went on, "and I for one would like to hear what he's detected."

"Who asked you, fancy pants?" Bartlett said.

Burr looked down at his trousers and smiled as if considering a defense of the fanciness of his pants. Other voices piped up, though, and he held his tongue.

"Sí! Let him speak!" said Ernesto the liveryman.

"Hear him out!" said Señor Diaz, the manager of the DeBarge House.

No one was joining in from the east side of town, so I threw in a "Let him talk!" and promptly swiveled my head this way and that as if looking for the yahoo who'd just yelled.

"There's no need to keep waiting for the sheriff to get to the bottom of all this," Diana said. "As acting marshal, Deputy Compton has the authority to hold an inquest right now."

Compton gave the lady a forlorn look. He clearly wasn't sure she was right—and maybe even hoped she was wrong.

"Do it, Flip!" someone called out.

"Shut up!" someone called back.

"Don't tell my husband to shut up!" a woman shouted.

"Oh, *you* shut up!" another woman shouted back.

"No, *you* shut up!" the first woman replied.

"I wasn't telling *him* to shut up!" the second man said. "I was telling *her* to shut up!"

"Wait," the first man said. "Who were you telling to shut up?"

"The stranger, jackass!"

"Who are you calling a jackass, jackass?"

The women, meanwhile, were still telling each other to shut up. As they went back and forth, more hollering broke out, and within seconds it seemed like every single person in town was screaming something.

But then one voice rose up over all the rest, and *everyone* shut up.

"I! Call! This! Inquest! To! Order!"

It was Cornelius Hale, the carpenter/undertaker. He was still standing at the back of the marshal's office, smoldering wood and heat-warped metal all around him.

"Now see here, Hale..." Haney began.

"You can speak if you're asked to testify, Clayton," said Hale. He couldn't bring himself to look the rancher in the eye—it was clear he might back down if he did—and instead, he turned toward Compton. "Call your first witness, Deputy."

Compton gulped so hard it looked like he was trying to swallow a toad. Then he cleared his throat and straightened his spine and ran his hands through his hair, trying to smooth down the wild cowlicks of a man yanked from his bed and thrown into utter chaos.

"Thank you, Mr. Mayor," he said, answering a question I didn't even know I'd had: who was in charge in DeBarge on paper?

The deputy turned to my brother.

"I should call you, right?" he whispered.

Old Red nodded.

"I call Mr. Gustav Amlingmeyer," Compton announced.

"Alright, then," my brother said. He stepped forward with absolutely no show of trepidation. He's usually the shy, quiet type who'd rather chew glass than open his mouth in mixed company. But once he gets to deducifying, he's a different man altogether.

He turned slowly for a moment, taking in the fifty or sixty people staring back at him in the early morning light. Then he began.

"We got three things all tangled up together here: the marshal's murder and the burning of his office and another matter all but a couple of ya don't even know about yet."

A murmur ran through the throng.

Old Red ignored it.

"It's quite a knot. But I think I know which thread to pull to untie it." He looked over at Compton. "Deputy…"

"Huh?" Compton said, obviously not expecting to get pulled into the testimony so quickly himself. "Yes?"

"Last I knew of, you had hold of Alf Hinkle's things. The this and the that I found on his body yesterday. Where'd it all go?"

"I locked everything up in the marshal's office last night."

A tight, humorless smile unfurled itself beneath Old Red's bushy mustache.

He was hearing what he'd expected to hear.

"Would you mind checkin' to see if it survived the fire?" he said. "And bring it on out here if it did?"

"Yeah. O.K. Sure."

A confused Compton trudged off toward the half-burned office. The east side crowd parted to let him through.

"I'll tell y'all what should be in there, case you ain't heard the gossip," Old Red said. "One bottle of Dr. Faraday's Female Remedy and four-hundred thirty-seven dollars cash money."

There were more murmurs, this time mixed with a few snickers.

"I knew Hinkle was crooked," a man near me grumbled to no one in particular.

My brother whirled around and jabbed a finger at him.

"That's a trout in the milk, mister!" he snapped.

"Uhh…what?" the man said.

"'Circumstantial evidence is occasionally very convincing,'" Old Red lectured, "'as when you find a trout in the milk, to quote Thoreau's example.'"

He wasn't quoting Thoreau, of course. He was quoting Holmes—trotting out a little throwaway line from "The Adventure of the Noble Bachelor." One I never cared for much, actually.

The man nodded as if my brother had said something profound. Then he cocked his head and furrowed his brow.

"Wait," the man said. "What?"

But Old Red had moved on.

"Yes, Marshal Hinkle had a big ol' roll of bills on him when he went out to the Sweeneys' place the other night," he said, turning in a slow circle to address everyone present. "But that don't mean it was some kinda rake-off from rustlin'. Say it was. And say the Sweeneys killed him."

"Hey!" Ed Sweeney barked.

Old Red ignored him.

"Why, they'd have taken the cash off his body, wouldn't they? So nope. Whoever shot the marshal didn't know he had that money. It didn't have nothin' to do with why he was killed."

"So Hinkle and Eduardo there argue in town," Bartlett said, jerking his chin at the line of Sweeneys glaring back at him. "And later, Hinkle heads out to the Sweeneys' rancho with more than four-hundred dollars and gets shot in the back. And the Sweeneys didn't have anything to do with it and Hinkle wasn't crooked and he just had the money on him in case he decided to stop for a cream soda on the way." He shook his head. "Doesn't sound like 'trout in the milk' to me. Sounds more like you've got bats in the belfry."

Haney chuckled behind him, and the laughter spread through his riffraff—always eager for a signal what to do with themselves—before making the jump into the townsfolk around me.

"You want proof," my brother said. "Fair enough. Let's see if I can't get ya some."

He turned toward the marshal's office—and Deputy Compton, who was returning with Hinkle's flat-brimmed campaign hat in one hand and a rolled-up gun belt in the other. The hat was crown down, and as Compton passed me, I could see the cash nestled inside it beside Hinkle's badge and the little brown bottle of medicine.

"You saved the marshal's hat, too, did you?" my brother said with a smile.

"Well...yeah. I thought I might keep it," Compton replied shyly. "And his gun belt and Colt. Alf didn't have any family around here, and I figured we wouldn't bury it all with him, and

Mr. Hale said it was O.K., so I didn't think it would do any harm to—"

Old Red held up a hand. "No need to explain. It's fortunate, you keepin' that hat. I got me some thoughts about it."

Compton had stopped before him, and my brother leaned forward to peer down at the hat.

"And what's in it, too."

He reached out and lifted up the stoppered bottle.

"There is absolutely no reason to drag that into this," Ed Sweeney snarled.

A few feet from him, his mother blushed beet red.

"Ed's right," she said. "That's private. If you have any sense of decency, you won't speak of it. It has nothing to do with Alf Hinkle's death anyway."

"I'm afraid I have to disagree with you, ma'am," Old Red said. He gave the bottle a little shake. "I believe if it weren't for this, Alf Hinkle would still be alive and we wouldn't have spent the last half hour keepin' his office from burnin' down."

Yet again, there were murmurs all around. I heard a "What?" and a "Ridiculous" and another "Bats in the belfry" and all manner of variation. The common theme being that my brother was crazy.

He didn't convince anyone otherwise with what he said next.

"Ed...how long have you had your hat?"

Ed blinked at him. "My hat?"

Old Red nodded. "Yes, sir. Your hat. It looks...new-ish, I'd say. It's got a little character to it, but it ain't been sun-bleached, ain't been sweated through, ain't gone droopy. I'd peg it at...less than a year old?"

Ed shrugged. "Something like that. What the hell does it matter?"

A few women in the crowd gasped. A few men chortled.

"Language, please, Ed," my brother chided. "I ask because I can't help but notice how nice and round and flat the brim is."

He jerked his chin toward Deputy Compton—and, more specifically, what the young man held in his hands.

"Like the marshal's hat," Old Red said. "Exactly like it, in fact."

"Alright. We have the same *darned* hat," Ed growled between gritted teeth. "So?"

"So I reckon you bought your campaign hat the same place Marshal Hinkle bought his. Still got some in stock, in fact. I saw 'em there yesterday. In Francisco Martinez's general store."

"Stop this," Mrs. Sweeney said. In an instant, her round face had gone from dark red to chalk white. "You're working for me, and I'm telling you to drop it."

"Oh, let your man talk, Martina," Haney said with a smirk. "I think he's finally getting around to saying something interesting."

He was obviously enjoying himself simply because the Sweeneys just as obviously *weren't*. As usual, most of his men got the signal to chuckle along with the boss. But Bartlett, I noticed, didn't join in for once. He glowered at my brother sourly, his right hand curled into a fist on his hip—inches from the butt of his gun.

"What's your point, Mr. Amlingmeyer?" the mayor, Hale, asked. "Why does it matter where Alf and Eduardo Sweeney got their hats?"

"It matters for a couple of reasons, your honor," Old Red said. "One bein' that Ed there used to do his shoppin' where one would expect, given the lay of things around here. On the west side of town, in the store owned by his mother's cousin. A cousin so close to Mrs. Sweeney, in fact, when vigilantes was ridin' around hereabouts last year stringin' up rustlers, she sent her two youngest children to stay with him in town."

My brother turned until he faced Diana Crowe, who was watching him with an expression that somehow combined beaming admiration and bewildered trepidation.

"My esteemed colleague from the A.A. Western Detective Agency, Miss Diana Crowe, did some diggin' into that medicine yesterday. And she told me that Ed had asked about remedies for...you know...woman troubles over at...what's the place called?"

"DeBarge Mercantile & Sundries," Diana said.

Old Red nodded, then slowly moved his gaze in a circle, looking into the eyes of the men and women watching him.

"You all know it. That's the store across from Martinez's place. On the *east* side of town. Which set me to thinkin'. That's where Eduardo Sweeney, of all people, goes to look for something so private? Not to his own kin?"

"Amlingmeyer," Ed said. Four syllables. He packed a lot of meaning into them, though.

Don't go further, he was saying.

Shut your mouth now.

Or maybe *You're a dead man.*

Johnny had let go of his brother's rifle minutes before, but now he looked torn between grabbing it again, just in case, and shooting Old Red himself.

I reached down and lifted my Peacemaker from its holster a fraction of an inch to make sure it was loose and ready. I didn't feel loose and ready myself, but it was good to know my gun was.

"This here bottle of Dr. Faraday's did end up comin' from Martinez," my brother went on, ignoring the Sweeneys. "But Ed didn't buy it from him. Martinez told Miss Crowe that Marshal Hinkle got it. That's why it was on him when he headed out to the Sweeney spread with all that cash in his pocket."

There was a stirring in the far corner of the audience boxing Old Red in, and Martinez himself stepped forward. He'd been mixed in with the west side crowd, near the end of Haney's line, as far from the Sweeneys as he could be without joining the towns-people to the east.

"This is…this is…ludicrous," he said, voice cracking. "Are you accusing *me* of murdering Alf?"

"No, I'm not," Old Red said. He pointed at Martinez's bruised face. "Though I do suspect it was him who gave you that shiner and not Bartlett and his boys like you told us yesterday."

"What?" Bartlett said. "We didn't lay a hand on him."

Martinez gaped at the man in shock, then turned to speak pleadingly to his fellow townsmen.

"Alf and I were friends. You all know that."

"*Were* friends, yes," my brother said. "I don't think you'd have stayed friends, though. Not with him knowin' what you done."

"Stop," said Mrs. Sweeney. "Please."

Martinez didn't seem to hear her.

"You're insane!" he roared, whirling on Old Red.

"You're fully dressed!" my brother roared back.

"You're an imbecile! A fraud! A...A..."

Martinez stopped his sputtering.

"What did you say?" he asked Old Red.

My brother looked him up and down.

"You...are...fully...dressed," he said. "Shirt, shoes, full suit."

Martinez gaped down at his own clothes as if shocked to see them there himself. I'd noticed how he was dressed when he'd first showed up to help with the fire, but I'd committed the same sin Sherlock Holmes once accused Doc Watson of: I saw but I did not observe.

My brother flapped his free hand at the people around us.

"Haney's men—they're dressed. And the Sweeneys. Cuz they was all skulkin' around thinkin' a war was about to break out. But look at everyone else from around here. Nightshirts. Long johns. Nightgowns. House coats. No shoes. Or if they got shoes, no socks. And then there's you, dressed for business. Cuz if someone saw you out walkin' around with lamp oil or kerosene or whatever you used—I figure there's a dozen ways to start a fire stocked on your store shelves—you couldn't very well be in your pajamas."

Martinez turned away to talk to the townsfolk again. "Have you ever heard such poppycock? I didn't have any reason to burn down the marshal's office."

"Sure, you did," Old Red said. "Yesterday you told Deputy Compton here he could keep Marshal Hinkle's things in your safe. Ain't that right, Deputy?"

Compton jerked to attention like a man waking from a trance.

"That's right," he said. "He did."

"Only you didn't take him up on it, did you?"

Compton shook his head. "No. I locked everything up in Alf's desk instead. So I'd have it ready whenever the sheriff showed up."

Old Red nodded. "There you go. Martinez tried to get his hands on the evidence, and when he couldn't, he decided to destroy it instead. He just didn't count on me and my brother and Miss Crowe bein' out and about and spottin' his fire 'fore it could finish the job for him."

"He's ranting," Martinez scoffed weakly, his back still to my brother. "What's he even talking about?"

Old Red was still holding the Dr. Faraday's bottle, and he lifted it high for all to see.

"This," he said.

He let the bottle drop to the ground—then shattered the glass with a single stomp of his boot.

TWENTY-EIGHT
MESSAGE IN A BOTTLE
OR, OLD RED DOLES OUT SOME TOUGH
MEDICINE TO OUR EMPLOYERS

"OLD RED!" Compton gasped. "What are you doing?"

Other folks cried out in surprise all around us.

Old Red locked his eyes on me, his right foot still pressing down on what remained of the medicine bottle.

"Brother," he said. "If you don't mind."

I stepped out of the crowd and moved toward him. I could see Diana beyond him, her wide eyes asking me what he was up to. It didn't seem like the right time for a shrug, so I tried to get my reply across with a cocked eyebrow.

Damned if I know, it was meant to say.

As I came closer to Old Red, I could see a message in his eyes, too. It seemed to be a plea.

For god's sake, tell me I didn't just make a fool of myself, perhaps.

He lifted his foot and looked down.

Shards of brown glass and pulverized white pills were scattered over the sandy soil beneath his hovering heel. There was a little slip of curled, yellowed paper there, too: the Dr. Faraday's label.

And something else lay there, as well. Something that seemed to draw a sigh of relief from my brother. It looked like a cigarette.

Old Red planted his foot to the side, bent down, and picked up the tiny white tube. He held it high, showing it to the townspeople. Then he handed it to me.

"What the hell is that?" Ed Sweeney said.

His mother seemed to have a guess. She was glaring at her cousin, Martinez.

There were markings on the little doodad, I could see now. Writing.

It wasn't a cigarette after all.

"It's a note," I said. "It was rolled up and stuffed in the bottle."

"Well…let's hear it!" Clayton Haney called out. He'd struck me as a dour, sour man, but now he was grinning with glee. His enemies' humiliation had him as giddy as a kid on Christmas morning.

I looked at Old Red. This was what he'd called me over for: He could deduce next to anything except what the letters R-E-A-D add up to. But did we really want to do Haney's bidding and shame the very family we were working for?

My brother nodded.

"It's proof," he said.

I unfurled the paper and took a moment to let what I saw there sink in.

"Some of it's in Spanish," I said, speaking loudly for all the crowd. "But I'll do my best."

I read this aloud:

Mi alma, mi reina, mi sirenita,

Stay strong! All is not lost! You are being sent away, but I will find you, and together we will escape and make a new life. Mi corazon arde por ti para siempre.

F.

Ed was raging before I even got to that last bit of Spanish or the "F." for Francisco Martinez.

"I should have killed him! I should have killed him!" he bellowed, raising his rifle.

Once again, his brother Johnny jumped in front of him. This time he ripped the Winchester from Ed's hands—and spun around to face Martinez with it.

His mother, my brother, and Deputy Compton all shouted the same thing.

"Johnny! Don't!"

Martinez yelped and hurled himself toward the crowd, trying to squirm his way through it. His neighbors pushed him away, sending him stumbling backwards. When he regained his footing, he tried to dive between the last two men in Haney's line, but they shoved him back, too.

"Stick around, Señor," one of them said. "Show ain't over."

Martinez staggered back with a moan. After a few steps his legs gave out, and he fell to his knees and started sobbing.

"I've been wondering where that pretty little chiquita Maria was," Bartlett said. He shook his head at Martinez. "She's what... fifteen? *Fourteen*? And your own cousin's daughter?" He snorted, then looked over at Johnny Sweeney. "Well...you gonna use that thing or not?"

Johnny was holding the rifle low but straight, the stock across his right hip, the muzzle pointed at Martinez.

"Think, Johnny," I said. "You'd just be handin' Haney what he's wanted since ya found the marshal dead: a Sweeney blamed for murder. And this time he'd have sixty witnesses."

Johnny glowered at Martinez a moment. Then he lowered the barrel of the Winchester.

A murmur of relief went around the crowd. Or maybe it was a murmur of disappointment.

Old Red turned toward Mrs. Sweeney.

"The...uhh...trouble with your daughter," he said. "It began when you sent her and her brother Miguel to stay in town last year."

Mrs. Sweeney nodded.

"After you learned she was...you know...that there'd be a young one, you made her tell you who was responsible."

The woman nodded again. "Sí." She frowned at Haney and

Bartlett. "When we heard that those two were bringing in more cutthroats, getting ready to come for those of us they hadn't already driven out or killed, I told Maria we'd be sending her into town again to keep her safe. She was distraught, panicked. I knew she'd been having..physical difficulties. The kind women understand. Seeing how hysterical she became about returning to the home of my cousin…" She shifted her glare to Martinez, the fire of fury flashing in her eyes. "I finally realized how we had been betrayed."

"So you went to Alf Hinkle with it," Old Red said. "That's what your argument with him was really about, wasn't it, Ed? Why you couldn't tell the truth about it before. You two was workin' out what to do about your sister. You wanted justice, maybe retribution. But the marshal talked you into keepin' it quiet. Gettin' Martinez to pay to send Maria away. Avoid scandal. Save the girl's good name."

"That's right," Ed said. "And now it's too late for that, damn you."

My brother turned away from him. Usually when he's closing in on answers, he's as eager as a bloodhound straining at the leash. But his expression now was pensive, grim.

"And you," he said to Martinez. "You just couldn't leave the girl alone, could you? When the marshal came to see you, he mentioned that she was having a tough time carryin' the child. So you gave him some medicine…and tried to slip her that note."

"You don't understand," Martinez whimpered. "We are in love."

He was still on his knees, and Mrs. Sweeney took a quick step toward him that set him back on his haunches cringing and crying.

"You are sick! Crazy! Maria thinks you are disgusting! Eduardo isn't the only one who would like to see you shot down like a rabid dog! But I said no. I said we would bring it to our friend Marshal Hinkle. And in trying to help us, he died."

For a moment, the only sound was Martinez's weeping and

the desert wind from the west whistling through the ruins of the marshal's office. Then, Old Red spoke to Deputy Compton.

"Well, there you have it. Marshal Hinkle was the Sweeneys' middleman, but not for sellin' stolen cattle. He was tryin' to do his job, as he saw it. Keepin' the peace. Ed Sweeney had no reason to kill him. Quite the opposite. Hinkle was helpin' the family through a terrible time."

"Yeah," Compton sighed. "That sounds like Alf."

Mrs. Sweeney and Ed and Johnny and the men lined up beside them—they just scowled at my brother.

He'd done what he'd been hired to do: prove Ed didn't murder the marshal. And now our clients looked like they'd gladly murder *him*.

"Quite a show the A.A. Western Detective Agency puts on," Bartlett said. "Makes me almost sad you're not on our payroll anymore. Your new bosses certainly got what they're paying for… and more."

He glanced over his shoulder at Haney, who didn't seem nearly so gleeful now that the Sweeneys were off the hook for Hinkle's murder.

"Let's go," he said. "It's been fun watching the Sweeneys squirm, but—"

"I ain't done testifyin', Bartlett," my brother said. "There's still the little matter of Marshal Hinkle's hat."

Slowly, slowly, slowly Bartlett turned his head to meet Old Red's gaze.

"What?" he said.

My brother threw a little nod at the still-sniveling Martinez. "Ed and the marshal both bought their hats from him, remember? And…well, you might have noticed I ain't no slick fashion plate like some fellers. No spats or stick pins on me."

I peeped over at Diana and Burr. The dude had been watching Old Red with a look of confounded awe, but now a little half-stifled smile slipped through his bemusement.

"But the flat brim and dimpled crown on them hats…" my

brother went on. "Even a plain-dressin' workin' man like myself would find that a right interestin' look. Distinctive, you might say."

"So?" Bartlett said.

"So…Ed Sweeney comes into DeBarge on family business, then a few hours later, in the dead of night, a man in a campaign hat rides out of Cañada de los Vaqueros headed toward the Sweeney place, and he's shot in the back by men with rifles. Men who were in the rocks a few dozen yards off the trail, drunk on Kentucky rye."

"So?" Bartlett said again, turning the word into a guttural growl.

He knew where my brother was headed. And he was warning him not to go there.

"So," Old Red said, "it's so very obvious there's hardly any deducin' to do."

My brother turned toward Compton but kept his eyes on Bartlett.

"No one set out to kill Marshal Hinkle that night, Deputy," he said. "They were there to kill Ed."

TWENTY-NINE
THE GRUBBY DETAILS
OR, OLD RED PULLS MORE ANSWERS OUT OF A HAT, AND IT BRINGS EVERYTHING TO A HEAD

THERE WERE gasps and mutters from both groups of townspeople bunched up behind the marshal's office, and someone from amongst the Sweeneys—Ed himself, I saw when I looked that way—lurched forward with a startled "What?"

But Deputy Compton just nodded, looking less shocked than chagrined.

"Of course. That's why they didn't take the money in Alf's pocket. They weren't there for that. It had nothing to do with him."

"Exactly," my brother said. "They just wanted Ed dead."

He was still looking at Bartlett.

"That's a lot of bullshit to get from a hat," Bartlett said.

"Oh, it ain't bull…and it ain't just from the hat," Old Red said. "For one thing, we found a bottle of rye whiskey where the back-shooters laid up waitin' for Ed. The deputy here can testify to that. Special stuff, it was. From Kentucky. Not stocked by any saloon or store in town. And I happen to know that two of your men recently robbed a specialty liquor drummer outta Denver."

Bartlett snorted, a disdainful, dismissive sneer on his face but his eyes cold and wary.

"Now you're just making things up," he said.

Old Red shook his head. "Nope. I am makin' deductions based on evidence. Like the drummer's business card and wallet. Which I found with the killers' bodies."

Suddenly it wasn't just Ed Sweeney letting out a stunned "What?" It seemed like everyone in DeBarge was saying it except for me, my brother, and Bartlett.

Old Red went on talking though it was impossible to hear him over the clamor.

"...snuck out to get a gander at the wagon the Sweeneys hauled into town yesterday," he was saying when folks finally quieted down to listen. "I had a hunch they was bringin' young Maria into town in it. Secret-like, so they could slip her out on the next stage, maybe. Or just make sure Martinez didn't try to talk to her while they holed up at the DeBarge House. That hunch was on the money, too. If you look in the back of that wagon, you'll see pillows and blankets for keepin' the young lady comfortable. And you'll see your boys Konrad and Knute, Bartlett. Reekin' of whiskey with cut throats. Cuz you liquored 'em up and did 'em in."

There was another uproar all around—even some of Haney's men turned to each other with a startled "Jesus!" or "What the hell?"—but Bartlett was ready for it.

"If the Karlsvik brothers are dead," he shouted over the hubbub, "it's obvious the Sweeneys killed them! They were gonna sneak the bodies out of town in their wagon!"

"That's a goddamn lie!" Ed roared.

"And now they have the gall to blame us for killing two of our own men!" Bartlett went on.

"You *had* to kill 'em, Bartlett," Old Red said. He kept his voice calm and quiet, forcing the crowd to quiet again to hear. "Them two was wild, drunken fools—and they could link you and your boss to Hinkle's murder."

Haney stepped up to stand next to Bartlett.

"This...is...ridiculous," he said, flapping a big slab of a hand

at my brother. "He's got no proof. No witnesses. Nothing but...
crazy theories."

My brother kept his eyes on Bartlett.

"Where's your pal Jody?" he said. "Strange that your right-
hand man wouldn't be here for the big showdown."

Bartlett clamped his mouth tight.

"I did find me some evidence on them Karlsvik boys. Other
than that wallet, I mean," Old Red continued. "One of 'em had
hair in his fist. I think he reached back and pulled it straight outta
the man slittin' his throat. Scraggly, scruffy little things. Like they
was from a grubby little beard."

Bartlett just kept glaring back at him, but I noticed the men
lined up alongside him and Haney eyeing each other uncertainly.

Diana and the dude noticed it, too.

"Deputy Compton," Burr said, "I have little personal knowledge of criminal matters, of course. But I believe there's a tech-
nical term for someone who knows the details of a murder but
doesn't divulge them."

Flip slowly tore his gaze away from Old Red and replied with
his usual quick wit and air of command.

"Huh?" he said.

Diana provided the answer for him.

"An accessory, Mr. Burr."

The dude snapped his fingers. "That's it. Thank you, Miss
Crowe. Correct me if I'm wrong, but can't accessories be charged
with murder even if they didn't take part in the killing?"

"They can be hung," Diana said.

Burr nodded. "Yes, that's right, isn't it? They would be consid-
ered conspirators, and they would die alongside those who actually committed the crime."

"Are you...threatening me?" Haney snarled.

"Certainly not," Diana replied. "We weren't talking to you at
all, in fact."

Her eyes darted to the left and right, running up and down the
row of gunmen squared off against the Sweeneys. Before, they'd

always been a homogenous blob, other than the Karlsviks. Ten interchangeable faces with the same smirk, the same sneer, the same scowl. Whatever expression Bartlett and Jody put there. But now I saw individuals—men wearing their own fear and doubt and resentment.

They were a rough-looking bunch of toughs, but there was something the Sweeneys had—and the Double-A Western Detective Agency, too—that they didn't: We were in this thing together. They were each in it alone. And they were starting to see it.

I gave them one more nudge.

"Not much loyalty your bosses got for you boys," I said to the Bartlett men closest to me. I slowly moved my gaze to the next man over, then the next, then the next, and so on. "They kill a couple of ya, then expect you to keep your neck in the noose with 'em when they're caught. Even if you get outta this today, you'll have to wonder when they'll decide it's too dangerous to leave *you* alive, given what you must know."

"Oh, shut up, Amlingmeyer," Bartlett said.

"I'm not gonna...stand here and...be insulted," Haney drawled.

He turned and started to lumber away.

But then someone moved in the opposite direction—stepping toward me and the rest of the crowd.

It was the man at the far western end of Haney's line. A skeletal fellow in a yellow duster.

"Bartlett and Jody took the Karlsvik brothers out with them a couple of hours before the fire," he said.

"Keep your mouth shut, Carlyle," Bartlett snapped at him.

The gaunt man kept going.

"Bartlett said they were going to scout around town. Bartlett and Jody came back. Konrad and Knute didn't."

Another man—a stubble-faced fellow in a poncho—stepped out of line to join Carlyle.

"And Jody's face was bleeding," he said. "Like some of his beard had been yanked out."

"Faraday!" Bartlett bellowed.

Faraday just glared back at him.

Another man stepped out of line beside him.

"Bartlett put a bounty on the Sweeneys," he said. "First of us to bag one would get two hundred dollars. The Karlsviks got drunk and went after Eduardo. But they got the marshal instead."

"They thought that was pretty funny," the cadaverous man, Carlyle, added. He jerked his head at Bartlett. "But I guess *he* didn't."

"You spineless, back-stabbing son of a bitch," Bartlett spat at him.

"You're one to talk about back-stabbing," another of his men scoffed—right before he whirled around and wormed his way into the crowd.

One, then two, then three, then four more gunmen did the same, turning their backs on Bartlett and darting off. Haney, meanwhile, distanced himself from the man more smoothly, silently sliding backwards one slow step at a time.

Old Red took all this in with an expression of gratified wonderment upon his face.

"Well, Deputy," he said, "I suppose I'm just about done with my testimony. There's just two more questions that need askin'."

Compton was standing beside him looking like Lot's wife— stiff, still, wide-eyed, and white as salt.

"Oh?" he managed to say. I don't think he could've gotten out two syllables just then.

My brother looked squarely at Haney.

"Did you know about the bounty on the Sweeneys?" he said.

Haney froze.

"Me?" he said. "Of course not."

Bartlett looked like he wanted to chew up his own teeth and spit out the broken shards. "He knew," he muttered in disgust. "You think the money was gonna come out of *my* pocket?"

The rest of his gang—or what used to be his gang, more like —had continued to peel off and hightail it, each desertion inspiring another.

No one stood beside Bartlett anymore. And only one man remained behind him…and even he was moving away.

"You need to…stop talking," Haney said, taking another big step back. "I'll get you a lawyer. The best. You'll…come out alright."

Bartlett barked out a bitter laugh. He glanced first to the right, then to the left, appraising the townspeople watching the show. Mixed in among them were the men who'd be on his jury.

None of them were looking back at him with sympathy. On every face was hatred or contempt or both.

"It's a good thing I don't have to rely on you, Haney," Bartlett said. He turned his head to the side and raised his voice to a booming holler. "Now! Show 'em they're covered!"

A round figure popped up on the roof of the blacksmith's shop beside the marshal's office. It was as if the squat, smoke-grimed building had suddenly sprouted a big, bulbous weather vane. One with a rifle.

"Dammit!" Old Red said. "Before I could even ask…"

I knew then what his last question was: Where was Jody? And none of us liked the answer.

Bartlett must have sent him off to get a bead on the Sweeneys when it looked like there'd be a final faceoff. And now there was one. Not the one Bartlett was expecting, but having the high ground was about to come in handy all the same.

"I want two saddled horses! Brought here! Now!" Bartlett shouted over the townsfolks' cries of surprise.

He wrapped a hand around the butt of his pistol and started to slide it from its scabbard.

"Then we're gonna settle accounts here," he said.

"Now just…hold on there…Frank," Haney said.

"Oh, I'm 'Frank' now, huh?" Bartlett snarled. "Shut up, Haney. This isn't about you anymore."

He pointed his gun at my brother and gave him a spite-filled smile.

"Jody! The Sweeneys try anything, kill their mother!" he said.

His eyes moved to the right—to Diana—and his smile grew wider. "Anyone else tries to stop us, shoot the lady snoop."

Up on the rooftop, Jody laughed. Even from a distance I could see the raw, red flesh on his right cheek where either Konrad or Knute had wrenched out a fistful of scrubby beard.

"She makes a real pretty target, Frank!" he called out. "I've already drawn a bead on her sweet little—"

There were two blasts in quick succession, almost simultaneous, and the side of Jody's head exploded in a spray of blood and brain. Before he could even fall, there were two more gunshots, the bullets thumping into his chest as he pitched forward and fell off the roof.

There were screams all around as the townspeople scattered. I went for my gun, and Compton and Old Red beside him did the same. Bartlett was distracted, glancing back to see what had become of Jody, and that gave us a chance.

Not much of one, though. We were no gunfighters. The second it took for us to wrap our hands around our pistol grips may as well have been a thousand years.

When Bartlett looked our way again, none of us had our Colts clear of our holsters.

Yet when the gunfire came, it didn't come from Bartlett. Ed Sweeney had been itching to shoot for the last quarter hour—for the last few *years*, more like—and he was quick to grab his chance when it finally came. He fired again and again. Bartlett jerked back, dropped his gun, and spun. More shots came from the Sweeneys—Johnny and the rest joining in—and ragged red splotches pocked Bartlett's back as he tried to stagger away.

"Stop! Stop!" Compton shouted.

But the gunfire didn't slow until Bartlett was a bloody heap on the ground.

Another body lay sprawled just beyond his. A big man laid out on his back, eyes pointed at the sky.

I walked over and knelt beside him, but there was nothing to be done. Clayton Haney was dead, too.

"What a shame. An innocent bystander," Ed said. "Too bad for him he was behind Bartlett."

He glanced around, searching for more threats. But the rest of Bartlett's men had stampeded along with the crowd, and he holstered his gun.

Old Red turned toward Diana—who was flat on the ground with Burr atop her. When the shooting started, the dude must have tackled her to keep her out of the crossfire.

My brother only let the sight of the gentleman stretched out over the lady throw him for a second. Or maybe two.

"Are you alright, miss?" he asked.

"I'm fine, Gustav. Thank you," Diana said. She looked up at Burr. "Which means you can get off now."

The dude opened his mouth to reply, then froze for a moment, obviously deciding against whatever he'd been about to say.

"Of course," he said instead.

He pushed himself up and offered Diana his hand.

"Are *you* alright?" Johnny Sweeney said, lowering his Winchester and stepping toward his mother.

She reached out to steady herself with a hand on his forearm.

"I can't believe it. Haney...Bartlett...it's finally over." She looked past Johnny at Old Red. "Thank you, Mr. Amlingmeyer."

"Wasn't just me, ma'am," my brother muttered.

He turned to give me a little nod, then did the same for Diana. And for the dude, too, to my surprise.

"But...*is* it over?" Deputy Compton said slowly. He had a dazed look on his face, and the first time he tried to slide his gun back into its holster, he missed. "I mean..." He pointed up at the roof of the blacksmith's shop. "...who shot Jody?"

"That's a good question," Old Red said. For some reason he looked over at Diana again.

"Indeed it is," the lady said. And left it at that.

The townspeople were starting to return by then, flowing in from the alleys and back lots they'd fled to a minute before, no longer two separate groups but one big herd of nervously murmuring humanity.

"Sorry, Flip," my brother said as the first gawkers crowded in around the bullet-riddled bodies. "Looks like you're gonna have to hold another inquest."

"Oh," the deputy groaned, pressing his fingers to his forehead. "Oh."

He sat himself down on the ground and looked like he was about to cry.

THIRTY
PROPER INTRODUCTIONS
OR, WE FINALLY MEET OUR GUARDIAN ANGELS, AND IT'S A DEVIL OF A SURPRISE TO ME

THERE WAS INDEED ANOTHER INQUEST, but that one went a bit more smoothly. For one thing, it was held indoors, in one of the town's cantinas, rather than beside smoking rubble. For another, no one got shot before it was over. The shootings during the first inquest were ruled either self-defense—in the case of Jody and Bartlett—or accidental, in the case of Clayton Haney. Then the sheriff, who'd timed his arrival just right to miss all the carnage, banged his makeshift gavel—a shot glass— declared the proceedings concluded, and asked that his "gavel" be filled with tequila.

Despite the happy ending for the Sweeneys, Ed stayed true to his churlish nature and spurned us at every turn. He couldn't forgive us for the public humiliation we'd brought upon his family —even though drawing out the truth about his sister had saved his neck—and if he spoke to us at all, it was to remind us that there was a stage out of town each day. Yet his mother paid us the $519 we were owed: $20 for the two days we were on the Sweeney payroll along with the agreed-upon bonus of $499 for clearing Ed of Marshal Hinkle's murder. That Haney had ended up dead in the process was thrown in as a sort of gratuity, I suppose.

It never was nailed down exactly who shot the man: The three slugs pulled from him were .44/.40s, which could've come from half the pistols and rifles fired in the shootout. When asked if any of those bullets were theirs, Ed and Johnny and the other Sweeney men would reply with something along the lines of "Who can say?" or a simple "Ask me no questions, I'll tell you no lies" shrug.

We did get an answer on who shot Jody, though. One we didn't mention at the inquest. It came our way maybe fifteen minutes after the shooting stopped. The Sweeneys had already retreated back to the DeBarge House Hotel, and the bodies were being hauled off to the mayor's carpentry shop for boxing. Flip Compton went with the corpses still in a daze he might be in, to this day, while the gawkers—a few weeping over Haney but most obviously unsure what to feel—had drifted off when it became clear the show was over. Francisco Martinez had slipped away somewhere in there, too. And he kept right on slipping after that: We later learned he bought a horse from Ernesto's livery, hopped atop it, and lit out, never to return.

That left me and Old Red behind the marshal's office with Diana and Burr.

My brother turned toward the lady with a look of shy chagrin on his pinched face.

"I got something to tell you, Miss Crowe, and you got a some-thing or two to tell me," he said. "Usually, I'd say 'ladies first,' but in this instance, I reckon it oughta be me."

Diana crossed her arms and regarded him warily.

"Alright," she said. "Go ahead."

Old Red took a deep breath and cleared his throat and twitched a bit and generally looked like a cat working up to cough out a hairball.

"I'm sorry," he said. "You are our partner, and the last few days I have not treated you with the respect you're due. I will... correct that."

I fought the urge to fall to my knees and cry, "Hallelujah!" Miracle of miracles, my brother was apologizing, and doing it rather well.

Diana smiled and unfolded her arms. She'd been steeling herself for Old Red's usual sourness but had been served up something sweet instead.

"Thank you, Gustav," she said. "I owe you an apology, as well. As I think you've already guessed…"

My brother frowned, and the lady quickly corrected herself.

"…or, rather, *deduced*," she said, "Mr. Burr's presence in DeBarge is no coincidence. My father sent him. He's working for the A.A. Western Detective Agency."

Burr tipped an invisible hat to Old Red.

"How do you?" he said.

My brother gave him a brusque, unamused nod, then focused on Diana again.

"Why didn't you tell us?" he asked.

"I didn't know about it until I saw him here. That was when you and Otto were out at the Sweeneys' ranch with Deputy Compton. You'd run off without telling me again, and…"

Diana searched for the proper word, then gave up and shrugged.

"You pissed me off," she said.

Burr pretended to be shocked.

"My dear Miss Crowe, ladies do not get 'pissed off,'" he said. "They become displeased."

"*I* get pissed off," Diana replied with an arched eyebrow. "As you well know."

The dude conceded the point with a small bow.

Old Red scowled again. Burr obviously had the kind of easy, bantering rapport with Diana he would've liked to have himself. Instead, the closest he'd ever come to easy bantering was his back-and-forth squabbling with me.

No wonder he was scowling.

"When you picked that fight with me and Otto," he said to Burr, "that was no mistake. You were testin' us."

"Quite so," Burr said. "I wanted to see what kind of protection you two could provide Miss Crowe…and might need yourselves. I studied up on you on my way here…"

He paused to give me a nod.

"I read your latest contribution to *Smythe's Frontier Detective*. A ripping tale."

I nodded back. "Thank you, sir. You are obviously a man of excellent taste and discernment."

My brother rolled his eyes. When he thinks of the magazine I write for and "ripping," it isn't a compliment. It's what he's inclined to do to the pages.

"Entertaining as it was, however," Burr went on, "I couldn't be sure it was an accurate reflection of your abilities, particularly in the pugilistic arts. So I arranged a demonstration."

"And what did you think?" I asked.

The dude smiled apologetically and waggled a hand.

Old Red went back to scowling.

"You've been sendin' telegrams to Ogden, ain't you? Reportin' to your father," he said to Diana. "What's his excuse for not tellin' us about the company we'd have here?"

"If it's any consolation, I'm pissed at *him*, too," the lady replied. "From the beginning, he wanted to send someone to... look out for his investment in you. I thought I'd convinced him that the only person who could manage that without antagonizing you was me. Obviously, I was wrong. About a lot of things. You know how obsessed the colonel is with secrecy. Once he had his mind made up, he was going to act. On his own." She shrugged and sighed at the same time. "We all have a lot to learn about how to behave in a partnership."

"Don't blame your father, Miss Crowe," Burr said. "After you left Ogden, he got word that Haney was hiring more toughs, ruffians, thugs. It alarmed him. That's when he got in touch with me. He thought I'd have more freedom of movement in town than you since no one would know I was there on the agency's behalf."

Old Red nodded thoughtfully. He was scowling up a storm, to be sure, but all in all, he was taking it better than he would have once upon a time. The lady was doing more swearing than him, and he didn't look tempted to draw his gun on anybody.

"And I suppose you'd have more freedom than the other two, as well," he said to Burr.

The dude widened his eyes. "You know about them?"

"Of course, he does," Diana said. "I told you he'd figure it out sooner or later."

Burr grinned back at her. "That you did."

"You know, I hate to be the odd man out here," I said, "but who the hell are 'the other two'?"

"The coyotes," my brother said. "The ones who saved us from gettin' shot by Ed Sweeney when we snuck out of the hotel."

He turned toward the scrub-pocked, gently rolling hills of the desert and put a hand to his mouth.

"You can come out now!" he called. "No need to keep hidin'!"

For a moment, the only sound was the whistling of the low wind through the ruins of the marshal's office and the shrill cry of a distant hawk. Then I heard the muffled thud of trudging footsteps, and two figures emerged from behind a cluster of prickly pear.

One was dark-skinned and long-haired, wearing a blue shirt and moccasin boots, and a breechcloth over the front of his trousers.

The Apache I'd fought in the canyon the day before.

With him was his friend who'd done most of the talking. "Señor Nadie." The bear. Who, of course, wasn't a bear at all, I could see now. But I could also see why, when spied from the corner of your eye, he might remind you of a grizzly. He was a strapping black man clad in a shaggy buffalo coat and flap-eared beaver hat of the kinds once favored by cavalrymen on long winter campaigns.

As the two men approached, I also realized why they'd kept themselves hidden and taken no credit for picking Jody off the roof. An Apache and a Negro traveling together would attract the wrong kind of attention in town—the kind that would have some men itching for an excuse to grab their guns. And should said Apache and Negro kill a white, even to save others, those same itchy-fingered men might just reach for ropes.

The Indian waved a hand at Diana, who was beaming back at him.

"See?" he said to his companion. "I told you Nachita would be fine. She's been shot at so many times the bullets don't even try to hit her anymore. They know not to bother."

The black fellow gave Diana a smile, then looked over at the dude with considerably more coolness.

"Burr," he said.

"Sergeant," Burr replied, touching his fingertips to his brow in a mock salute.

"I see y'all are acquainted, but me and my brother ain't been introduced," I said. "Not with real names, anyway…right, Cochise?"

The Apache beamed at me. "It's a good name. I was just borrowing it."

Diana held a hand out toward the men. "Otto and Gustav Amlingmeyer—Ira Hoop and Eskaminzim."

"It's a pleasure, fellas," I said. "Assuming, that is, you ain't plannin' on startin' another fight with us."

Hoop had stopped with his heels together, his back straight, and his arms hanging straight down. He looked like he was standing at attention.

"Sorry about that," he said. "The colonel sent us here to look out for you, and we decided to see how much help you'd need from us in a scrap."

Eskaminzim laughed. "I'm not sorry. It was fun." He jabbed a pointed finger at me. "But next time I'm not going to let you win!"

"Yeah, well…we'll see about that," I said, though I was certainly in no hurry for a rematch. I had to hope no more heretofore secret agents from the Double-A popped up, as every one that did, seemed intent on going toe-to-toe with me.

"You two know Col. Crowe from the army?" Old Red asked Hoop and the Apache.

Hoop nodded.

Eskaminzim grinned and jerked his head at his companion.

"First, he and the old man tried to kill me," he said. "Then they made me a scout."

"Ira and Eskaminzim also worked for father when he was with the Southern Pacific Railroad Police," Diana said. "Whenever men with their particular skills were needed."

"And I didn't work with the Railroad Police, exactly," Burr threw in, "but they had the opportunity to observe *my* particular skills up close from time to time. I suppose the colonel thought they might come in handy."

"They already have," I said. "Everyone's did."

I turned to Old Red. Up to then, he and I had 'Holmesed and Watsoned' on our own, without anyone to back us except for, on occasion, Diana. My brother's not the most sociable man in the world. Hell, he's not the billionth most sociable man in the world. But now, it seemed, we suddenly had our own posse. Would he accept the help?

Old Red met my gaze—and read my mind.

"Mr. Holmes didn't have no gang of nursemaids," he grumbled.

"And just think about what happened to him," I replied.

I thought the words might sting, but my brother didn't wince. If anything, the rigid frown he'd been wearing the last few minutes seemed to soften.

"I have been, Brother," he said. "I have been."

There was a moment of awkward silence then, no one knowing what to say now that the introductions were out of the way.

"So," Diana finally said, "what next?"

She was looking at Old Red.

"Well, miss, first I reckon we oughta help Flip wrap things up here," he told her. "After that, I'm headin' back to Ogden…to kick your pa's ass."

My brother's bushy mustache lifted a bit.

Somewhere under there, he was hiding a little smile.

"Then," he said, "we should see if he's got another job for us."

A LOOK AT BOOK SEVEN:
HUNTERS OF THE DEAD

SHERLOCK HOLMES MEETS THE OLD WEST IN THIS FAST-PACED MURDER MYSTERY THAT UNEARTHS MORE THAN JUST FOSSILS.

The A.A. Western Detective Agency takes on a new case in 1894 Wyoming, a land of bandit gangs and rustlers, when a group of scientists come to town in the hopes of rustling up something very different— dinosaur fossils.

With Big Red and Old Red Amlingmeyer on protection duty, Old Red's obsession with Sherlock Holmes is forced to take a back seat. Until a human body is shockingly discovered during an excavation, that is.

As the mystery deepens, these cowboy detectives must put their sleuthing skills to the test to catch a killer stalking their client's dig site.

With death lurking around every corner, can the Double-A Western Detective Agency catch the killer before it's too late?

AVAILABLE OCTOBER 2023

ABOUT THE AUTHOR

Steve Hockensmith's first novel, the western mystery hybrid *Holmes on the Range*, was a finalist for the Edgar, Shamus, Anthony and Dilys awards. He went on to write several sequels—with more on the way—as well as the tarot-themed mystery *The White Magic Five* and *Dime* and the *New York Times* bestseller *Pride and Prejudice and Zombies: Dawn of the Dreadfuls*. He also teamed up with educator "Science Bob" Pflugfelder to write the middle-grade mystery *Nick and Tesla's High-Voltage Danger Lab* and its five sequels.

A prolific writer of short stories, Hockensmith has been appearing regularly in *Alfred Hitchcock* and *Ellery Queen Mystery Magazine* for more than 20 years. You can learn more about him and his writing at stevehockensmith.com.

Made in the USA
Las Vegas, NV
18 January 2024

84566407R00152